ADRIANA PRIDEMORE

As always, thank you to my husband.

You are my muse, my critic, and my cheerleader.

CONTENTS

SAFE HOUSE

"Whitney, wake up." She felt Philtzer shaking her shoulder. "Whitney Martindale? Hey, Whit! We're here."

Stiffly, she sat up, letting Philtzer's jacket slide off her onto the floor. She shoved her dark hair from her face and blinked at the glaring light shining through the windshield. Slowly, she stretched. Everything was cramped from being curled up on the passenger seat of the cargo van. Philtzer had acquired it to help them escape from Germany, but it wasn't built for comfort.

"Where are we?" Her voice was hoarse from exhaustion.

"Safe house in Le Havre, France," Philtzer explained as he gathered his things. "Come on. We need to get everyone inside." He was out of the van before she could get her fuzzy brain working.

She grabbed his jacket from the floor and pulled it on. Even though it was late spring, Whitney shivered. She wrapped the jacket tightly around her and looked around. They were across from the docks. She tried to read the sign on the big building across the street, but her French was terrible. All she managed was 'Port', but she couldn't decipher the second word. Feeling slightly culture shocked, she turned and stared up at the building they had come to. It stood on the corner, rising above its neighbors with balconies wrapped around every fourth floor. It looked like an apartment building.

"Hey, Whit?" Philtzer poked his head around the side of the van. "Come here."

She hesitantly moved toward the rear of the cargo van.

"Can you sit here and make sure no one disturbs the truck while I grab the others?"

"What others?" Whitney blinked at him stupidly.

"Hamilton, Sophia, and Sandra." Philtzer glanced up and down the street, but no one paid them any attention. They looked like a furniture delivery truck. "We're gonna need the extra hands to carry the coffins in."

"Wait, what?"

"Coffins? You know, the boss and Rami?" Philtzer pointed to the sky. "It's daylight."

"Oh. Right." She felt stupid. Of course, they couldn't just get out of the truck and walk inside; they were vampires.

"It's okay," Philtzer grinned and ruffled her hair, "you'll catch up after some sleep."

"Ha. Ha." Whitney shoved his hand away and tried to smooth her hair back down. "Why are you always so cheery? Is it a werewolf thing?"

Philtzer chuckled and jogged toward the door. Whitney sat down on the bumper and waited. The van rocked slightly as the others moved around inside. She heard a rapping on the roll-up door behind her head.

"Hello out there?" Thomas Sun-Dancer called.

"Philtzer is getting the others," Whitney said without turning. She knew he could hear her through the metal. Werewolves had very good hearing.

The van rocked again, and she began to wonder what they were doing in there. Ten minutes later, Philtzer was back with Sandra, Hamilton, and Sophia. Whitney moved out of the way so he could reach the door.

Sandra stepped over beside her. "You okay?"

Whitney gave her a very sarcastic thumbs up, and Sandra put a reassuring arm around her shoulders.

Philtzer banged on the door once with his fist. "You ready in there?"

"Hold on," Thomas replied. The truck bounced as something heavy inside fell. After a moment, the door rolled up. Thomas stood beside a large, tarp-wrapped, oblong shape strapped to a dolly. He panted, "Rami first."

Behind him, Unkhabami stood holding a blanket. She was also panting. Whitney suddenly put it all together. It was Rami's coffin strapped to the dolly. He was still so weak from his fall off the cliff that his coffin would have had to be moved with him still inside. Rami was no small man. It would have taken the strength of Thomas, Unkhabami, and Madraeus to lift him.

Sandra and Whitney stood back to let the others lift Rami's coffin down.

"Come on, us mere mortals will get the doors." Sandra pulled Whitney toward the apartment building. The others followed, and between the five of them, they got Rami's coffin through the door and into the elevator.

"Thank goodness for elevators," Sophia panted as the doors closed.

Whitney and Sandra went back out to the truck to wait for them. Whitney stood with her arms crossed, staring up into the cargo area where a second coffin waited with Madraeus inside.

"Well, you did it," Sandra said as she elbowed Whitney. "You tamed the beast."

She knew Sandra was referring to Madraeus' beastly rampage through the German village. He had killed hundreds, and they had sent Whitney in to stop him. Not because she had any special skills, but because everyone was convinced that Madraeus loved her. They believed he would never hurt her.

"Not exactly tamed." Whitney shivered, remembering the moment when he charged her with his fangs out, ready to kill.

"Pacified then?" Sandra offered.

"Yeah, I guess." Whitney shrugged, remembering how he had fallen at her feet.

"Alright, round two," Philtzer said as he and Thomas strolled up behind them with the dolly. Thomas hopped up into the back and pulled the dolly up into the cargo area. Together, they lifted Madraeus' coffin onto the dolly, wrapped a tarp around it, and strapped it down. Hamilton and Sophia returned in time to help lift it out of the truck. Then, as a group, they headed into the building.

The elevator was rattly and cramped with six people and a coffin. Whitney was fast becoming the victim of another claustrophobia attack. When the doors finally slid open, she shot out of the elevator but stopped and looked around in confusion.

"That way, number six." Philtzer pointed down the hall to the left.

Whitney left them behind as she hurried to the apartment. Behind her, she could hear the heavy sound of the wheels on the carpet as they wheeled Madraeus along. She opened the door and stood to the side. Thomas maneuvered the dolly around to get it through the door. As he passed, he glanced at Whitney's pale face.

He winked at her reassuringly. "Almost there."

Thomas grunted as he angled the coffin to fit in beside Rami's, taking up most of the living room floor. Philtzer and Hamilton had already unwrapped the tarp from around Rami's coffin. Sophia was pulling the drapes shut to ward off the sun.

Whitney realized in just a moment she would be face-to-face with Madraeus again. She winced, thinking of how he had kissed her while they'd hidden in the coffin together. Overwhelmed by conflicting emotions, she had scrambled away from him as soon as the lid was lifted.

This is going to get awkward fast. Dreading the meeting, Whitney muttered, "Couldn't you just leave him in there?"

Thomas grinned. "He can hear you, you know."

Whitney flushed.

"You might want to leave some room in your mouth for the other foot." Philtzer laughed as he helped Thomas remove the dolly straps from around the coffin.

"Come on," Sandra motioned her toward the hallway, "I'll show you around." She grabbed Whitney's shoulders and steered her out of the room.

The safe house was a tidy little apartment with three bedrooms. Each was decked out with two sets of bunk beds. The closets were fully stocked with clothing in a range of sizes. The windows all had blackout curtains and were tinted for extra protection from the sun. The living room had sliding glass doors that led to the balcony.

"This is our room." Sandra opened the door and gestured for Whitney to enter. "You, me, and Sophia are sharing. Hamilton, Thomas, and Philtzer have that one," she pointed to the room next door and then to the one across the hall, "and that one is for Madraeus and Rami."

Whitney eyed the bunk beds. "What about Unkhabami?"

"Probably with Rami or in here." Sandra shrugged. "We came here right after Philtzer showed up. Hamilton is the only one who speaks French, so we sent him out for groceries, and Soph and I got the house sorted out. Your bags are there, and the shower is at the end of the hall."

Whitney turned and smiled sadly. "Thank you, Sandra."

Sandra looked around and shrugged. "We got everything as ready as we could."

"No, I mean thank you for coming with me."

"Yeah, what else have I got to do?" Sandra snorted. "The dead don't have many hobbies. I sure as hell wasn't going to stay home with your grandma and listen to her rant and rave about her baby being out with monsters."

"I don't blame you," Whitney laughed, but her smile faded quickly enough. Her grandmother hadn't wanted her to come to Europe at all. Defying her weighed on Whitney's heart.

When Sandra saw the shadow steal over Whitney's face, she sighed and walked over to Whitney's suitcase. "Why don't you shower and sleep? Everything is better with sleep."

KEEPING SECRETS

Whitney's sleep was not as restful as she would have hoped. She had dreamt of the mine, of Rami's broken body, and of Madraeus coming at her with his fangs out, ready to rip her to shreds. She jerked awake and looked around. She couldn't remember where she was. Bunk beds stood on either side of the room. Someone snored in the bed above her. Slowly, everything came back to her, including the memory of Madraeus holding her close and keeping her calm as they crossed the border from Germany, hidden in a coffin... *and then he kissed me.*

Whitney groaned. She had no idea what to do about her relationship with her boss. He had saved her life multiple times, but he had also murdered a bunch of people. He had been the most gentle, caring, and protective man she had ever met, but he was also terrifying and dangerous. Everyone insisted that he loved her. *But how can he? How can he love and kill? How can I still want to be around him?* Her life had been filled with death and danger ever since she had taken the receptionist job at InfiniCorp. Any sane person would run screaming, and yet she hadn't.

Am I messed up in the head? she wondered. She wasn't sure who she could ask for advice. *It's not like therapy covers relationships with supernatural beings.*

Whitney whimpered, covering her face with her arms.

There was no way she was going back to sleep, not with all those thoughts running around in her head. She wondered if anyone else was awake. The bunk across from her was empty, but the blankets were messy, so someone had to be up.

She quietly slipped out of bed, trying not to disturb her bunkmate. She took a quick peek. Unkhabami was sprawled across the top bunk with her feet propped up on the railing and her mouth hanging slack as she snored. Whitney smiled. The priestess deserved her rest. Unkhabami had worked to the point of exhaustion as she tried to heal Rami. Not to mention the fact that the priestess' intensity had always scared the crap out of Whitney, and she did not want to face an angry, tired were-cat.

Whitney dressed as quietly as she could. It occurred to her that she should call her grandmother. *She's probably worried sick!* She knew she was in for a lecture, but she couldn't just let Grammy worry and wonder what had happened to her. They hadn't parted on the best of terms. Her grandmother hadn't approved of Whitney's association with monsters.

And yet she worked with Madraeus when Cecelia had kidnapped me, Whitney huffed.

Whitney slipped out and moved quietly down the hallway, smiling at the noise spilling out of the kitchen of yet another werewolf mealtime.

"I'm not washing all those dishes." Sophia stood just inside the kitchen door with her hands on her hips. "I did them last time, but this one is your mess."

Whitney reached out to tap Sophia on the shoulder, but the werewolf turned around before she could touch her.

"Good afternoon," Sophia said. "You didn't sleep long."

"I didn't?" Whitney had no idea what time it was. Living with vampires and werewolves had destroyed all hope of a normal schedule.

"It's only been about three or four hours."

"Oh, really?" Whitney felt like it had been days. "I was wondering, is there a phone?"

"Why?"

"I was just thinking about calling Grammy."

"What are you going to tell her?" Sophia asked.

"I don't know. She's gonna be mad no matter what I say."

Sophia shrugged. "At least she cares."

Whitney sighed. "She begged me not to come here."

"Considering how your life has been playing out lately, can you blame her?"

"No, but I just wish she would understand. This is all hard enough without her constantly telling me I'm getting in over my head. It's not like I planned all this."

"None of us planned to be here," Sophia said as she looked back into the kitchen.

Whitney winced. Sophia's introduction to the world of the Races had been violent and traumatic, and then she'd been lied to and manipulated into Cecelia's army.

"I'm sorry for what happened to you, Sophia," Whitney said softly, "but I'm glad you're here with us now."

For a long moment, Sophia was quiet. When she turned back, she nodded. "Thank you. I'm sorry about what happened to you too."

Whitney gave her a sympathetic smile.

"There's a burner phone by the couch," Sophia said. "You can use it without being traced."

"Thanks." Whitney found the phone Sophia had mentioned and stepped out onto the balcony to call her grandmother. The sea breeze coming off the harbor across the street flipped Whitney's hair across her face as her grandmother answered.

"Hi, Grammy." Whitney tried to sound cheerful so she wouldn't worry her. "Just wanted to check in."

"Where are you? Are you okay?" Elizabeth Martindale sounded close to tears. "I've been so worried!"

"I'm fine." Whitney winced as she realized that she had said 'I'm fine' a lot lately, and she had never been fine any of those times. "We're in France and headed to England soon. Everyone is good. Rami is safe and..." She almost mentioned Madraeus' rampage but stopped just in time. That was the last thing that she needed her grandmother to know about. Elizabeth had begrudgingly dealt with vampires and werewolves out of necessity, but there was no way she would be okay with Madraeus wiping out a whole town.

"And?"

"What?" Whitney shook her head, wishing she had planned her conversation better. "Sorry, I got distracted. Everything is fine."

"Whitney Elizabeth Martindale, I have known you a long time. What aren't you telling me?"

"Nothing, just the usual crazy work stuff." Whitney cringed as she said it. 'Crazy work stuff' when you worked with vampires and werewolves was a whole new level of bonkers. "How are things at home? No trouble, right?"

"No." Elizabeth knew exactly what she was asking. "None of Cecelia's minions have bothered me."

"That's a relief."

"I did have a visit from Agent Milner."

The balcony floor fell away, and Whitney plummeted into full panic. "Milner? What happened? What did you say?"

"We had a very candid conversation."

"Oh, Grammy," Whitney whispered. "Please tell me you kept the Races' secret?"

Silence greeted her question.

"Grammy?"

"I'm sorry, Whitney." Elizabeth sighed. "I told you that you shouldn't be mixed up in this. It's time for the authorities to handle this."

"Grammy, what have you done?"

"I did what I thought was right. For you and for all of us. I love you, and if you won't listen to me, then I have to do what is necessary to protect you. You can hate me if you want, but I did this because I love you."

"Oh, Grammy!" Whitney gasped. "I could never hate you! I just..." Whitney thought about all the possible repercussions. "I just wish you hadn't—"

"Whitney?" Sandra called from the living room. "You want coffee?"

"Grammy, I have to go. I love you."

"Whitney, wait!"

Her grandmother's desperate plea for her to stay on the line echoed in her head as she ended the call. Her hand dropped to her side as she stared out at the ocean, wondering what she should do. She should warn everyone that the FBI might be beating down their door any minute, but she couldn't endanger her grandmother by ratting her out.

"Whitney?" Sandra came out onto the balcony and whistled. "Nice view!" She gazed around at the ships and the glittering waves before looking at Whitney. "Hey, you okay?"

Whitney shook her head. "My grandmother had a 'candid conversation' with Agent Milner."

"What!" Sandra glanced back toward the living room and lowered her voice. "Did she tell him anything?"

"I'm pretty sure she told him everything." Whitney rubbed her forehead. "I have to warn them, but if they know that my grandmother was the one that spilled the beans about the Races, then she'll be in danger! You know their rules about secrecy."

"That particular sword hangs over my head daily," Sandra snorted.

Whitney knew that Sandra had been allowed to live only because of her friendship with Whitney, but on the condition that she never let anyone know about the Races.

"Honestly," Sandra shrugged, "does it really matter?"

"Sandra!" Whitney gaped. "This is my grandmother we're talking about!"

"That's not what I meant!" Sandra rolled her eyes. "Milner already had files on the Races. He's already on their trail. What could your grandmother have told him that he didn't already know?"

"Before, he only suspected. Now he *knows*." Whitney shook her head. "What if the council goes after her? What if Milner comes here?"

"I doubt he knows where we are now."

"If she mentioned that the Hares are meeting us at Devon, we could be screwed!"

Sandra laughed. "Honey, we're already screwed. We have enough problems with the snake demon and your boss being crazy. We'll deal with the FBI when we have to. But right now? I say keep it to yourself. No sense starting something if it might just go away on its own."

"But what about the council?"

"Pretty sure they're too busy with the whole Cecelia army thing to consider one mortal who may or may not have said something they shouldn't have.

Whitney considered Sandra's logic. "You're right. "I'm just tired of secrets."

"Come on, coffee will help."

Whitney could only nod.

TO TELL OR NOT TO TELL

They found Philtzer and Thomas sitting at the kitchen table, surrounded by the remains of a very large meal.

"Hey, girls!" Philtzer looked up and smiled. "What's shakin'?"

"Do you ever stop eating?" Sandra muttered.

"Not if we can help it!" Thomas grinned.

Whitney managed a smile as she sat down. It never ceased to surprise her how much she liked these two werewolves. They were absolutely lethal and completely childish, but definitely some of the best men she'd ever met.

Maybe I could tell them about Milner, she thought.

Philtzer's gaze turned serious as he looked at Whitney. "You okay?"

"Me? Um, sure." Whitney wondered if he had heard her conversation on the balcony. Guilt flooded through her. She quickly started digging through the culinary debris on the table.

She grabbed the last croissant and took a bite. She could feel Philtzer watching her.

Philtzer started to ask her something, but Sandra interrupted, "Anyone heard from Mrs. Myers?"

Whitney shivered as she remembered Cherry, the pink pixie, freezing time long enough for them to make a run for it before the FBI raided Mrs. Myers' house.

"Talked to her yesterday. FBI had a lot of questions but no clear connection to any of us except through work, so I think she's off the hook," Thomas said.

Whitney wondered if her grandmother had made the connection for Agent Milner since she wasn't exactly fond of Mrs. Myers. Whitney threw Sandra a worried glance, but Sandra kept her expression bland.

Philtzer noticed Whitney's expression and bumped her with his elbow. "Hey, don't worry. Myers has been dodging the authorities for a couple thousand years."

"And we took everything with us when we left," Thomas patted Whitney on the back, "so the FBI won't have anything to go on."

The croissant turned to dust in her mouth as the enormity of the mess she was in overwhelmed her.

Philtzer elbowed her again. "Don't look so worried. We're making headway."

Whitney gaped at him. "Headway? Everyone you know has been attacked, the FBI is tracking us, Madraeus went nuts and wiped out a whole town, Cecelia is who knows where, keeping who knows how many people locked up as food for her army, the snake demon from ancient Egypt who created vampires is about to break loose and wreak havoc across the planet, people are dying! That's not headway! That's everything going to crap!"

"Well," Thomas snorted, "when you put it like that..."

Philtzer laid a hand on her arm. "Look on the bright side. You're still alive."

Sandra poured two cups of coffee and set one in front of Whitney, "Yeah, remember, you're the bright spot of hope for the whole world."

Whitney moaned. In all the terrifying drama of saving Rami and trying to stop Madraeus' killing spree, she had forgotten what Unkhabami and Myers had said, that she was somehow the key to stopping a supernatural world war.

"Whit, it's okay," Philtzer said, seeing her fallen expression. He grabbed the seat of her chair and pulled her around to face him. "This is going to work out."

Whitney stared at him. Her chin quivered.

"We know where Cecelia is headed. We know what she wants." Thomas muttered, "Thanks to the bunnies."

"The bunnies," Whitney repeated, thinking about John and Barbie from the Ancient Society of the Three Hares. Barbie was not too bad. She had been straightforward, even though she was clearly terrified. But John? He was another matter. Whitney hadn't liked him at all. He was creepy and secretive. *Although, what should I expect from a secret society?*

Despite her feelings about John, the Hares had shown up offering a shortcut to stopping Cecelia, but they needed Madraeus to do it. No one was happy about working with the Hares. Their society had existed for centuries as a way to hunt down and stop the monsters of the world, and they had trapped a lot of vicious creatures from folklore and legends. The Hares considered any member of the Races a primary target.

"I have a question." Whitney turned her cup in a slow circle. "If Cecelia is going around freeing all the creepy things the Hares locked up, where are they?" She looked up at Philtzer. "In the mine, I just saw normal vampires and werewolves."

"Normal?" Sandra snorted.

"You know what I mean." Whitney waved her hand vaguely. "What happened to the other things?"

"Maybe they didn't care about Cecelia's plan and ditched out," Sandra said, crossing her fingers.

"We're not that lucky." Thomas sighed. "Rami told me about the little alp demon they beheaded in the abbey, and then there's the ghouls that attacked Unkhabami's village. I'm sure there're probably more."

"So, do we have to go around and hunt all these things down again?" Whitney asked.

"Maybe," Thomas shrugged, "but one thing at a time. Bunny problem first."

"Where're the rascally rabbits now?" Whitney asked. "I thought they wanted Madraeus' help."

"They went on to Devon." Sandra hopped up to sit on the counter. "Said they wanted to fortify their defenses while we convince Madraeus to help them."

"So? What did Madraeus say about it?" Whitney looked to Philtzer. "Is he going to help?"

Thomas and Philtzer exchanged a look.

Whitney didn't miss the wariness in their expressions. "What?"

"We're not really sure how to put this," Philtzer began, glancing at Thomas.

"We didn't tell Madraeus about the Hares," Thomas blurted.

"Or Rami," Philtzer added.

Whitney glared at them. "What?"

The werewolves looked at each other again, and Thomas answered, "I couldn't tell Madraeus. He was so upset after we picked you guys up that I didn't want to make it worse."

"And Rami was still recovering from his fall in the ravine," Philtzer added. "We wanted to give him a chance to get better first."

Whitney dropped what was left of her croissant onto her plate. "So, when are you gonna tell them?"

Before they could answer, Hamilton came in carrying two cloth shopping bags in each hand. Thomas took the opportunity to dodge the question by helping him with the groceries. Philtzer busied himself with cleaning up the table.

Hamilton glanced suspiciously at Philtzer and caught the scowling expression on Whitney's face. He looked back at Philtzer. "What'd I miss?"

"These two were just confessing why they're avoiding telling Madraeus about the Hares."

"Ah." Hamilton nodded and turned back to unload the sacks. "Honestly, I don't blame them. I don't want to tell him either."

Philtzer looked at Whitney and pointed to Hamilton as if to say, *See?*

"Cowards," Sandra muttered under her breath.

"Nope." Philtzer shook his head. "Just been the messenger too many times."

Thomas shrugged. "You were the one that was supposed to talk to him anyway, remember?"

Whitney turned pale as she gaped at them both. Before coming to rescue Rami, everyone had decided that she was the one to talk to Madraeus about helping the Hares. Despite the fact that the Hares had tried to kill him multiple times over the centuries, they were all convinced that Madraeus' feelings for Whitney would allow him to listen to reason. Whitney was still unconvinced.

But then again, there was that kiss, she thought.

Thomas grinned. "Madraeus has already proved that he won't kill you."

Whitney rolled her eyes. "Oh, that's great logic."

"You can do it, Whit." Philtzer blinked at her hopefully, giving her his best puppy dog eyes. "He'll listen to you."

"I think it's a moot point," Hamilton interjected quietly, making all eyes turn to him. "I'm not sure if we should tell Madraeus."

"I agree with Hamilton," Unkhabami said from the doorway. The others fell silent.

Whitney turned to look at her. She was so tall that she towered over the room. Whitney pulled out Philtzer's chair and offered it to Unkhabami. The priestess nodded her thanks and sat down.

Thomas leaned back against the counter. "Okay, I'll bite. Why?"

"I've been thinking." Hamilton let his gaze wander over them all. "Rami said that Madraeus is acting odd. He's usually calm and in control. The Hares said the snake demon that Cecelia is after has some influence over the vampires he'd created."

Thomas nodded. "The Hares said that Madraeus was a first-generation offspring from Apep."

"You think the snake is messing with Madraeus?" Sandra asked.

Thomas blew out a long sigh. "It would explain why he went crazy."

Hamilton nodded and crossed his arms. "It stands to reason that if the snake can communicate its wishes, it can probably hear what is going on too."

Philtzer lost all of his playfulness. "You mean, it's listening?"

"The Hares said that Cecelia is listening to the 'All Psycho Snake Radio', so why not Madraeus too?" Sandra said.

Unkhabami looked around the table at them all. "If we tell Madraeus, the snake will hear and Cecelia will know."

"Not the most ideal situation." Hamilton sighed, exchanging a look with the other werewolves.

A grim silence settled over the kitchen.

"What if Madraeus goes all wacky again?" Sandra looked around the room. "Then what?"

Philtzer nudged Whitney's chair with his toe. "Whitney'll sort him out."

"Pfft!" Whitney shot him a nasty look.

He grinned and looked at Unkhabami. "Any predictions?"

The African priestess closed her eyes and began muttering under her breath. "There are many confusing images. There is darkness and a grove surrounded by a rock wall. There is blood. Everything is blurry, but I see Whitney Martindale..."

"Me?" she squeaked.

"Yes." She opened her eyes. Unkhabami suddenly looked old. "You will be the key."

"What's that even mean? I don't want to be the key to anything." Whitney looked at the others, feeling a weight settle back onto her shoulders. She felt the same when they told her that she was the only one who could possibly stop Madraeus.

Thomas crossed his arms. "Be that as it may, that doesn't solve the Madraeus problem."

"Well, what are you going to do?" Sandra scoffed. "Lie to him?"

"No, not lie." Thomas shook his head. "Just don't tell him the whole truth until the very last minute."

Whitney shook her head. "That's not going to go over well."

"What about Rami?" Philtzer asked. "Do we tell him?"

"Does anyone know if he is first-generation?" Sandra looked around the group. "How do we know that he isn't listening to snake radio too?"

"He is not." Unkhabami raised her chin. "I would know."

"Maybe. Maybe not," Sophia huffed. "Men are all about keeping secrets."

"Not me!" Philtzer grinned. "I'm an open book."

Sandra ignored Philtzer and pressed her case. "What if Rami is hearing Apep too but not telling anyone?"

Silence filled the kitchen as they all realized the implications of both Rami and Madraeus hearing Apep.

"I vote we say nothing to Madraeus or Rami until we know for sure," Hamilton said, raising his hand.

One by one, they each raised a hand in agreement.

"That's settled. Now, how do we get them to go to Devon?" Hamilton crossed his arms and looked at each of them, but no one had an answer.

CONFESSION

Madraeus woke slowly, dreading consciousness. It had been bad enough that he had relived his rampage in his dreams, but being awake meant facing the consequences, and he wasn't sure he could. How could he ever make up for the near extinction of an entire town? Not to mention the pain he'd caused those closest to him.

On the other side of the room, he could hear Rami sleeping. Rami was like a brother, and he had almost lost his life because Madraeus had failed to stop Cecelia sooner.

Everyone has suffered because I have failed. Those people in the mine, Sophia, Whitney...

He lay still, staring at the ceiling. It wasn't actually a ceiling; it was the bottom of the top bunk. It was only a couple of feet above him, but at least he wasn't still in the coffin. He hated spending time in those damn boxes. It was confining and demeaning, but now it was worse. From now on, every time he used one, he would think of Whitney.

He closed his eyes, reliving their trip across the border as they hid together inside his coffin. He could feel her body rocking against him as the van bounced along. He could smell her scent and her fear. He opened his eyes. She had been terrified. Her time in the mine had given her a terrible fear of dark, closed spaces, especially when she was locked in with a monster.

That's what I am, a bloodthirsty monster. He sighed and rubbed his forehead. *How have I made such a mess of things?*

He had been the head of the Council of Races for hundreds of years. He was not prone to making decisions based on emotional reactions. But when Cecelia had shown up in his hotel room and told him that Rami had been killed by the village police, he had lost his mind to rage and grief. His quest for revenge had nearly wiped out the entire town. Madraeus covered his face with his hands. It had all been a lie.

Cecelia had lied just to provoke him. Rami had survived to reveal the truth. Guilt and self-loathing seized his chest. Why had he believed her? Cecelia loved to lie. He remembered going to the ravine to see for himself. He'd found Rami's blood on the rocks and rage had overwhelmed him. He didn't remember much after that.

Madraeus sat up and swung his feet off the bed. He braced his head in his hands. He should have looked closer. He should have been more thorough. Why hadn't he? Then he remembered.

The voice.

That hissing demon in his head that urged him to destroy. He hated that voice. It tended to show up when he was around

Cecelia, and it never ended well. Usually, he could ignore it, but this time it had been so loud. It had taken over every thought in his head.

A hissing laugh echoed through his mind, sending a shiver down his spine.

Madraeus wasn't normally prone to fear, but right now he was scared, really scared. He didn't want to hear that voice again. It was the Dark Ages all over again. Back then, it had made him savage. Back then, he hadn't cared about the damage he'd caused. There had been nothing to care about, but now? Whitney's face floated through his mind.

He couldn't go back to that savagery, but once again, he was killing under the influence of that voice. What if it took over again?

Then you will wear more than jussst the blood of a few ssstupid villagersss, the voice laughed.

Madraeus glanced down at the dried blood still covering his shirt. With a snarl, he ripped the shirt off and threw it across the room.

The voice laughed again.

"How many more will die if I don't get control?" Madraeus whispered.

All of them!

Madraeus moved to cover his face again and noticed his hands were shaking. He clenched them into fists. He had to do something. He had to find a way to lock out the voice.

You can't get rid of me, the voice hissed in his head.

Madraeus shot to his feet and stumbled forward a couple of steps.

You are mine, it hissed again.

"No!" Madraeus muttered. He pressed the heels of his hands into his temples.

You have alwaysss been mine.

"No!" Madraeus growled.

Mine.

"*No!*" Madraeus snarled. Without realizing it, his fangs had elongated and his hands curled into claws. His breath came in short gasps. He caught sight of Rami across the room and locked onto him like a lifeline. He had to regain control. He stared at his hands, forcing them to relax, then he deliberately retracted his fangs. Closing his eyes, he concentrated and slowed his breathing.

The hissing voice laughed at his efforts.

Through the door, he heard the sound of voices and laughter. He could hear Philtzer and Thomas. No doubt the others were there too. He couldn't face them like this. He had to get away before he hurt someone.

Ignoring the hissing laughter in his head, Madraeus rummaged through the wardrobe and dresser for clean clothes. Quietly, he pulled on a fresh shirt and pants.

He looked toward the door. He knew he couldn't go out the front door of the apartment. He would have to go past everyone, and he couldn't handle their questions right now. They wouldn't understand. He needed to leave.

He glanced at Rami once more to make sure he was still asleep before moving to the window. Night had fallen; he could feel it. Living for more than 1,700 years provided a certain awareness of the sun's position. He pulled the curtain aside and opened the window. He climbed out onto the balcony that ran around the entire building. It was no trouble to follow it along and then drop down to the lower section of the building. In moments, he was standing on the street.

He stopped long enough to get his bearings. He knew where he was. Although he hadn't been to Le Havre in about twenty years, he remembered it well enough. A cool sea breeze, laced with the remnants of rain, ruffled his hair. He closed his eyes and turned into the wind, letting it caress his face. The night sounds of Le Havre seemed somehow subdued, but maybe that was his imagination. He took a long, deep breath and opened his eyes. He turned and headed for the end of the block. Street lamps illuminated the corners and intersections, reflecting off the numerous puddles. The rest of the street was in shadow, which suited him fine.

Yesss, out into the night! Let'sss hunt!

He concentrated on ignoring the hissing voice. He met a few people as he continued up Rue Saint-Jacques. It was late enough that most people were already home eating but hadn't come back out yet to join friends for a bit of nightlife. He turned onto Rue de Paris and walked on. It wasn't long before the lighted stone walls of the Cathedrale Notre-Dame du Havre came into sight.

He stopped and stared at the ancient church. It stood nearly unchanged by time and war, unlike the buildings that surrounded it. Melancholy washed over him as he realized that he was the same. He had lived for so long, and only the things around him changed. He hadn't. He was still a press-ganged soldier, still the same lost soul Brother Edwin had found outside of the monastery.

Ssstill my creation.

Madraeus stopped. *My creation?* The world fell away, and memory flooded in. He was standing in the dark, on guard duty in Cyrene, listening to the sounds of the night. A rustle in the shadow of a crumbled building drew his attention, then something big launched out of the darkness, knocking him to the ground. Could this demon in his head be the thing that created him?

The voice in his head laughed at his reaction to this revelation.

Yesss... You are mine and alwaysss have been.

"No!"

Madraeus squeezed his eyes shut, trying to think of something else. He had gained control when he saw Rami. He tried to concentrate on Rami, but the voice just laughed. Whitney's face floated into his mind. *Yes. Whitney.* He would think of her.

She will be mine.

"Never!" Madraeus snarled. He would protect her at any cost.

Madraeus gazed at the cathedral, standing tall and forbidding before him. He needed help. Whitney had once asked if he would burst into flames if he stepped into a church. He knew he wouldn't, but right now, he didn't care if he did. Right now, he saw it as the path to salvation. Brother Edwin's teachings about faith had helped him before. If it worked once, it would work again.

It won't help, the voice hissed.

Madraeus clenched his jaw against the voice. He checked the street, but there were only a few tourists milling about and taking pictures. Desperate to be rid of the voice, he hurried across the street and up the stone steps. He pushed through the heavily carved wooden doors and stepped into the cavernous interior. Slowly, he looked around. Tall stone pillars stood sentinel along each side, rising up to the vaulted ceilings that towered over the wooden pews. At the far end, the stained glass windows lay hidden in shadow. Ornately carved wooden alcoves and stone statues lined the perimeter. It was beautiful.

Even though he seemed to be the only one in the cathedral, he cautiously started up the aisle. He moved silently along the benches and rows of chairs until he came to the front.

Madraeus stared up at the crucifix standing just to the left of the altar.

You are praying to the wrong god.

Was he just fooling himself, thinking that faith could save him? It wasn't the first time that he'd been wrong about the Church.

"Your Bishops promised me freedom from my sins if I freed the Holy Land," he murmured, staring up at the image of Christ.

They lied to you.

He thought of the political machinations behind the Crusades. "I was naive."

Naive no longer. Thisss world isss already corrupt.

Madraeus squeezed his eyes shut.

Embrace your power! Let the Darknesss in!

Madraeus shook his head, trying to shut out the hissing.

We will crush the Light and rule from the Darknesss!

"No," Madraeus whispered.

Take what isss rightfully yoursss!

His knees hit the cold stone floor.

You are mine. You alwaysss have been.

"No!" Madraeus' snarl echoed back to him, mixing with the laugh inside his head.

"Is there something wrong, my son?" a soft voice asked in French.

Madraeus' eyes shot open and was surprised to see the floor only inches from his nose. He stared in horror at the stones. He could feel his control slipping. Out of the corner of his eye, he could see the hem of a priest's robe.

Kill him.

Madraeus squeezed his eyes shut again, struggling for control. He flinched as a gentle hand touched his shoulder.

"It's alright, my son. You are safe here." Those gentle words worked like magic, draining the tension from Madraeus' body. The priest's compassion flowed around him, allowing him to retract his fangs and gain some control.

"Excuse me, Father," Madraeus answered in French. He averted his face as he sat up. "I didn't mean to shout."

"It is alright." The priest smiled and reached a hand down to help Madraeus up. "I wish all my parishioners would be as enthusiastic when they prayed."

"It's more desperation than enthusiasm."

"Church is a good place for the desperate." The priest motioned Madraeus to the nearest seat. "I am here if you wish to talk."

Kill him.

Madraeus sat down abruptly. He clenched his fists to stop the shaking.

The priest peered at him closely and asked, "What troubles you, my son?"

Madraeus squeezed his eyes shut. "I have done things."

"We have all done things, but you are here." The priest shrugged. "It proves you are not beyond help. No one is beyond hope, my son."

You are.

"I am. I've killed so many." Madraeus whispered, looking away. He couldn't hold the priest's gaze. The priest remained silent, and Madraeus waited for the man's condemnation.

MISSING

Whitney stood outside the girls' bedroom for a long time, working up the courage to enter. After their meeting in the kitchen, Unkhabami had asked not to be disturbed and retreated to their room. It was now well after dark, and the priestess had yet to come out. Whitney raised her hand for the tenth time to knock but dropped it again.

She needed to speak to the priestess. Whitney had questions that only Unkhabami could answer, but she was afraid to ask them. Unkhabami scared her. The High Priestess of the Paka-Watu was terrifyingly intense. The way she looked at a person, Whitney shivered, it was like having layers of your soul peeled away. Whitney dreaded ever coming up against her were-cat side.

And yet, Unkhabami had a softer side. When Cecelia had sent ghouls to destroy Unkhabami's village, she had fought to save her people, nearly losing her life in the process. Whitney thought about how desperate the priestess had been to find

Rami. Unkhabami had been filled with terror at the idea that he might die.

Whitney stopped and cocked her head, trying to decide if a vampire could die or if it was die again. She shook her head, realized she was stalling again, and raised her hand.

"Just come in." Unkhabami's voice purred from the other side of the door.

Whitney froze. She felt like she'd been caught looking for Christmas presents. She grimaced and turned the handle. The door swung open, but she didn't move from the threshold.

"Whitney, I could hear you standing out there being indecisive for the last ten minutes."

"Sorry." Whitney clasped her hands behind her back and looked down at the woman sitting cross-legged in the middle of the floor.

"Come in."

"I don't want to disturb you." Whitney took a step backward. "I could come back later."

"Whitney Martindale," Unkhabami growled, freezing her in her tracks. "You came to say something. Say it."

Whitney had learned long ago not to argue with her. She was a seer like Whitney's boss at the temp agency, Mrs. Myers, but she wasn't nearly as motherly. She wished Mrs. M. were here to ask instead of the priestess.

Whitney edged into the room, and the door swung shut behind her, making her jump.

"Why are you so skittish?" The priestess peered at her. "This is not your first time speaking to me."

"I know." Whitney tried to rally her courage, but it didn't work.

"Come sit."

She moved over and sat down cross-legged with her back to her bunk.

"You came for a reason, little one?" Unkhabami stared hard at Whitney.

"Umm." Whitney bit her lip. "I did."

"And?"

Whitney picked at the threads of her jeans.

"The questions will never be answered if you keep them to yourself," Unkhabami purred.

Whitney's gaze shot up to find the priestess smiling fondly at her.

"Do not look so surprised." Unkhabami laughed. "It does not take a seer to know when someone is troubled. I was the High Priestess of my village," she began, but Whitney interrupted.

"Was?"

"The village is gone." Sadness filled her eyes. "Only a few children survived the ghouls. The others are dead. Our village is no more." The pain and worry in the priestess' eyes were beyond anything that words could help.

"I'm sorry," Whitney whispered. Unkhabami inclined her head, accepting the condolences. They sat in silence for a moment, and then Whitney asked, "Where are the children now?"

"With another village. They will start new lives." The priestess stared at her hands.

Whitney's heart went out to her, thinking how hard it must be to lose everything like that. "And what about you? Will you start a new life in another village?"

"I do not know." The priestess looked up, and Whitney gasped. The seer's eyes glowed with power and sadness. "So much of the future is mist. I have been trying to see all day, but everything is clouded."

"I'm sorry." Whitney sighed. "Maybe I should come back later then."

"No." Unkhabami held up a hand to stop her. "I welcome the distraction. I cannot force the future to reveal itself, and I should not try. Please, ask me your question. Hopefully, I will be of more help to you."

Whitney opened her mouth to ask but then closed it again. The priestess' gaze was so intense that it was hard to form sentences.

"You want to know what I saw this morning? When I said you would be the key?"

"Actually, no." Whitney stopped her. "I don't think I could handle knowing what's coming. If I knew, I probably wouldn't have the courage to keep going."

"You are wise," Unkhabami laughed. "Not many are wise enough to *not* ask."

Whitney smiled. "Well, sometimes I'm not as dumb as I look."

"Then what is your question, little one?"

Whitney watched the power fade from Unkhabami's eyes, and then she was simply a woman waiting to help. It made it a lot easier to talk. Whitney grabbed a pillow and hugged it close before speaking.

"I was wondering about the visions that Madraeus said he's been having. He said that when we were in the garden and he was charging at me, ready to kill, he had a vision of me dying by his hand, and that's what stopped him." Whitney explained hesitantly. Unkhabami nodded her understanding and motioned for her to continue. "He told me in the mine that he'd seen visions of my futures. He also told me that you had performed a ritual that allowed him to find me in the mine."

"Yes. His visions are a side effect of the ritual." Unkhabami frowned. "I warned him there would be consequences."

"What consequences?" Whitney whispered.

"He may have flashes of your futures here and there. He will never be completely separate from you ever again."

Whitney sat forward. "Is he always going to see my future?"

"It is likely, yes."

"Will he see that we are going to be lying to him about the Hares?" Whitney whispered, afraid that he might hear her in the next room.

"I cannot say. Seeing is complicated." Unkhabami spoke hesitantly, choosing her words carefully. "One second of indecision can change everything. Things shift and move. Nothing is constant or true."

"But you used it to find me last time." Whitney stared at the priestess.

"Prophesying is not to be undertaken lightly. I warned Madraeus of this, but he insisted. He manipulated my ability to see into the future based on his intent."

"He must have been pretty intent then."

"He loves you," Unkhabami stated bluntly. "His intentions did not waver."

Whitney blinked. She started to speak and found she couldn't. Unkhabami studied her for a moment, then sat back and shook her head sadly.

"You do not believe that he loves you."

Whitney swallowed the fear in her throat. "I don't know how he could."

"Because of what you are, or because of what he is?"

"He killed all those people," Whitney whispered. "How can he kill like that and love?"

"Why did he go on the rampage?" Unkhabami asked, and a little glow of power came back into her eyes.

Whitney could barely find her voice. "I don't know."

The priestess shook her head. "Then you will never understand."

Whitney sighed and rested her chin on the pillow. She wasn't sure what to say to that, and luckily, a knock at the door saved her from answering.

"Sorry to interrupt, kids!" Philtzer said as he opened the door and stuck his head into the room. "But Madraeus is gone."

"What?" Whitney was off the floor and halfway to the door before he could answer.

"He's not in his room."

"What if he's freaking out again? We have to find him before he does something terrible!" She pushed Philtzer backward out the door. "How did he leave? Didn't Rami see him?"

Whitney glanced into the open door that led to Rami and Madraeus' room. Unkhabami glided past them to Rami's bedside.

"He's still asleep," Philtzer whispered as he pulled the door shut.

"Then how?"

"Out the window." Philtzer shrugged as if it wasn't a new thing for his boss to escape out a window.

Probably isn't, Whitney thought.

"Van is still downstairs," Thomas said as he came down the hallway. "He's on foot."

"He could be anywhere!" Whitney looked back and forth between the two werewolves.

"We'll have to track him." Philtzer looked at Thomas. They played a short game of Rock-Paper-Scissors, then Philtzer sighed and started to strip. "Don't worry, Whit, I got a nose like a bloodhound."

"Great." Whitney tried to smile as Philtzer shifted and led them to the door.

FOUND

"THOU SHALT NOT KILL." The priest sighed as he folded his hands and looked toward the stained glass window above the altar. "It is one of the Ten Commandments. As a child, I always thought that it would be the easiest Commandment to keep." He looked at Madraeus again. "Unfortunately, as an adult, I know now that it is one of the hardest."

Surprised, Madraeus looked up to find the priest smiling sympathetically.

"I've killed men too." The priest shook his head. "More than I'd like to admit. And every night I see their faces. I feel the weight of their deaths on my soul. I was a soldier and there have been many wars in my lifetime," he explained. "There are times we often find ourselves in situations that are not of our choosing. We find ourselves doing things that we don't want to do, or things we shouldn't do because our choices are not our own."

Madraeus shook his head. "That doesn't make it right."

The priest sighed. "No, it doesn't, but it makes a difference."

"But does it make enough of a difference?" Madraeus rubbed his forehead.

"I believe so." The priest shrugged. "We cannot always pick and choose our reasons. I have killed out of survival and because I was ordered too."

"What about out of rage or grief?" Madraeus stared up at the crucifix again.

For a moment, the priest was quiet, but then he sighed, "God knows what is in your heart, and He has already forgiven you, but now you must forgive yourself."

Madraeus stared down at his hands. "I don't know if I can."

"Often we feel unredeemable," he said as if reading Madraeus' thoughts. "But there is always a way back."

Madraeus sighed. "I'm not so sure."

"You are here, yes?" The priest smiled. "That is the first step away from the darkness. The first step onto the path of light. The path of salvation and redemption."

So long ago, when Madraeus had been lost and hurting, Brother Edwin had taken him in and said something similar. Edwin had taught him about salvation. It had changed him. His kindness had saved Madraeus and brought him to the light. When Cecelia's father, enraged at his daughter becoming a monster, destroyed the monastery at Lindisfarne, Madraeus had struggled against the desire for revenge. As the old monk lay dying, he had extracted a promise from Madraeus that he would save Cecelia from her darkness.

But it hadn't worked out so well. Instead, Cecelia had pulled him back down into the shadows. Madraeus had succumbed to his own savage tendencies for centuries until he had met Mary. She brought him back to the light and became his wife. He had managed to find peace until Cecelia had murdered Mary and her entire family. He could have returned to the darkness then, consumed by vengeance, but he had pledged his sword to the church and stayed on the path of redemption.

But now, he had fallen. Again. Madraeus had returned to the darkness in that tiny German village when he believed Rami had been murdered. He had traveled too far down that dark path.

"I should have stopped," Madraeus muttered.

The priest answered quietly, "You are only a man."

The naiveté of that statement almost made Madraeus laugh out loud.

"No one is perfect." The priest looked around and leaned closer. "Don't tell anyone I said this, but God isn't as infallible as we all think either. Look at the difference between the Old and New Testaments. In the Old Testament, nothing He did worked to put Man on the right path. He had to change his mind and try a new way. That is the New Testament."

Madraeus searched the older man's face.

The priest smiled. "I'm just saying that if God couldn't get it right every time, then you probably won't either. So, be gentle on yourself. Forgive and just do your best."

Madraeus stared at the priest, not realizing that his eyes showed every bit of fear he'd been trying to hide. "What if my best isn't enough?"

"Then you look to God for strength. His shoulders are much bigger than yours or mine." The priest gestured toward the stained glass window. "'Put on the full armor of God, so that you can take your stand against the devil's schemes.' Ephesians 6:11."

"Odd choice of verse." Madraeus frowned at the priest. "I would have thought—"

"The Lord is my strength?" The priest smiled. "I could have used that one, but you are a soldier, yes? And soldiers never stop fighting. I feel that you have a lot of fighting yet to do, and if you are going to fight, then fight wearing the armor of God."

"Are you telling me to become a soldier of God again?"

"Again?" The priest looked at him curiously.

"It was a long time ago." Madraeus shook his head and looked away.

"Ah." The priest folded his hands and stared up at the window.

"What if..." Madraeus rubbed his face and sighed. "What if my fight conflicts with a vow?"

"Is the vow reasonable and good?"

"Once, I would have said yes, but now?" Madraeus shook his head, thinking of the damage Cecelia had caused over the centuries. "Now, I'm not so sure. I kept the vow for years, but it just seems to make things worse."

"Sometimes we must change how we deal with things just as God changed his way of dealing with Man. Perhaps, you should try a different way as well." The priest looked back at the window. "Perhaps a different way will take you toward the light and not away from it."

Madraeus looked down at his hands and sighed. "Perhaps."

"I will warn you," the priest's tone caught Madraeus' attention, "dragging yourself back to the light will not be easy. From the look on your face earlier, I think you know that already."

Madraeus let his eyes stray to the spot where he had fallen to the floor.

"You will do better with help. Friends, loved ones, family." The priest reached out and squeezed Madraeus' forearm reassuringly. "I am here, too, if you need me."

"Thank you," Madraeus nodded. "I—"

His answer was cut short by the doors crashing open. Madraeus shot to his feet and pulled the priest behind him. His fangs came out and his eyes darkened in readiness to do battle with the intruders, but it was unnecessary. In the doorway, Whitney stood framed against the darkness. She was panting and pale. At her side stood a black wolf, and behind her stood Thomas, alert and ready for a fight.

Madraeus relaxed, retracted his fangs, and straightened.

Whitney started forward slowly.

Madraeus turned back to the priest. "My apologies, Father."

"I see you still have a soldier's reflexes." The priest chuckled, then looked over Madraeus' shoulder at the trio coming up the aisle. "Ah, the friends and family."

They stopped a few feet away. Philtzer sat down and started to whine as he stared up at his boss. The priest looked from one worried face to another. He reached up and squeezed Madraeus' shoulder. "I believe that you are in good hands." His gaze centered on Whitney. "You cannot be so far gone if a woman like that comes rushing to find you with so much worry in her eyes."

Madraeus looked back at Whitney. Her face was drawn and filled with fearful concern. Her eyes switched from him to the priest. It was clear that she wasn't understanding their conversation. They were still speaking in French.

The priest smiled. "Love can be a wonderful balm to the soul."

"Love?" Madraeus searched Whitney's expression. "Can she love me after all I've done?"

"No one worries that much unless they love." The priest patted him on the arm. "Go home. Be loved. It will heal you more than my preaching at you." He chuckled and offered his hand to Madraeus. "Be at peace, my son."

"Thank you, Father." Madraeus shook the priest's hand, turned and bowed in the direction of the altar, and then walked down the aisle toward Whitney, Thomas, and Philtzer.

"You alright, boss?" Thomas stepped forward.

"Yes." Madraeus suddenly realized that he hadn't heard the voice while he'd been talking with the priest. He glanced back at the priest who sat gazing up at the stained glass window. Madraeus turned back to his friends. "Yes. I am now." He reached down and ruffled Philtzer's fur. The wolf jumped up and started to wag his tail. "Let's go."

As soon as they stepped out into the night, Whitney punched him.

"What was that for?" Madraeus gasped, rubbing his shoulder.

Whitney cradled her hand and hopped around in pain, making Thomas laugh. Madraeus glanced at him, then looked back at Whitney.

"You disappeared again!" Whitney cried, rubbing her knuckles and glaring at him. "Not a word! Just poof, gone!"

Philtzer growled under his breath, and Thomas stopped laughing.

"We didn't know where you went! We had to get Philtzer to track you down!" Whitney gestured at the black wolf. Her tears glinted in the light of the street lamps. "We thought—"

"You thought I'd gone crazy again?" Madraeus looked at each of them. They had been right to worry. Slowly, he stepped toward her. He reached out and wrapped his hand around her sore one, massaging her knuckles. "I'm sorry. I needed to clear my head. I needed to get some control."

Whitney reared back and searched his face.

The intensity of her gaze sent a shiver of apprehension through him. "What's wrong?"

She opened her mouth to answer but stopped and shook her head. "Nothing. We should get back. The others are worried." She pulled her hand free of his grasp and walked away down the street.

Every time Whitney hid things, it always turned disastrous. Madraeus glanced at Thomas. "What was all that about?"

Thomas refused to look him in the eye. He turned and hurried to catch up with her.

"Am I missing something?" He looked down at Philtzer.

The wolf laid his ears back and whined.

"Don't suppose you want to transform and tell me?" Madraeus frowned, but Philtzer only growled at him. "Guess I'll have to wait then."

Apologies

Whitney walked quickly down the darkened street. She could hear Thomas catching up to her, but she wanted to be alone. From the moment that Philtzer had announced that Madraeus was missing, she had felt nothing but dread and terror. Her fear had grown as they searched for Madraeus. The idea that he could be rampaging through the streets on another killing spree had almost frozen her to the spot. She never wanted to face him down like she had in that garden. She never wanted to see that kind of evil on his face again. However, she also knew they couldn't just wait and see if he was going to freak out and kill again; they had to go looking for him. She didn't know if she was more afraid for his would-be victims or for Madraeus himself. When he had come out of his rampage last time, he had clung to her as if afraid she wasn't real. Vulnerable and scared Madraeus was almost as terrifying as out-of-control, angry Madraeus.

"Hey! Whit?" Thomas called after her as she crossed yet another street.

She sighed and kept walking. She wasn't ready to talk yet. She was still coming down from the terror-induced adrenaline rush.

She heard him running up behind her. "Whitney!"

"What?" she snapped, turning to face him.

Thomas took one look at her expression and held his hands up in surrender. "Just wanted to tell you—"

"What?"

"You're going the wrong way." Thomas pointed back to where Philtzer and Madraeus were waiting at the corner.

"Oh." Her shoulders slumped. "Sorry."

"Hey, it's okay." Thomas grinned. "Been a helluva night."

"Are there any other kinds anymore?" Whitney muttered.

Thomas snorted. "Doesn't seem like it."

"Were your lives always like this?" Whitney glanced toward Madraeus. "Or just since you met me?"

"Just since you," Thomas said.

Whitney stumbled to a stop.

He elbowed her. "I'm kidding." They started walking again. "It's usually not quite this intense. Cecelia is really going all out this time."

"That's not very comforting."

"There is one thing, though."

"What?" She couldn't take much more.

"We really need to teach you how to punch."

"Oh, shut up." Whitney took a swing at him and missed.

"Told ya." Thomas grinned.

They rejoined the others and turned down the right street. Whitney refused to look at Madraeus even though she could feel him watching her. She had no idea what to say to him. She hadn't spoken to him since the kiss in the coffin. Her reaction had left things awkward between them. Chasing him down and punching him hadn't alleviated that awkwardness. His comment about needing to gain control hadn't helped either. She couldn't help wondering if he was listening to Apep in his head.

As they neared the safe house, Philtzer growled and yipped at Thomas. He took off, bouncing and running. Thomas grinned and shot after him.

"Couple of puppies." Madraeus shook his head. "They'll never grow up."

Whitney watched them race and smiled sadly. "I wish I could be as carefree with all this going on."

Madraeus sighed. "As do I."

She hadn't meant to strike up a conversation with him, not yet.

"I am sorry, Whitney," Madraeus said quietly. "I didn't mean to worry you."

"Worry me?" Whitney scoffed. "You scared the crap out of me!"

"That was not my intention."

"Exactly what was your intention?"

"Whitney," Madraeus sighed.

"No, tell me." Whitney stopped and grabbed his arm, pulling him around to face her. "What did you think you were doing?"

"I already told you, I needed to clear my head."

"You could have cleared your head back at the house."

Madraeus suppressed a shiver as he thought about the voice. "No, I couldn't have."

Whitney crossed her arms. "Yes, you could have."

"No. I couldn't." Madraeus growled. His expression turned peevish. "Besides, now you know how it feels."

"How what feels?"

"You disappeared on us after Justin attacked you. It scared us all."

"You're going to compare that to this? That was totally a different situation."

"How?"

"Seriously?" Whitney threw up her hands. "I took off once to the gym to clear my head. There wasn't even the remotest possibility of me killing anyone! You, you rampaged through a whole village, then disappeared!"

Madraeus stepped closer, but she was too angry to back up. "I wasn't planning on killing anyone!"

"We didn't know that!" Madraeus glared at her, but she forged ahead anyway, refusing to be intimidated. "If you were Mr. Stable and Calm, then why sneak out?"

"Mr. Stable and Calm?" Madraeus snorted. "I am the head of the Council of Races. I *am* stable and calm!"

"Yeah, right. That's why you went out a window." Whitney rolled her eyes. "Look, I know something else is going on."

"What are you talking about?"

"I know you think you can handle whatever is going on with you, but you can't. Not alone."

"Just what do you think is going on with me?"

Whitney closed her mouth with a snap. She hadn't meant to mention their suspicions about his mental state. She shook her head and turned away. "Nothing."

"Wait a minute!"

She didn't respond. She just kept walking. She hurried ahead to the safe house, hoping to leave him behind. Once inside, she planned on hiding in her room, but he was right on her heels. Before she could reach the elevator, he grabbed her arm and spun her around.

"We're not finished," he snarled.

Fortunately for her, the elevator door slid open, and she was saved from responding by Rami exclaiming, "You found him!"

Unkhabami stepped from the elevator. Her gaze slid from Whitney to Madraeus and down to where his hand still held her arm.

Madraeus let go of Whitney and turned to Rami. "You're up."

"Yes, I am nearly back to normal." Rami sent a grateful glance at Unkhabami.

"I'm glad."

"We were worried," Rami said as Madraeus stepped into the elevator.

"So I've been told." Madraeus glanced at Whitney as she followed Unkhabami into the elevator. She moved until the priestess was between her and Madraeus.

They returned to the apartment in awkward silence. Once inside, Rami sank down onto the couch with a sigh of relief.

Madraeus searched his friend's face and apologized, "I'm sorry. I did not mean to worry you."

Rami gave him a short nod that seemed to sweep away the entire matter. Whitney envied him the ability to just let it go.

Whitney noticed Philtzer as he came down the hallway, still buttoning his shirt. He grinned at her as he disappeared into the kitchen.

"So, what happened?" Rami looked from Madraeus to Whitney.

Neither spoke. They just glared at one another across the room.

"You should have seen me!" Philtzer said from the kitchen. "I was amazing!" He came into the living room, holding a bag of cookies. Philtzer launched into an embellished version of how they had tracked and found Madraeus.

Thomas came in and handed a bottle and two glasses to Madraeus and Rami. Hamilton and Sophia joined them a moment later.

As Philtzer's story got more outlandish, Thomas tried to rein him in and steer the story closer to the truth. Between bites of cookie, Philtzer argued for his hero status in the story.

Whitney hovered by the door, watching. She couldn't bring herself to sit down with them. She was still too angry at Madraeus and, if truth be told, more than a little scared.

She watched him and dread filled her. If he was being manipulated by the snake demon, everyone here could be destroyed. Then again, if Madraeus learned they were lying to him, he would see it as the ultimate betrayal. Who knows how he would react to that? Whitney's heart stumbled as she looked around at Philtzer, Rami, Thomas, Hamilton, Sophia, and even Unkhabami. She couldn't bear the thought that any of them could die. Her gaze strayed back to Madraeus. She couldn't stand the thought of losing him either.

Madraeus felt her watching him and turned. He said nothing. His eyes bored into her, promising that he would find her later and finish their conversation. Whitney jumped as Sandra appeared by her side.

Sandra glanced from her to Madreaus. "Come on. Let's get some tea."

Whitney let Sandra pull her into the kitchen, grateful for the excuse to postpone that confrontation.

NEXT MOVE

MADRAEUS SAT LISTENING TO Philtzer embellish his part in the search. He really didn't think it needed that much drama. He'd gone to clear his head, that was all, and yet everyone was turning it into a near apocalypse. Especially Whitney.

He turned and caught her watching him.

He growled under his breath. *Mr. Stable and Calm indeed.*

Rage built in him as he thought of those words. She made it sound like he had jumped out the window just so he could wash the streets with blood. Madraeus scowled. *After all the times she'd disappeared or led us on some merry chase because she'd gotten some stupid idea in her head, she has the audacity to lecture me about disappearing?*

The worst part was that she was right. He had left because he hadn't felt in control. He had been scared that he would lash out and hurt someone. Perhaps he shouldn't have disappeared out the window. Perhaps he should have told them he needed air and walked out the front door. All he'd done was put everyone on edge. They'd be watching him now, waiting for any sign that he wasn't in control.

He looked around the room, trying to see if they were watching him. He waited for the covert glances and suspicious gazes, but they were too caught up in Philtzer's antics. He turned to glare at Whitney again, but she was gone.

Madraeus frowned. What had she meant about knowing something was going on with him?

She couldn't possibly know about the hissing voice that plagued him. Maybe she just meant the incident in the village. But if that was it, then why had she walked away and refused to talk to him about it?

"Madraeus!" Rami poked him with the toe of his shoe.

His attention snapped back to the conversation. "What?"

Rami raised his eyebrows. "Thomas said that Lady Douglas called."

Thomas perched on the arm of the chair that Hamilton was sitting in. "Lady Douglas was attacked assassination style."

"Is she...?"

"She's fine." Thomas grinned. "No one in their right mind should try to sneak up on her."

"Cecelia isn't in her right mind." Madraeus shook his head. "What about the others? The rest of the council?"

"Everyone loyal to the council was hit." Thomas shrugged and looked down. "Some dead. Some not. We can't go back to Denver. They came after Hamilton and Cody and burnt my place to the ground."

"Lady Douglas was pretty pissed about your little party in Germany too," Philtzer said, gesturing with a cookie.

Madraeus couldn't bring himself to say anything about his rampage, not without making them all question his sanity, so he remained silent.

Philtzer continued, "But with all the other attacks happening, she's changed her tune."

"In what way?" Madraeus could feel the hair on the back of his neck prickling as a sense of doom rose in his chest.

Philtzer grimaced. "Think 'The Purge' but with the Races."

"She plans to wipe out anyone who is against the council." Thomas clarified, "Anyone who supports Cecelia or her ideas, that is."

"She cannot!" Rami muttered. "She will start a war."

"I agree with her." Unkhabami sat forward.

Madraeus stared at her in shock. "What?"

"My village has been destroyed by ghouls. All gone. Nothing left but ashes." Unkhabami gazed at Madraeus steadily.

Madraeus could see in her eyes that there was so much more to her story. There was also a warning not to ask about it. Madraeus bowed his head, honoring her pain. "I am sorry, Priestess."

"I destroyed them." Unkhabami smiled slowly, showing her teeth. "Cecelia will pay for their deaths, I promise you. And anyone who supports her will share her fate."

Madraeus raised an eyebrow. He couldn't remember the priestess ever getting involved in a conflict outside of her territory. Madraeus wondered if Cecelia knew what she'd unleashed when she'd upset Unkhabami.

If Unkhabami and Lady Douglas are both on the warpath, Madraeus thought, *the Races may not survive the immediate future.*

"Oh, and Whitney got arrested by the FBI," Philtzer blurted with more than a little of his normal mischief.

"What?" Madraeus snapped.

Thomas raised his hand sheepishly. "In her defense, they came looking for me."

"You?" Madraeus stared at the werewolf. "Why?"

"I didn't do it on purpose." Thomas shook his head. "Police tracked down my plates. Must have gotten them on the mountain when we were escaping from the mine. They came to the office looking for me, and Whitney was there looking for you."

Madraeus' heart leapt at the idea that Whitney had come looking for him, but he had to put the thought aside as Thomas continued.

"She lied about seeing me, and of course, that made them suspicious, especially when the cop noticed the bites and bruises on her arms. So, they arrested her."

"Whitney!" Madraeus bellowed. "Come in here."

Silence answered Madraeus' command, followed by urgent whispering in the kitchen.

Thomas and Philtzer exchanged a wary look, then they both looked to Rami. He gave them a nod as if to say, *It will be all right.*

"Whitney!"

The sound of the kitchen chairs sliding across the floor seemed extra loud.

Whitney poked her head around the corner. Her face was a mask of wariness.

"Come here," Madraeus growled and instantly regretted it. Her expression changed from apprehension to anger in the breadth of a heartbeat.

"Don't order me around!" she said as she came fully into the living room. She crossed her arms and glared at him. "I'm not your dog!" Whitney, realizing what she said, glanced around at the werewolves. "No offense."

"None taken." Philtzer grinned and turned to watch his boss' reaction.

Madraeus couldn't help but admire the sparkle in her eyes. She always glowed when she argued with him. It was part of the reason he'd felt alive again after so many centuries. After the kiss in the coffin, he had been afraid she'd lost it. Something opened inside his chest, and the rage and grief he'd been feeling eased. Madraeus took a long, deep breath, then asked calmly, "You were arrested?"

Whitney lifted her chin defiantly. "Yeah, so?"

Out of the corner of his eye, Madraeus caught Philtzer grinning and frowned. "And...?"

"And... it's sorted." Whitney flushed. Madraeus narrowed his eyes as she stumbled over her explanation. "Mrs. M sent a pixie in."

"Which pixie?" Madraeus asked.

"Cherry."

Madraeus groaned. He could only imagine what kind of chaos Cherry had left behind. "And you just walked out of the station?"

"Well, first we stole all the files on the Races, then we left." Whitney waved her hand in the air like it was no big deal. "It's fine."

"Files?" Madraeus looked to Rami, who shrugged.

"Pretty detailed ones," Sandra said from the doorway behind Whitney. "You should probably worry about Agent Milner."

Whitney threw a worried glance at Sandra.

Madraeus asked, "Do they know where you are right now?"

Whitney thought of her grandmother and paled. "Um..." She shrugged and gestured at Thomas and Hamilton. "They got me a fake passport."

Madraeus wondered at her sudden color change but turned his attention to the werewolves. At that moment, Hamilton's phone buzzed. He pulled out his phone as he hurried out of the room.

Madraeus sat back and rubbed his forehead. "We need to get this situation under control."

"Agreed," Rami's deep voice rumbled as Hamilton came back in.

"Good news," he wiggled his phone at them, "paperwork's done. We can make the channel crossing tomorrow night."

Vhitney's tone caught Madraeus' at-
'n time to see her exchange a worried

ntil nearly midnight."

ne coffin this time." Thomas grinned

Not really." Hamilton winced at the look Madraeus gave him. "We won't arrive until around nine in the morning. Sorry, boss."

"It's fine." Madraeus sighed, resigning himself to another long trip in a box. "Why are we crossing the channel?" Madraeus looked from Hamilton to Rami, just missing the pointed look that Thomas sent Philtzer.

"Heading to England next!" Philtzer chirped.

"What's in England?"

Philtzer shrugged. "More red pins."

Philtzer's unusually short answer set off an alarm bell in Madraeus' head. "Is that all?"

"Yeah." Philtzer shoved a handful of cookies into his mouth.

Madraeus glanced around the room, but no one would meet his eyes.

"We should get packing." Thomas stood and shooed Sandra and Whitney into the hallway.

Rami sighed. "I am not looking forward to another coffin ride, but it cannot be helped."

After that, the room emptied rather quickly, leaving Madraeus sitting alone.

That was odd, he frowned.

He wandered out onto the balcony and stared down at the dock. He replayed the scene in his mind, trying to find the reason for the mood shift, but he couldn't find it. For some reason he got the feeling that they were keeping something from him, but why? And what could it be? It was just like Whitney in the street earlier. Something was definitely wrong.

TRUCE

Whitney tossed and turned for hours.

After the scene in the living room, she had managed to avoid Madraeus long enough to get to bed without another confrontation, but it hadn't given her any peace. Her mind kept replaying the scene in the garden. No matter how hard she tried, she couldn't get the picture of Madraeus in all of his terrifying glory out of her mind. She tried to think about something else, but his image kept intruding.

Finally, she fell asleep reciting multiplication tables. She was bad enough at math that it kept her mind off Madraeus, but it didn't last.

Whitney woke suddenly. Ripped from sleep by another nightmare, she sat panting and clutching the blankets. Her eyes traveled slowly around the dark room. She could hear breathing. In her logical mind, she knew it was just Sandra or Sophia, but deep down, her primal instincts were urging her to run. Breathing in the dark could only be a predator.

With shaking hands, she pulled the blankets back and slowly slipped her feet to the floor. Someone in the room turned over. It was innocent enough, but it set Whitney's heart pounding. Forcing her limbs out of paralysis, she crept toward the door. Holding her hands in front of her, she moved slowly until finally her fingertips brushed against the wood. She almost cried out in relief as she found the doorknob. Quickly, she slipped out into the hallway and let out a shuddering breath. The hall was filled with the soft glow of light from the living room.

She inched her way toward the light, hoping that someone was up, but the living room was empty. The TV in the corner was on, but the sound was so low it was almost inaudible. The screen displayed the latest news from Germany. Whitney stared at the pictures of Madraeus' handiwork and shook her head.

How are we ever going to get past this mess?

Whitney glanced around, wondering who had been watching the TV. The door to the balcony was open, and a cool breeze wafted in, making the curtain flutter. Maybe they'd gone outside for some air. She hoped it was Rami. She had always found comfort in the giant's presence. Silently, she drifted toward the balcony door. She stepped out into the cool darkness and looked around. She couldn't see anyone.

Maybe they're in the kitchen, she thought.

She heard something move behind her. She spun around and caught a glimpse of a shadowy figure. Whitney yelped and dodged away but miscalculated her surroundings. She tripped over a chair and fell into the corner, knocking over a potted plant. She scrambled around, trying to get her feet under her, but she only managed to scatter the potting soil across the balcony. She nearly screamed when the figure bent over her and grabbed her by the upper arms. Whitney thrashed around, trying to break free. It was her nightmare all over again. But instead of trying to attack her, the figure merely pulled her to her feet.

"Whitney! Calm down. You're fine. You're safe. Whitney!"

Whitney stopped struggling and looked up to see Madraeus' face only inches from hers.

"Are you all right?" he asked quietly.

She knew she should say yes but found herself shaking her head instead.

"My poor Whitney," Madraeus sighed and pulled her into his arms. He held her protectively just like he had after Justin had attacked her, and for a moment, she didn't care that he was a vampire. She didn't care that he'd murdered sixty-six people in the mine. She didn't care that he had killed so many in Germany. She only cared that someone was there to take care of her.

The tears came quickly. She cried and cried until she started to feel stupid for crying, and then she cried some more. All the while, he just held her. He stroked her hair and whispered comforting words, just as he had weeks ago in her apartment after Justin had killed her friend. She didn't notice how long she stood there blubbering, but finally her well of tears ran dry.

"I'm sorry." She sniffed and blinked away the droplets stuck on her eyelashes. "I got your shirt all wet, again."

"It's all right," Madraeus muttered into her hair. "I don't mind."

Whitney backed out of his arms and turned toward the balcony. She reached out and wrapped her fingers around the cold, metal railing as she tried to calm her nerves. Across the road, she could see the ships in the harbor bobbing up and down.

"You really should see about that bell." Whitney tried to laugh as she rubbed away the tears that clung to her face. It seemed like a lifetime ago that she'd told him he needed to wear a bell so he couldn't sneak up on her.

"I'll see what I can do." He smiled sadly. "I didn't mean to scare you."

"Don't flatter yourself," Whitney scoffed. "At the moment, a kitten would scare me."

"Completely understandable," Madraeus said as he moved up to the railing beside her. "Kittens can be terrifying."

Whitney glanced at him, wondering if this was one of those rare moments when he was trying to be funny, but his expression remained serious as he stared out toward the harbor.

Silence stretched out between them. She debated asking him if he was scared of cats.

"What are you doing out here?" He turned toward her. "Are you spying on me? I don't intend to slip away again if that's what you wanted to know."

"I'm not checking up on you." Whitney sighed and rubbed her eyes. "I didn't even know you were out here."

After a moment, he took a step closer to her. "Then why are you up?"

She refused to answer.

"Look at me," he commanded softly, and after a moment, she slowly turned.

In the dim light from the street lamps, she couldn't see his eyes, but she felt the intensity of his gaze, nonetheless.

"Bad dreams again?"

She peered at him suspiciously. "How do you know I was having bad dreams?"

"I've seen that look on your face before."

"Oh." She turned back to stare at the ships.

"Do you want me to make you some cocoa?"

The question caught her off guard. She looked at him sharply.

"You said it helped with bad dreams."

She stared at him. "I can't believe you remembered."

"I remember everything," he murmured.

The flickering light from the TV glowed through the door and caught her eye. She tipped her head toward it. "Is that why you're out here? Because you're remembering?"

"Are you accusing me of having an attack of conscience?"

"No. Yes." She shook her head and stared out at the harbor again. "I don't know."

"I have a conscience, Whitney."

"I know you do."

"It's not like I wanted to kill an entire village!"

"Then why did you?" She looked at him and was startled to see the pain on his face.

"Damn it!" He slammed his fist into the railing, making it vibrate. "I wish I could explain."

Whitney let go and stepped back.

He turned and caught her by the upper arms. "Don't run from me."

"I'm not running." She wanted to, but his expression was so desolate that she knew she couldn't go. "Truth is, whatever is going on with you scares the crap out of me."

"Me too," he muttered. He gave her shoulders a gentle squeeze and slowly let her go.

She wasn't sure what to say to that. He had always been the strong leader, completely unshakable. The thought of him being as scared as she was sounded so impossible that she almost blurted out what she knew about the Psycho Snake Radio. She managed to stop the words from passing her lips.

"Madraeus," Whitney began but stopped. She wasn't entirely certain what she wanted to say.

"I know." He spoke like a man walking on thin ice. "I'm sorry. I'm scaring you again." He looked up at the stars and sighed. "That's all I ever seem to do."

"That's not true," Whitney whispered. "You've saved me time and again. I mean, yes, sometimes lately, you scare me, but..." she reached out and touched his arm.

He looked down at her hand and covered it with his own. "Shall we have a truce then?"

"A truce?"

Madraeus looked up into her eyes. "I'll try to stop scaring you if you stop digging at me."

"I'm not digging at you," Whitney blurted.

"You know what I mean." He held out his hand. "Truce?"

Whitney stared at it, then reached out and shook it. "All right."

His thumb brushed back and forth across the back of her hand while his eyes held hers. "Come with me?"

"Where?"

When she hesitated, he added, "I won't hurt you. I will never hurt you." He gave a gentle tug and started for the balcony door. She followed him. He led her into the living room and over to the couch. He gestured for her to sit, then grabbed the blanket from the back of the couch and tucked it around her. "Stay."

Without waiting for her protest, he left. She glanced over her shoulder and saw him disappear into the kitchen. The continuing coverage on the TV caught her attention. She couldn't stand to watch it, so she began looking for the remote. By the time she found it tucked down between the cushions, Madraeus was back.

"Sorry, it's not cocoa." He handed her a mug and sat down about an arm's length away. "There was no chocolate. I hope just milk will work."

"Thank you." She took the cup but stopped before taking a sip and stared at it.

"What's wrong?"

"Last time you made me cocoa, I conked out for almost two days." She watched him suspiciously and was gratified to see him squirm a little.

"Well," he smiled slyly, "this isn't cocoa."

Whitney snorted at that minor distinction, and that made him really smile for a moment. Whitney liked it when he smiled. He seemed less intense, less world-weary.

He sobered and looked down at his hands. "You needed the rest, and I needed you safe."

"And this time?" She watched him over the rim of the cup.

They stared at each other.

His voice was barely a whisper. "You still need the rest, and I still need you safe."

Whitney swallowed past the lump in her throat. "I doubt I'll be getting much more sleep tonight."

"You could sleep out here," Madraeus offered.

"Here?"

"I promise not to bother you."

Whitney bit her lip. She was far too tempted to say yes. Sleeping on the couch with the lights on and the TV going would definitely make it seem less like the mine. But could she sleep with Madraeus sitting there, too?

Madraeus slid closer. Whitney pulled her knees up. He leaned forward and took the empty cup from her hands. He set it on the end table behind her. He was so close. He turned his face toward her. She could feel his breath on her cheek. She watched him, thinking of the kiss they'd shared in the coffin. She wondered if he was going to kiss her again. His gaze bored into her. She felt like she was in a trance. The room felt much warmer than it had a moment ago. He touched her shoulder and gave a gentle push. Obediently, she slid down onto the throw pillow that sat against the armrest. He hovered over her. His lips parted. The air buzzed and hummed, and she found herself wishing he *would* kiss her again. He swayed closer, but then he pulled back. He tucked the blanket up around her and smoothed her hair back.

His voice sent a shiver over her skin. "Go to sleep, Whitney."

She felt a sudden desire to make him stay beside her, but he was already sitting at the other end of the couch. She closed her eyes, trying to get a hold on her emotions and thinking that this was going to be a long night.

LISTENING

The journey across the Channel was uneventful, completely uncomfortable, but uneventful.

They had split up the group to make crossing into England less suspicious. Thomas and Philtzer once again became delivery men, driving a truck with two coffins inside. Sandra, Hamilton, Sophia, and Whitney split into pairs to cross, and Unkhabami opted to cross on her own.

Madraeus had once again debased himself to traveling by coffin. Cramped and filled with painful memories, Madraeus hated it.

He wanted nothing more than to be out and free. However, even if he did get out of the coffin, he was still confined inside the cargo area of the van. It would make things complicated if the crew noticed someone getting out of the back of a vehicle that supposedly only contained two corpses. When he could finally feel the gentle sway of the ferry as it moved out into open water, he lifted the lid and sat up.

Rami's coffin sat across from his, but the lid was still closed. He knew Rami would choose to sleep, gaining a little extra healing time, but still, he willed the lid to open. He desperately wanted to talk to Rami about Whitney.

But then he *would* have to talk to Rami, and he wasn't sure he wanted to hear what Rami would say, so he willed the lid to stay closed.

Madraeus rubbed his face. He didn't know what he wanted anymore.

Yes, he did. He wanted to go back to his peaceful existence of managing InfiniCorp and putting out fires for the Races. He wanted to be done with this soul-racking pain that had consumed him since meeting Whitney. And yet... he didn't want to give up Whitney. He wanted to take her somewhere quiet and just be, but who knew if that would ever happen.

Sitting on the couch next to her while she slept last night was both heaven and hell. To have her so close, and yet, not be able to do anything about it had been torture. Like a pathetic fool, he had spent most of the night watching her sleep. She had been afraid, and yet, she hadn't left. She'd stayed in the living room with him. That had to be a good sign. Unless it had nothing to do with him, and it was just because she needed the company to keep away the nightmares.

Madraeus sighed. Thinking along this line would drive him crazy. This was going to be a long trip. Perhaps it would go faster if he slept through it. He slid back down into his coffin, wishing that he'd thought to bring a book.

Sometime after sunrise, Madraeus felt the van stop. The door rattled as it rolled up. He heard everyone file into the back. The door rolled down again. Once more, the van was in motion.

"I am not sitting on a coffin." He heard Whitney say. "It's creepy."

"Then sit on the floor." Sandra's logical response followed.

"You'll be sorry." Hamilton's voice came from near the foot of Madraeus' coffin. "Trust me. In a few minutes, your butt'll be numb."

"I'm still not sitting on a coffin," Whitney grumbled, making Madraeus smile. Originally, he had not thought her willful, rebellious attitude an asset, but he was beginning to appreciate her stubbornness. "How much longer?"

"Couple of hours."

Madraeus wondered where they were going. He hadn't been able to get a straight answer out of anyone before leaving Le Havre.

"Any thoughts on how we're going to—" Whitney's question cut off abruptly.

Madraeus frowned. *What was she going to ask?* Madraeus strained his ears, but he couldn't hear anything else. Silence stretched out for minutes, but still he couldn't detect any hint of what was going on. Suspicion and rage built in his chest. *What are they trying to hide from me?* Somewhere deep in his mind, he heard a hissing laugh. He closed his eyes and tried to bury it.

"Are we going to stop for food?" Sophia broke the silence.

Sandra laughed. "You sound like Philtzer."

Sophia snorted. "That ferry food wasn't exactly filling."

"I'll agree with that." Hamilton chuckled. "They thought Philtzer and Thomas were going to clean them out."

"I wish I had your metabolism," Whitney said, "but not your appetite."

"It does get annoying," Sophia complained. "I used to barely eat. Now, all I do is look for food. It's like my whole day is nothing but one long fridge raid."

"Just one of the many joys of becoming a werewolf?" Sandra asked.

"Yeah, right." He could almost hear Sophia rolling her eyes.

"My butt is numb," Whitney grumbled.

"I told you!" Hamilton laughed. "Come on. Sit up here."

"Dude! He's in there." Whitney hissed.

"So?" Hamilton laughed. "It's not like he's dead. It's not a real coffin."

"Eww!" Whitney's reluctance was almost comical.

Madraeus growled. It was bad enough being stuck in this coffin, but to be the subject of a conversation that he couldn't participate in was irritating.

"Would it make you feel better if we asked him first?" Hamilton's voice shook with barely controlled laughter.

"No!" Whitney barked. "It's fine. I'll sit."

Madraeus knew that he couldn't actually feel when she sat on the coffin, but he knew she was there, nonetheless. Slowly, he reached out a hand to where he thought she was sitting and touched the lid. He closed his eyes, wishing he could really touch her, but he knew he had to wait. He had to make the fear fade from her eyes. Last night had been a good start, but then again, what if she couldn't handle the idea of being loved by him?

The hissing voice rose from deep in his mind, laughing at his plans and stealing his confidence. He clenched his fists. He would not, could not, let that voice control him again.

He thought back to the cathedral and the little round priest. What had he said that had made the voice fade? He couldn't remember the exact moment when it had faded, but he did remember the words he had used. *Put on the full armor of God, so that you can take your stand...* He didn't fully understand it, but he wished he had some kind of armor to shield him from its hissing influence. The voice hissed again, and Madraeus began to mutter every prayer he could remember.

Madraeus didn't notice time passing until suddenly someone was knocking on his coffin lid.

"Hey, boss?" Philtzer knocked again. "You awake?"

"Yes." Madraeus dragged his thoughts back together again.

"We're here," Philtzer called.

"Where is here?" Madraeus reached up and pushed the lid open. He glanced around. The rear door of the truck was closed. Rami was sitting up, watching them.

"Hotel on the edge of Exeter, near Broadclyst." Philtzer sat down on the end of Rami's coffin. "We managed to get a couple of connecting suites. The girls get one, and we get the other. Lucky for us, they both have balconies. Easy escape routes."

Philtzer shrugged. "Everyone else headed in already, but it's still daylight."

"Great." Madraeus glanced at Rami.

"You want us to try and get you inside? Or you wanna wait until night?"

"People do not normally bring coffins into hotels," Rami rumbled.

"Modern hotel?" Madraeus asked, and Philtzer nodded. "Parking garage?"

"Nope."

"Is it at least cloudy?" Madraeus asked hopefully. They might get away with an overcast sky and hoods.

"Nope." Philtzer was enjoying this too much. "Bright and sunny."

"Lovely." Madraeus sighed and rubbed his face. "Guess we'll wait here for a while."

"Brought you a deck of cards." Philtzer grinned and reached into his pocket. "Want me to bring you anything else?"

"We'll be fine." Madraeus took the card deck with less than good grace.

"Cool." Philtzer stood and brushed off his pants. "I'll come get you later. The others should be in by then."

"Others?" Madraeus looked up at the young werewolf.

"Yeah, Cody and Malcolm and a couple others." Philtzer shrugged and reached for the door. "Duck and cover." He waited only a moment for them to hunker down and close their lids before rolling up the door.

Madraeus waited to hear the door close again, then opened his coffin and sat up. He looked over at Rami. "Why are the others coming?"

"If I remember correctly, there were quite a few pins clustered around Broadclyst. I believe we will need the help."

"More than likely," Madraeus agreed, but deep down, the hissing voice whispered that they were coming to stand against him. Madraeus stared at the cards, willing the voice away. Slowly, he began to shuffle the deck. As he did, one of the cards slipped out and landed on the floor. He reached out and picked it up. It was the ten of spades. He stared at it and then looked at Rami. "I think we should send Whitney home."

"Why?" Rami sat up a little straighter.

Madraeus looked back down at the ten of spades. "I think it would be safer for her. Something's coming. Something that I don't want anywhere near her." Madraeus shuddered as he heard the echoing hiss in his mind. "Something bad."

"We cannot send her away." The sadness in Rami's tone caught Madraeus' attention. The giant sighed. "You have not been yourself, my friend. Your reaction in the village is evidence of that. She brought you out of your rampage. If you lose control again, we will need her."

"No! You're not going to use her like that again!"

"We may have no choice, my friend."

"No!" Madraeus snapped. "Never again!"

"Can you promise me that you will not lose control again?" Rami snapped at him.

Madraeus stared at his friend. It wasn't often that Rami lost his temper.

The hissing laughter filled Madraeus' head.

"I will not lose control," Madraeus said, although he wasn't sure if he was speaking to the voice or to Rami. "I'll do whatever is necessary to keep her safe."

"And that is why we need her to stay."

ENGLAND

WHITNEY LOOKED AROUND THE girls' suite. The room looked like a food court had exploded. Thomas had found a Chinese takeaway, Philtzer had raided a fish 'n chip shop, and Sophia had found a pizzeria. The result was nearly every item on the menu from all three places ending up in their hotel suite.

Whitney sighed, "I'm stuffed."

"Me too." Sandra blew out a long breath and slouched back against the couch. "Do you think we finally filled up the puppies?"

"Yeah," Whitney snorted as she scooped empty boxes into a trash bag, "for the next five minutes."

"I think you have to be rich to be a werewolf," Sandra mused.

"Why?"

"How else can they afford all that food?"

Whitney chuckled. "Good point."

"What about them?" Sandra nodded toward the door leading to the other suite. Through the open door, they could see Madraeus and Rami talking quietly with Unkhabami.

Whitney sobered. "I don't know. They had bottles of blood at the safe house. Maybe they brought some with them."

"Now whose practical side is scary?" Sandra smirked.

"What do you mean?" Whitney turned to look at her.

"You. Being so casual about carting around bottles of blood."

Whitney shrugged. "Occupational hazard."

Just then, the wolves came through the door carrying several duffel bags.

After dropping the bags onto the bed, they started to check through their supplies. Whitney watched Thomas unpack and repack a medical bag. Philtzer laid out a pile of weapons that included knives, crossbows, swords, and a wicked thing that looked like chains with handles.

"How did you get all that through customs?" Sandra asked.

Thomas didn't even look up. "We didn't have to."

It was a sobering thought to realize that they had weaponry available wherever they went. Whitney shot a worried glance at the other room and hoped they wouldn't have to use it on Madraeus.

She looked back at Sandra and whispered, "Do we have a plan yet?"

Sandra shook her head. "We have to wait until the last possible minute."

"When is that?" Whitney hissed.

"I don't know." Sandra covertly peered at Madraeus

Whitney picked up a wadded-up food wrapper and threw it at Philtzer. It sailed past his leg, but even missing, she still managed to get his attention. He looked at her with his eyebrows raised. She couldn't ask him outright without Madraeus hearing her, so she tried sign language. She jerked her thumb toward the other suite and gave him the *Well?* expression.

"What?" Philtzer mouthed, cocking his head, looking completely confused.

Whitney rolled her eyes and gestured toward Madraeus again. Philtzer gave her a blank look. Realizing he was doing it deliberately, Whitney wrinkled her nose and wished she was close enough to kick him. He grinned at her.

"When are you going to tell him?" Whitney mouthed.

"I'm not," Philtzer mouthed. "You are."

Whitney mimed choking Philtzer, which only made him laugh. Thomas stopped adjusting the contents of the medical bag and looked at them both questioningly. Philtzer and Whitney both tried to silently express their side of the argument.

"What are you doing?" Madraeus asked.

Everyone froze mid-mime. In unison, their heads turned. Madraeus stood in the doorway to the other suite, watching them. Whitney could only compare the look on his face to that of a suspicious parent. She swallowed but couldn't find her voice. Nor could she look away to beg Philtzer or Thomas for help.

As the expectant silence wore on, the suspicion on Madraeus' face deepened. Whitney began to panic.

"We were talking about what happens if we find Cecelia," Sandra blurted.

Whitney watched Madraeus run his gaze over them all. Unfortunately, Sandra's excuse didn't erase the suspicion in his eyes. He crossed his arms and leaned against the door frame. "Really? And what conclusions have you come up with?"

Sandra looked from Whitney to Philtzer and then back to Madraeus. "We haven't made it past volunteering each other to talk to you."

Whitney felt her jaw drop as her gaze snapped to Sandra. She couldn't believe how brazenly honest Sandra was. Slowly, she looked back at Madraeus and was shocked to find a smile hovering at the edge of his lips.

"Am I that scary?" Madraeus asked dryly.

"Yes," Sandra said without hesitating.

The smile almost made it to his lips.

"Then shall we all talk? That way, no one has to face me alone?" He looked from Sandra to Philtzer to Whitney.

"What are we talking about?" Rami's voice called from the other suite.

"Apparently," Madraeus said over his shoulder as he flicked a look at Philtzer again, "we are asking about what happens when we find Cecelia."

"Good." Rami appeared in the doorway behind Madraeus. "We need a plan."

Rami prodded Madraeus farther into the room. Philtzer and Thomas moved the piles on the bed aside and sat down. Rami sat with Sandra on the couch, and Whitney sat down on the floor at Rami's feet. Madraeus took the desk chair and sat across from them all.

No one said anything for a long time. Everyone was waiting for someone else to speak first.

Madraeus took pity on them all and asked, "Do we know where Cecelia is?"

"Um," Philtzer looked at the others before continuing, "not really."

"We're still looking," Thomas added.

Madraeus propped his elbow on the arm of the chair and rested his chin in his hand. "So, you are wondering what to do *if* we find Cecelia?"

More uncertain looks were exchanged, and Whitney tried to squash the panic that was growing in her chest. He didn't look like he was buying their excuse.

"You have always told us she is your responsibility," Rami rumbled.

Madraeus met each of their gazes in turn before sighing. He rubbed his hand across his chin thoughtfully. "No more."

"Pardon?" Rami shifted slightly, bumping against Whitney's shoulder.

"I will no longer take responsibility for her. I renounce my vow." Madraeus spoke clearly, looking only at Rami.

Silence followed his declaration.

Rami whispered, "You are sure?"

"Yes." Madraeus nodded. "If you see her, kill her."

Whitney's eyes grew huge.

"She has caused enough pain. I should have seen that centuries ago."

Madraeus looked straight at Whitney as he spoke. She felt like he was saying, *You were right*. In the mine, she had lectured Madraeus that he should have killed Cecelia a long time ago, but she'd been upset and locked in a cage. This was totally different. This was a death sentence. She glanced at the others. They were all nodding in agreement.

"You said there were several pins near here from our map?"

"Yeah." Philtzer jumped in with relief. "Quite a few."

"And do we know if they are friend or foe?" Madraeus asked.

"Umm, yes?" Philtzer grinned.

"Thanks, Philtzer, that's very helpful."

"We aren't sure yet." Thomas elbowed Philtzer. "It could be a combination."

A knock at the door interrupted any further explanation. Philtzer jumped up to answer it. He opened the door only a little, and after a brief conversation, he shut it again. He turned and sent a warning look at Thomas. "That was Sophia. They're downstairs."

Thomas glanced at Madraeus, then looked straight at Whitney. Her heart plummeted. 'They' had to be the Hares. All she could think was, *They can't be here now! We don't have a plan yet!*

"Who is here?" Madraeus glanced around the room.

"Um." Whitney knew he had picked up on the tense looks they were passing each other.

"Who's here?" Madraeus repeated. Rami shrugged, and Sandra shook her head. Whitney avoided his gaze with every trick she could think of.

Whitney tried to catch Philtzer's eye. She needed to know what to do, but he was watching Thomas. Whitney looked to Sandra next. She was watching Madraeus. Whitney stared at her, willing her to look over, and finally she did. Whitney raised her eyebrows, but Sandra could only shrug.

"Is there something going on that I need to know about?" Madraeus asked.

Reluctantly, Whitney turned to find that all of his attention was focused on her. His gaze was so intense that she found the words bubbling up in her throat, ready to spill out from fear. She swallowed them back with difficulty.

Thomas looked at Whitney and muttered, "They're coming up. It's now or never."

SURPRISE

"WHAT'S NOW OR NEVER?" Madraeus glared around the room.

No one would meet his eyes. Whitney looked at Thomas. Thomas looked at Philtzer. The hissing voice of suspicion raised its head once again. He was right. They were hiding things from him.

Thomas took a long breath and looked at Madraeus. "The answer to that question is complicated."

Madraeus' tone turned icy. "Then uncomplicate it."

Hesitant looks were exchanged again.

"Sandra was approached by a couple of individuals who were seeking your help."

"Why Sandra? If it were one of the Races, then why wouldn't they just come to me?" Madraeus frowned.

Philtzer shook his head. "It's not one of the Races."

"Who then?" Madraeus' eyes glittered.

"The Ancient Society of the Three Hares wants your help," Sandra blurted.

"What did you say?" Madraeus shot to his feet and snarled, not realizing his eyes had gone black.

Whitney scrambled to her feet.

Instantly, everyone was standing. Power and menace pulsated through the room. Philtzer and Thomas were both shimmering slightly as they got ready to shift.

Something deep inside of him shuddered as the tension reached a nearly unbearable level. Madraeus' eyes snapped to Whitney. She didn't say anything. She held his gaze, but her whole body was shaking.

She's afraid of me.

Madraeus heard the faint hissing laughter in his mind. He slammed his eyes shut. He would not allow the voice to control him, never again. He took a deep breath, willing his body to relax. He slowly opened his eyes only to find everyone in the room still watching him. Slowly, he sat back down in his chair.

"Perhaps you should start at the beginning." His voice sounded raw.

Cautiously, everyone took their seats. Sandra explained John and Barbie's request that Madraeus help them stop Cecelia.

Madraeus listened quietly, but he could feel his fangs elongating. The very idea that the Hares would come asking for help filled him with rage.

"They should all be destroyed," Madraeus growled.

Yesss! The hissing laughter echoed through his head again. He closed his eyes, forcing himself to remain calm.

"If they are locking up the scary creatures like the ghouls," Sandra gestured toward Unkhabami, "doesn't that make them the good guys?"

"No," Rami and Madraeus said simultaneously.

"The Hares are just as evil as any of the creatures they hunt."

"So, if the good guys are the bad guys, and the bad guys are the bad guys, then who are the *actual* good guys?"

"I think that's us," Whitney sighed.

"Well, that's not good. I've seen your track record of being a good guy," Sandra snorted, looking at Madraeus.

Madraeus glared at her but said nothing. She was right. He wasn't exactly an angel.

"Do we know why the Hares have chosen this moment to ask for aid?" Madraeus asked.

"Apep." Sandra nodded. "Egyptian demon that tries to consume the world with darkness. His venom makes vampires."

Madraeus flashed back to that night in Cyrene again. He could hear the rustling in the dark, something shooting out of the shadows, and knocking him to the ground.

"They said they have Apep locked up here in Broadclyst, and they know Cecelia is coming here next," Sandra continued, "but they don't have enough manpower to stop her. That's where you come in."

"What do you think, boss?" Philtzer asked after Sandra fell silent.

"Why didn't you tell me sooner?" Madraeus eyed them suspiciously.

They don't trussst you, the voice hissed.

"Don't you trust me?" Madraeus looked down at his hands.

"The Hares said that Apep is able to keep in contact with his victims," Sandra added.

"In contact how?" Madraeus asked without looking up.

"We're calling it the Psycho Snake Radio," Sandra smiled in spite of the situation. "We think it's like hearing voices."

Not just voices. The Voice. Madraeus found that he couldn't look at any of them. He felt that somehow, they would see it in his eyes. They would see the shadow of the snake lurking inside him. The room faded away. He could hear the others talking, but he didn't know what they were saying. All of his attention was focused on the truth slithering up out of the darkness. A truth he didn't want to believe. The moment he admitted that Apep was the voice in his head, he heard the sibilant laugh again. He shuddered. He wanted to scream, *No!* He wanted to jump up and pace, but he couldn't. Slowly, he lifted his gaze to find Whitney watching him.

She knew. Or at least she suspected. She had hinted as much that night in the street. Sadness washed over him.

That's it then, he thought, *I will never have her. It's over.*

It didn't matter what happened to him now. The priest had said that love could be a balm to the soul, but losing it was death.

"Madraeus?" Rami called his name, bringing him back into the conversation.

"Did you know?" Madraeus's voice was flat.

The giant shook his head. "This is the first I have heard of it."

"We did not want to risk telling you," Unkhabami said from the doorway, "either of you."

Rami looked up at her. "Why?" The hurt was evident in his voice.

"Apep might have influence over its first-generation offspring," Thomas explained. "We didn't know if either of you are affected. So, what's the verdict? They'll be here any minute."

Madraeus felt like the words were being dragged out of him. "We stop Cecelia. Even if it is with the Hares."

"The enemy of my enemy is my friend?" asked Sandra.

"No," Madraeus growled. "Allies, maybe, but never friends."

"Well," Philtzer rubbed his hands together, "let's get this party started."

"You're messed up in the head," Sandra muttered as they filed into the other room to meet the Hares.

"Come on, babe," Philtzer grinned, "you're having fun and you know it."

"I'm buying you a dictionary for Christmas." Sandra shook her head. "You need to brush up on your definitions of fun."

Philtzer's grin widened.

"What are you smiling about now?" Sandra frowned at him. "I just insulted you."

"Nah, you just said we'd be around for Christmas!" Philtzer laughed. "Shows optimism."

Madraeus let their conversation wash over him. All he could think about was how empty he felt. There wasn't even anger left. He blinked away the darkness and looked around. Everyone had left except Unkhabami and Rami.

Concern filled the giant's face. "You are hearing the voices too?"

Madraeus dropped his hands and looked at his friend. Madraeus slowly nodded.

"How bad is it?"

Madraeus sighed and looked up at the ceiling. "Bad enough."

"The village?" Rami asked after a moment.

"Yes." Madraeus sat forward and braced his elbows on his knees. "I heard it hissing in my head, urging me on."

"Has it ever been this bad?"

"Sometimes. Lindisfarne. Antioch. Paris."

"All times of great strife." Unkhabami nodded. "Apep's most recent capture was during the Revolution."

"I always thought it was Cecelia's demon infecting me." Madraeus shook his head. "Guess I wasn't far off."

Unkhabami nodded. "The Hares said that Apep's influence may increase as his prison weakens."

"Then he must be almost free," Madraeus huffed.

"Is it that strong?" Unkhabami whispered.

Madraeus nodded.

"Are you in control?"

"Sometimes." Madraeus shrugged. "That is why I went to the church. It's helped before."

"And now?"

Madraeus looked over his shoulder toward the other room. He could see Whitney standing with her arms crossed as if trying to hold herself together. "She helps."

"Whitney?"

Madraeus nodded. "I love her, Rami. But I can't be with her. Not like this. I can't endanger her again."

"She was the only thing that stopped you last time." Unkhabami sat forward and grabbed Madraeus' wrist. "You need her. And we need you."

"What about her?" Madraeus' eyes flashed. "She deserves to be safe. To have a life!"

"If Apep is free, none of us will have a life," Unkhabami hissed.

HARES

Whitney wrapped her arms around her waist and watched
the others as they waited for Sophia and Hamilton to bring the
Hares upstairs. She could sense their nervousness. Even Philtzer
wasn't immune. His normal cheerful demeanor seemed a little
too forced. Thomas was pacing and looking out the window.
Sandra sat quietly at the desk in the corner and watched the
door.

Whitney glanced over her shoulder. She could see Unkhabami sitting on the couch, speaking quietly to Madraeus and
Rami. Her expression was terrifying. Whitney shivered. If the
Priestess ever looked at her like that, she would probably die
from a heart attack.

She couldn't see Madraeus. What would he do when the
Hares came in? She knew he was angry. The power she'd felt
earlier coming off of him had been terrifying. It's no wonder
they'd picked him to be the head of the Council of Races. Whitney shivered again when she realized that she had faced down
that much power and survived. If she had been anyone else, the

idea that she could wield that much power over someone like Madraeus would be intoxicating, but instead, it just scared her.

"Whitney?" Rami's voice rumbled behind her. She turned to see him motioning to her to come back into the other room.

"Yeah?" Hesitantly, she moved toward him. Once in the room, she glanced at Madraeus.

"Please," Madraeus stared at Rami, "don't."

"I am sorry, my friend." Rami shook his head. "It is for the best."

"What's for the best?" Whitney's head swiveled, looking from one to the other.

"I am sorry, Whitney, but we need you again," Rami rumbled sadly.

"Need me for what?" Whitney took a step back.

"They want you to be my leash," Madraeus spat out.

"Leash?"

"What he means is that you have a calming influence on Madraeus." Rami frowned at Madraeus. "I want you to stay by him. Keep him from lashing out and losing control again."

"What?" Whitney shook her head. "I... I don't think..." She looked at Madraeus, and then back at Rami and Unkhabami. "I'm not the right one for the job."

"You are the only one for the job," Unkhabami snapped as she moved past them.

"But—" From the other room, they could hear the door opening. She recognized the voices of John and Barbie.

"Whitney, please?" Rami stood up, towering over her. "We need you." He reached out and held her shoulders. "Madraeus needs you."

"No!" Madraeus snarled. "She needs to be safe!"

Rami frowned at his friend. "She is safest standing next to you."

Whitney glanced at Madraeus. He came to his feet, but he wasn't looking at her. He was glaring at Rami.

Rami gave Whitney's shoulders a squeeze, then moved past her into the other room. Whitney and Madraeus stared at each other. She didn't know what to say, but there was something in his expression that tore at her heart and got her feet moving. She found herself standing in front of him.

Slowly, he reached out his hand and traced a finger down her cheek.

"I don't want to put you in danger."

Whitney stared up at him, and for once, all of his shields were down. Raw emotion swirled in his eyes, and in that moment, Whitney understood what Unkhabami had been trying to tell her. This man standing in front of her loved her completely and fully. He would do anything, kill anyone, to keep her safe.

Love. Love was the reason he had killed all those people. His love for Rami. And his love for her was just as dangerous.

Her knees suddenly felt like jello.

"Whitney?" Madraeus caught her by the elbows as she swayed.

She clutched his arms in a death grip. Whitney wanted to say something witty, or to laugh, anything to shift the mood. Instead, she murmured, "I'm okay."

"You don't have to do this."

"It's okay." She leaned her head into his chest, trying to control her knees. Her numb brain had no idea how to process her revelation. "I'm okay."

"Madraeus? Whitney?" Rami called from the other room.

Finally, Whitney lifted her head. She looked up at Madraeus and nodded. "I'm with you. I can do this."

"I don't want you to." Madraeus framed her face with his hands. "I want you to go home. Safe with your grandmother."

Whitney tried to laugh, "Are you kidding? Face one of her lectures alone? No way! I'm safer with you."

"Madraeus?" Rami called again.

"Very well." Madraeus nodded, and Whitney thought she saw a sparkle of pride in his eyes. "Let's be done with this." He moved past her toward the other room, and she followed.

As they came through the door, Whitney felt like she'd been hit in the face. Menace pulsed through the room, and it wasn't all from Madraeus.

John Danos and Barbie Calvin stood just inside the door, facing the werewolves. Barbie stood slightly behind John, although she was taller. Her blonde hair still looked frowzy. John had puffed up his short, round frame in an effort to look menacing, but his pudgy face and black framed glasses just made him look comical.

"So? Are we ready to leave?" John snapped at Madraeus.

Whitney felt her eyebrows go up. In front of her, Madraeus went rigid.

"This is how you ask for my help?" he snarled. In his anger, his accent thickened.

John flinched, but Whitney had to give him credit; he didn't back down. "I assumed it had all been explained."

"It may have been explained, but you should at least observe the dictates of common manners," Unkhabami snarled.

Whitney was surprised at the look of revulsion on John's face as he looked at the priestess. Out of the corner of her eye, she saw a subtle shift in the way that Madraeus was standing. Sensing danger, she reached out and grabbed a handful of his shirt. She felt a twinge of guilt for wrinkling his pristine dress shirt, but when he leaned back into her hand, she knew that she had made the right choice.

Barbie glanced toward them and must have sensed the danger as well. She stepped forward quickly to make amends. "Please, will you help us?" She blinked at Madraeus. "I know that the Hares have wronged your people over the centuries, but right now we have a common goal, and time is running out."

"Barbie!" John grabbed her arm and pulled her backward.

"No." She ripped her arm out of his grasp. "I've told you, I'm done. You can act superior if you want, but I want to stay alive!"

Whitney felt a little of the tension leave Madraeus as he asked, "Why is time running out?"

"Cecelia is here."

Her admission rattled the room. Whitney could feel the others exchanging looks, but she didn't dare take her attention off Madraeus, not with the way that John was glaring at him.

"What makes you so sure?" Rami rumbled.

"As we explained to the others," Barbie gestured at Thomas and Sandra, "Cecelia is attacking each of our Warrens. She is murdering every Hare and freeing their charge."

"And you think she is headed here next?" Madraeus asked.

"She's been everywhere else. She's closing in on Devon," John answered reluctantly. "Devon is the largest concentration of traps."

"Why?" Philtzer demanded.

"Like attracts like." John sneered, glaring at all of them. "Apep draws them here like a magnet."

"So, Apep is here?" Rami sounded as if he hoped that he was wrong.

"Yes," Barbie nodded, glancing nervously at Madraeus.

"And you want my help to do what?" Madraeus asked.

"We need you to protect the Key," Barbie said.

"Key?" Madraeus prompted.

"The human whose blood keeps the prison locked," Barbie answered.

Madraeus glared at Barbie. Whitney had the feeling that he understood a lot more about what a key was than she had. Barbie looked away. She couldn't hold Madraeus' gaze.

He blew out a long breath. "Take me to this Key."

"Wait a minute!" John stepped forward. "You're suddenly a bit too keen! How do we know that you aren't under the demon's influence?"

Philtzer threw up his hands. "Oh seriously! Dude, you came to us!"

"That doesn't matter!" John snapped. "I must guarantee the safety of the Key."

"If I were not in control," Madraeus' voice was deadly quiet, "your throat would have a gaping hole in it right now and the rest of you would be decorating the walls of this room."

Barbie backed up from Madraeus, but John continued to glare at him. No one else moved. Whitney's fist tightened in Madraeus' shirt.

Finally, John nodded. "Fine." He turned and yanked open the door.

Madraeus reached for his jacket. His sudden movement made Whitney jump, and she let go of his shirt. As everyone filed out behind John, Madraeus gestured for Whitney to go out before him. As she stepped around him, she looked up into his face.

"You're scary."

"Hmm." Madraeus gave her a mischievously evil smile and followed her out.

THE WARREN

Hair on the back of Whitney's neck bristled as they walked down the hall to the elevator. Primal instinct took over, urging her to run from the dangerous predator behind her. But she knew that Madraeus wouldn't hurt her... at least she hoped he wouldn't.

She slowed her pace a little, trying to make sure that they didn't have to ride in the same elevator as John and Barbie. Luckily, they ended up with Philtzer and Thomas. The first few minutes were awkwardly silent until Philtzer grinned.

"Barbie is cute."

"Philtzer," groaned Thomas.

"I'm just saying." Philtzer held up his hands.

The werewolf laughed at his friend and winked at Whitney. She glanced at Madraeus. He was watching Philtzer with an amused, yet tolerant expression.

"Try to control your hormones," he sighed.

Philtzer gave him a winning smile. Madraeus shook his head. The bell dinged, announcing their arrival. Madraeus turned his attention back to the door.

Leave it to Philtzer to be inappropriate to break the tension, Whitney smirked and stepped out into the lobby.

The Hares had already left in their car, so the rest of them piled into the back of the truck. Whitney climbed in, then stopped and looked around. She knew Sophia and Philtzer had claimed the seats up front. Rami, Unkhabami, and Sandra were sitting on Rami's coffin. Thomas stood against the wall, waiting to shut the door. Hamilton slid to one end of Madraeus' coffin and patted the spot beside him. She still didn't like the idea of sitting on someone's coffin. It was like walking on someone's grave.

Her hesitation got her a poke from behind. She turned to see Madraeus climb in behind her.

"Don't worry, I'm not in it this time," he whispered in her ear as he slid past her to sit down by Hamilton.

They both looked up at her expectantly. Her face reddened as she realized that Madraeus must have heard her comment on the way here. She tried to ignore their amusement at her expense and moved over to sit down gingerly beside him.

Thomas pulled the door shut. He banged on the wall a couple of times to signal Philtzer they were ready to leave. As the truck bounced into motion, Whitney shifted uncomfortably.

"Are we going to have enough time to deal with this mess before the sun comes up?" Rami asked Madraeus. "It is already ten."

"I don't know." Madraeus shrugged. "Depends on if Cecelia is close, if she's in a hurry, if she has her army organized…"

"Maybe we're catching her unaware?" Sandra offered, holding up crossed fingers.

"I doubt it," Madraeus answered.

"She's been several steps ahead of us for a while now." Thomas grabbed a strap hanging from the side of the truck to steady himself as the truck turned a corner.

"I would imagine that comes from the snake listening in through our heads," Rami scoffed.

"She can't have known the Hares would come to us, though, right?" Whitney looked up at Thomas, but he shrugged.

Madraeus looked at Rami and asked quietly, "Are you hearing it too?"

The giant sighed. "There have been quiet whispers, but it has not gained my attention to the same degree as you. Perhaps I am not as important or as powerful as you are. Or perhaps, I have not been under its influence as long. You do have more than 800 years on me."

It's no wonder its influence is so strong, Whitney thought. *He's had to listen to Apep whispering in his ear for more than a thousand years.*

Whitney turned to Madraeus only to find him sitting with his head down and his eyes closed. Her eyes traveled to his hands.

They were clenched into tight fists. Every muscle in his body seemed to be tensed. Random observations that she didn't realize she'd been noticing clicked into place. Every time he started to lose control, he closed his eyes. He was fighting for control right now.

She shot a desperate look at Thomas as she reached out and grabbed Madraeus' wrist. He flinched. Faster than she could move her hand out of the way, his other hand covered hers. She winced as his grip became painful.

"Madraeus?" Rami's deep voice rumbled as he leaned forward.

"I'm all right," Madraeus rasped. His grip on her hand loosened a little.

"This is going to be a long night," Thomas muttered as the truck began to slow down.

As soon as it stopped, Thomas rolled the door up and hopped out. Whitney peered out the door, trying to see where they were, but it was too dark. Madraeus still had a hold on her hand, so she stayed where she was while the others stepped out into the night. She could feel him shaking.

Madraeus finally opened his eyes and looked at her sadly. "You were right not to tell me. Now that he knows where I am, Apep wants me to kill the Key."

"You're not going to, though," Whitney stared at him, "right?"

"I don't know," he whispered.

She searched his face and said with more confidence than she felt, "I trust you. You're a good man. You'll do the right thing."

He stared at her without agreeing and then stood, pulling her up with him. He jumped down out of the truck and reached back to help her out. They walked across the parking lot to where the others were waiting.

John and Barbie stood near a Gothic iron gate that led to the yard of a huge church. The gate was lit on either side by archaic-looking lanterns, making it look creepy. Faint light from distant street lamps cast scary shadows across the churchyard. Whitney shuddered as they followed the Hares inside.

The church wasn't much more inviting than the gate. Above the main door, set in stone was the symbol of the Three Hares, three rabbits chasing each other so that their ears formed a triangle. Whitney couldn't even begin to guess how old it was, but it looked ancient. Tall, thin windows that looked like stained glass lined the walls and were grouped into sets of three with an arch over each set. At the far end, a huge square tower rose into the night. The top was obscured by the darkness.

"If you will follow us," Barbie motioned to them, leading the way down a path along the side of the building to the far end of the church.

Rami started down the path with Unkhabami, but the were-wolves all fanned out across the grass and disappeared. Sandra glanced at Whitney, then followed Rami and Unkhabami. Madraeus reached out and grabbed Whitney's hand and pulled her along beside him. She wasn't sure if it was for her benefit or for his, but as they passed through an ancient cemetery, she was secretly glad of the contact.

They passed a huge stone cross towering over the gravestones, and Whitney had an absurd urge to cross herself. As they got closer to the back of the church, Whitney noticed a low stone wall encircling a grove of trees. It looked weird, but then again, everything tonight looked either weird or scary. The Hares led them around the back of the church to where a large bush grew up against the wall.

Out of the darkness, a voice challenged, "Who's there?"

Whitney looked around but couldn't see anyone.

"It's us!" John snapped impatiently.

"No need to be rude, John," the voice called back.

"Sorry, Willie!" Barbie called. She turned to say something to John, but he pushed her aside and reached for the bush. He shoved the foliage out of the way to reveal a door recessed into the stone.

At that moment, Philtzer appeared out of the darkness, straightening his clothes.

"Well?" Rami rumbled.

"There's about ten of them stationed around the perimeter. Too close in if you ask me. Thomas and Hamilton are running a circuit out beyond them. No sign of any of Cecelia's people, though. Sophia and I will do a quick run through the town."

Philtzer gave a quick salute before he disappeared into the darkness again. Madraeus turned away and stared up at the church. Whitney followed his gaze.

"You okay?" she whispered as John and Barbie began unlocking the door.

Madraeus turned back to her. His expression told her he wasn't okay at all, but he nodded and squeezed her hand.

"This way," Barbie called as she swung the door open and started down a stone stairwell. John stood to the side, glaring at them all. Rami and Unkhabami stepped forward to follow Barbie, but Sandra and Whitney both froze, staring at the darkness beyond the door.

Whitney felt sweat break out across her forehead. She couldn't go in there. It was too much like the mine. She glanced at Sandra and knew she was thinking the same thing.

"Something wrong?" John snapped impatiently.

"Is that a cave?" Sandra's voice sounded like she'd swallowed glass.

"No." John sounded petulant. "It is just the Warren."

"And what does that mean?" Sandra rasped.

"It's an underground workplace and living quarters," John answered grudgingly.

"So... like a basement?"

John huffed, "Sort of."

Despite John's impatience, Sandra turned to look at Whitney. Her expression said she was spooked, but not completely terrified. Madraeus squeezed Whitney's hand again, and she looked up at him. He knew why she was afraid, and his expression was reassuring. Whitney took a deep breath and nodded to Sandra.

"Are we ready now?" John crossed his arms.

"Yes. Fine. Go!" Whitney snapped. John's impatience was really starting to get on Whitney's already frayed nerves.

He led them down the stairs and through a twisting maze of corridors. The Warren was a lot more than a basement. It was an entire complex. Dozens of hallways and rooms led off from the main passageway. There were libraries, kitchens, and a lot of sleeping chambers.

"This isn't creepy at all," Sandra muttered as they caught up with the others. In a louder voice, she asked, "You guys live down here?"

"Sometimes," Barbie called over her shoulder, but John shushed her.

The farther they went, the more nervous Whitney felt. A gigantic case of claustrophobia swamped her. She had to fight against the panic. Before long, she had a death grip on Madraeus' hand, and she was sure that she needed him more than he needed her.

Finally, they reached a set of rooms that looked like a separate apartment. Barbie paused at a door near the far end and turned to face them.

"Where are we?" Rami rumbled, looking around.

"This is where the Key lives." Barbie's expression warned them that something significant was about to happen. "Try to remain calm," she said as she turned to open the door.

THE KEY

Madraeus could feel Whitney shaking as they walked through the Warren. He knew that being underground like this was scaring the hell out of her, but it did have one advantage: he was so focused on her that it blocked out the voice.

A detached part of him admired the organization of the Hares. It was obvious that they were diligent in their beliefs. Many of the rooms had odd, ancient-looking carvings burned into the doors. He assumed it was for protection, either to keep things out or keep things in.

The farther they walked into the labyrinth, the more Whitney clung to his hand. He glanced at her. Her breathing was quick and shallow, and her eyes were enormous. He hoped she wasn't going to have a full-blown panic attack.

Another scathing comment from John pulled his attention away from Whitney. He felt his fangs grow a little. He detested John's superiority and self-righteousness. He'd meant what he'd said back at the hotel; he would love to splatter John all over the walls.

Do it.

Madraeus' body tensed as the voice filled his head.

Thisss isss your chance. Wipe out the Haresss.

Madraeus clenched his jaw against the sound.

They are nothing. They dessserve to die.

"Try to remain calm," Barbie's words slowly reached him as she turned away and opened the door. Rami and Unkhabami were the first through the door, but they stopped immediately. Sandra sidled past Rami and entered the room.

"What the hell is wrong with you people?" Sandra's voice echoed out of the room.

Madraeus frowned and stepped forward, dragging Whitney along beside him. Rami moved to let him through.

The room had once been a bedroom, but it had been turned into a hospital room. Medical machines of all varieties beeped and hissed. Two nurses stood on either side of the bed, monitoring their patient. They looked up in alarm as the room filled with strangers. One stepped closer to the bed as if to protect its occupant.

"This is Grace." Barbie gestured toward the bed. "She is the Key."

Whitney leaned around Rami to see who was in the bed. She gasped and turned her face into Madraeus' shoulder. His arms came up around Whitney protectively. His eyes focused on the patient. His gut twisted. The thing in the bed could not be called a person. It was monstrous. Its skull was deformed, and the jaw misshapen. The brown hair that clung to its skull was sparse and straw-like. The hands were twisted and disjointed.

Kill that monssstrosssity!

For once, Madraeus was inclined to follow the voice's direction, but instead he rasped, "What is that thing?"

"That is what you get from a couple of centuries of inbreeding," Sandra snarled. She looked at John. "You said you used eugenics to keep the bloodline pure so the prison would stay locked." She flung her hand toward the bed. "Look what you've done, you sick bastard!"

"We didn't choose this!" Barbie stepped forward. "We didn't make her this way."

"No, you just let it keep going!" Sandra snapped. "That's just as bad." Sandra turned to Madraeus. Her eyes were filled with hatred and disgust. "You're right. They're not the good guys."

John lifted his chin. "We did what we had to for the sake of the world!"

"Much evil is done in the name of the world." Unkhabami shook her head and turned away from the bed.

"We are protecting the world from monsters like you!" John protested.

"We are not the monsters here." Rami shuddered. He couldn't seem to tear his eyes from the bed.

"What about her?" Sandra pointed to Grace. "Who is protecting her from monsters like you?"

"Her life doesn't matter!" The fanatical gleam was back in John's eyes.

"So, you just use her and throw her away?" Sandra shouted.

"I would use a hundred lives if it served our purpose!" John spat.

"How dare you!" Sandra shrieked.

"I should walk away right now and leave you all to rot!" Madraeus snarled. He let go of Whitney and took a menacing step toward John.

Yesss! They should pay! Dessstroy them all!

"No, please! We need your help!" Barbie stretched out a hand as if to stop him. "She's dying."

"Barb! Be silent!" John snapped. Barbie flinched at his tone, but her pleading eyes never left Madraeus.

"What do you mean?" Madraeus surveyed the machines again. He hadn't had much experience with medical equipment.

"She's a vegetable," Sandra whispered. "Those are life support machines."

"If you knew she was dying, why bring us here?" Madraeus stared hard at Barbie. Her expression became wary. Suddenly, he understood. "You didn't bring me here just to stop Cecelia. You brought me here to fight the snake. Didn't you?"

"We're barely keeping her alive." Barbie's voice shook. "Apep is going to get out. Soon."

"And you don't think you can handle it," Madraeus scoffed.

Barbi shook her head. "No. We can't."

"We can handle it." John raised his chin.

Barbie ignored him. "There are so few of us left."

"Why not just tell us the truth?" Rami asked.

"You are the enemy!" John hissed.

Madraeus didn't like the calculating look in John's eyes. He felt the hair on the back of his neck prickle. His lip curled as his fangs started to inch downward.

Kill him!

Madraeus took a step toward John. Whitney grabbed his arm to hold him back, but the contact sent a shock through his system. His world went black.

All around him, people screamed. The sound of falling stones was deafening. He cast around looking for the source of the danger. A massive reptilian head rose out of the darkness. The snake lashed out. Madraeus' eyes snapped to the object of its strike. Whitney!

No! He tried to run forward to save her, but he was frozen in place. All he could do was watch as the snake struck again and again. Its fangs pierced her neck, her chest, her face, her arm.

"No!" Madraeus screamed again, and the world cleared. He stood panting, staring at the spot where she had been. There was nothing there.

"Madraeus?" Whitney tugged at his arm. His gaze snapped to her. She stared up at him fearfully. He glanced around. Everyone was watching him, especially Joly John.

Hissing laughter filled his head. *Sssoon I will devour her. Her flesh will be mine.*

Rage shook Madraeus.

"You will not have her," he snarled.

You sssaw it yourself.

"Have who?" Whitney asked.

Chest heaving, Madraeus shook his head, trying to deny what he'd seen. What the snake whispered in his mind. His eyes flew to Unkhabami. He'd seen the future again. Whitney's future. Apep would be released. The snake demon would destroy everything. He would destroy Whitney.

Madraeus would do anything to prevent his vision. He grabbed Whitney by the arms. "You have to leave!"

"What?" Her expression clouded as she tried to keep up. "Why?"

"You have to go. Now!"

She winced as his grip tightened. "What are you talking about? I'm not going anywhere." She shook her head and tried to break his hold on her.

"You can't go!" Barbie protested.

"Rami, take her." He threw Whitney across the room into the giant's arms.

"Hey!" Whitney shouted as she landed hard against Rami's chest. Sandra grabbed her to keep her from falling.

"Take Sandra too. Get out, now! Get somewhere safe."

"My friend," Rami asked as he helped steady Whitney, "what has you so spooked?"

Madraeus knew he must look crazed, but it didn't matter. "Please! Just do it!"

Rami stepped toward him. His face filled with concern. "What is it?"

Unkhabami laid a hand on Rami's arm. "Do as he says."

The giant looked at her and nodded. He gathered the girls despite their protests and started for the door. Madraeus watched them go. He knew he should feel relief that she would be safe, but the voice wouldn't allow it.

I will ssstill find her.

"I will kill you first!" Madraeus muttered.

"What did you say?" John peered at him, and the zealous gleam flared in his eyes. "You're listening to him, aren't you? You're under the demon's influence!"

"Shut up, you fat little fool!" Unkhabami snarled. Her eyes locked onto Madraeus.

He held her gaze. His body shook as the voice hissed in his head.

You cannot ssstop me. She hasss come!

THE ARRIVAL

"Demon!" John threw himself at Madraeus.

Madraeus scowled and smacked him to the side. John landed in a heap against the wall.

Unkhabami sneered at the unconscious man. "You should kill him."

"I don't have time." Madraeus dismissed John with an impatient wave. "We have bigger problems."

Unkhabami wrapped her hand around Madraeus' wrist and closed her eyes. He kept still, uncertain what she was doing. Suddenly, she shuddered and opened her eyes. She stared at Madraeus, and for the first time in centuries, he saw fear in the priestess' eyes.

"What did you see?" he demanded.

Unkhabami's eyebrows rose, then lowered into a scowl. She looked away. "Nothing."

Madraeus peered at her, trying to reconcile her reaction with her words. As comprehension began to dawn, a bell clanged somewhere in the halls behind them.

Grace's nurses huddled closer to the bed, and one muttered something to Barbie. The other raised the bed railing and began checking all the monitors.

"What is the alarm for?" Madraeus and Unkhabami both looked to Barbie for an explanation, but she stood frozen where she was with her face drained of all color. "Well?" Madraeus demanded, but she continued to stare dumbly at them.

"Pull yourself together, girl!" Unkhabami snapped. "Did you think this was a game?"

Barbie flinched at her harsh words, and then slowly, like a puppet, she lurched forward. She tried a couple of times to speak but couldn't get the words past her fear. Finally, she croaked, "Attack."

"Weapons!" Madraeus grabbed Barbie and pushed her toward the door. The urgency in his tone finally reached her. She nodded and seemed to get herself back under control.

Madraeus and Unkhabami followed her out of the room and down the hall. She stopped a few doors down. She fumbled with the lock and then flung the door open. Once inside the armory, she grabbed the first sword she found.

Madraeus eyed her shaking hands. "You know how to use that?"

Barbie nodded uncertainly.

Unkhabami yanked a bow and quiver of arrows off the wall. "A few arrows to stop an army," she grumbled as she filled the quiver with as many arrows as she could find.

Madraeus grunted in agreement and turned to find a sword of his own. Madraeus took Barbie by the arm and shoved her back the way they'd come. "Close and lock the Key's room. Stand outside the door and don't let anyone past." He turned and led the way toward the stairs.

As they got closer to the exit, they could hear the sounds of fighting. Madraeus broke into a run, taking the stairs two at a time. He shoved the heavy wooden door aside. The bush that hid the door cracked and splintered. At his first glimpse of the churchyard, he knew the Hares had no chance. Cecelia's army outnumbered them ten to one.

There were pockets of fighting, but mostly it was just a crowd of spectators as nearly a hundred watched the Hares fight for their lives. He scanned the area looking for Philtzer and the others, but there was no sign of them. He fervently wished that they could have waited to engage Cecelia's army until more of his own people were here. More than that, he hoped that Rami had gotten Whitney and Sandra away safely.

Beside him, Unkhabami growled. He glanced at her, following her gaze. The priestess' eyes were locked on Cecelia. Dressed all in white, she glowed in the gloom. Madraeus smirked. She had always had a flair for the dramatic. Spark stood next to her in wolf form. Her white fur made her easily recognizable.

Madraeus caught movement in his peripheral vision and realized that Unkhabami had nocked an arrow and was aiming at Cecelia.

Ssstop her! The voice hissed in his head, and for a fraction of a second, he felt compelled to knock her bow to the side, but he resisted, allowing her time to shoot.

Cccecccelia!

The arrow flew true and should have pierced Cecelia's heart, but at the snake's warning, she moved. Cecelia threw them an annoyed glance. Apep's ability to read his thoughts and relay them would make winning this battle all the more difficult.

You can't defeat me.

"Take them!" Cecelia snarled, pointing at Madraeus and Unkhabami.

Her army surged forward. Madraeus heard Unkhabami snarl as she fired at anyone in sight. Madraeus gripped his sword tighter and waited for his first victim to get within range.

You can't fight them all.

Madraeus ignored the voice as his blade sliced through the nearest vampire and moved on to the next. Four lay dead behind him as Madraeus worked his way forward, slashing and stabbing, moving ever closer to where Cecelia stood. Victims of Unkhabami's arrows lay scattered across the churchyard. The Hares began to rally as they grasped onto the hope that Madraeus and Unkhabami had provided.

Dimly, Madraeus became aware of a change in the crowd ahead of him. The army began to shift and shout as they turned away. For a brief moment, he thought they were running, but then he realized the cavalry had come. From the far side of the churchyard, wolves and vampires surged forward, cleaving their way through Cecelia's army. He caught sight of Vivian, Malcolm, Cody, and Regina amongst many others. The entire churchyard erupted in battle. Screams and snarls filled the night as the factions collided.

Unkhabami's arrows ran out, forcing her to shift into a leopard and fight with teeth and claws. Once or twice, he caught sight of a familiar wolf, but in the mass of fighting fur it was impossible to sort out Cecelia's wolves from his own. Madraeus saw Philtzer and Sophia at one point, but then he lost track of them as two vampires attacked him. He managed to spit one on his sword, but the other tackled him from behind.

Madraeus landed hard in the dew-soaked grass, knocking the air from his chest. As he struggled to get out from under his attacker, he dropped his sword. The vampire slashed at him with a knife. He could feel deep gouges opening up across his back. Anger and annoyance flared up. Madraeus rolled to throw off his attacker and scrambled to his feet. Grabbing his discarded sword, he swung it in a sideways arch, catching the man across the torso. Blood gushed outward as the man tried to hold his organs in.

"Let me save you the trouble." Madraeus smiled as he stepped forward. The man's look of sheer terror made no impression on Madraeus as he brought his sword down, slicing the enemy vampire's neck in two.

He took a moment to get his bearings. All around him, the fight continued as he turned in a slow circle, looking for the telltale flashes of white, but neither Cecelia nor Spark could be found in the crowd. With a sinking feeling, he realized they were gone.

The Key! He spun around to stare at the church. He had gotten too far from the entrance to the Warren. No one was guarding it. Madraeus ran forward but stopped short as the deafening sound of stones breaking filled the night. The ground shook. The stained glass windows of the church began to crack, then suddenly shattered, sending shards of colored glass in all directions. All around the yard, the fighting staggered to a halt as all eyes turned toward the church. From inside, an eerie purple light glowed brightly for a second and then winked out.

Everything fell silent until something crashed against the main door of the church. Something big was trying to get out. The armies began backing away, confused by this new development. Except the Hares. They knew. Madraeus saw several run forward, but they never made it to the church. The thing inside broke through, splintering the heavy wooden door.

Apep was free.

SPECTATING

"Rami! Stop!" Whitney struggled against his grip on her upper arm as he dragged her along through the dark.

Rami hustled them up the stairs and out of the Warren. He only paused for a moment to look around before heading toward the lot where they'd left the truck.

"Ray wanted us to get to safety," Rami said without stopping.

"Where exactly do you think is going to be safe from this craziness?" Sandra asked from his other side. He had her by the arm, too.

"I do not know," Rami snapped, "but I have rarely seen Ray so panicked."

"But you said I was supposed to stay with him and keep him calm!" Whitney tried to pry his fingers loose. "How am I supposed to do that if I'm clear out here?"

They had just reached the huge stone cross in the graveyard when a wolf came bounding out of the darkness.

Rami stopped. "Thomas?"

The rangy-looking wolf shimmered for an instant, and then Thomas was sprinting toward them in human form. It occurred to Whitney that she was getting way too used to seeing naked men running around.

"Back!" He skidded to a stop on the wet grass and gestured back down the path. "Go back! Hurry!"

Rami didn't hesitate. Whitney felt herself being spun around and hurried back toward the church.

"I can run on my own, thanks!" Sandra finally succeeded in getting her arm free.

"This way!" Thomas bounded out in front of them, leading them toward the grove of trees inside the rock wall.

"What's going on?" Whitney panted as they climbed over the wall.

"Get down and be quiet!" Thomas pulled her behind a tree.

The dim light from the churchyard slanted through the trees. Whitney glanced around the little grove. The trees had been planted around a little pond. In the center of the water stood a statue. She couldn't make out the features in the dark, but it made the grove seem like some kind of shrine.

"Explain," Rami demanded as his eyes searched the churchyard.

"Cecelia is here," Thomas whispered as he peered out at the church. "She brought her army. There's about a hundred of them."

"A hundred?" Whitney gaped.

"Where are the others?" Rami whispered.

"Hamilton is warning the Hares, and Philtzer is bringing in our troops." Thomas grinned. Whitney could see his teeth shining in the dim light. "She won't know what hit her."

"Our troops?" Whitney turned to Rami.

"Cody, Regina, Malcolm, Marcus, and about twenty others. They came ahead while we were in Germany." Thomas shifted, trying to find a more comfortable position. "We wanted to be ready."

"That's it?" Sandra punched him in the arm. "Twenty against a hundred?"

"Closer to thirty." Thomas peeked over the wall.

"Why didn't you tell us?" Whitney reached out and punched Thomas in the other shoulder.

"Quit beating up on me." Thomas rubbed his shoulder with a hurt expression, although she knew they couldn't have hurt him. "It was a need-to-know basis."

"And we didn't need to know?" Whitney frowned at him.

"Madraeus and I did not need to know," Rami corrected.

"Snake radio." Sandra nodded. "So, now what?"

"Now, we wait." Thomas turned back to watch the churchyard.

"But weren't we leaving?" Sandra glanced at Rami.

"Leaving? Wait." Thomas frowned, looking at the three of them. "Why are you out here? Why aren't you watching Madraeus?"

"Madraeus freaked out and told us to leave," Sandra answered at the same time as Rami whispered, "Something has gone wrong."

"What's gone wrong?" Thomas looked at Rami.

"Shh!" Whitney grabbed his arm and pointed.

The Hares had formed a semi-circle around the entrance to the Warren. Out of the darkness on the far side of the church, a mass of people emerged, led by Cecelia with a white wolf trotting at her side. She stopped in front of the Hares and crossed her arms. They could hear her clearly even from across the yard.

"Give it up. You won't survive the night."

"She's confident," Sandra muttered.

"She is probably right," Rami whispered. "They are badly outnumbered."

One of the Hares shouted, "Neither will you!"

"Well, at least they are both being optimistic." Sandra shrugged, watching the standoff.

Whitney shook her head at Sandra's odd appraisal of the situation.

"We need to warn Madraeus." Rami's voice barely made a sound.

"I think he already knew," Whitney leaned close to Rami's ear. "He knew something was going to happen. That's why he sent us out."

Rami shot her a worried look.

Whitney poked Thomas in the elbow. "Where are the others?"

"Coming around behind them." Thomas' voice was barely a whisper as he made a circling gesture with his hand. An instant later, fighting erupted between the Hares and Cecelia's army.

Whitney watched as the Hares fought off the first group of attackers. Most of Cecelia's army just stayed where they were. "Why aren't they fighting?"

Sandra said, "I guess they don't think they need to."

"Look!" Rami pointed to the entrance of the Warren. The door stood wide open, with Madraeus and Unkhabami standing in front of it. They watched as the priestess nocked an arrow and let it fly at Cecelia.

"Did you see that? She missed!" Sandra gasped. "How could she miss?"

Her question went unanswered as Cecelia ordered the attack. Vampires surged forward toward Madraeus as more werewolves transformed and swarmed toward the Hares.

"We have to help them!" Whitney shot to her feet only to be pulled back down by Thomas.

"Sit down!" He pushed her back behind a tree. "You're gonna get yourself killed!"

Whitney squirmed in frustration but stayed behind the tree. She looked back to see Madraeus run forward, slashing and stabbing. Body after body slumped to the ground around him as he worked his way toward Cecelia.

"Holy crap!" Whitney gaped, watching him.

Thomas chuckled, "And he's not even trying yet."

"What?"

"Whitney, he wiped out almost an entire village on his own." His voice was filled with pride as he watched his boss. "This is nothing."

"And that doesn't scare you?" Sandra whispered.

"Not as long as he's on our side." Thomas craned his neck, trying to keep track of the battle.

"Is that them?" Rami gestured to the disturbance rippling through Cecelia's army.

"Yep," Thomas began to shimmer, "stay here." A second later, he was a wolf. He sprang over the rock wall and sprinted toward the battle.

The fight seemed to last forever. It was hard to tell who was winning. As she watched her friends fight, Whitney felt like her heart was going to beat itself to death. She tried to keep track of each of them, but it was fast becoming impossible. Her gut twisted as she saw Madraeus knocked to the ground. But then he was up again. She gasped as she watched him behead his attacker. She didn't know how much more of this she could watch.

"Isn't that John?" Sandra pointed toward the door of the Warren.

Whitney watched, thinking that he would join the fight, but he didn't. Instead, he slid along the side of the church.

"Where's he going?" Whitney had a sinking feeling as he disappeared around the corner.

"So much for zealots," Sandra snorted.

Barely a moment later, Cecelia dashed over and vanished through the door to the Warren. Whitney grabbed Rami by the arm. "Cecelia's in the Warren! We have to stop her!" She surged to her feet and started for the wall.

"Whitney!" Rami tried to stop her, but she was already over the wall. Sandra and Rami rushed out after her. They were halfway across the graveyard when they heard a rumbling from inside the church. The ground shook. The windows shattered, spraying them with glass. Whitney fell to her knees, covering her head with her arms. She felt Rami and Sandra hit the ground beside her. The entire area glowed with purple light, and the temperature dropped as if a cold wind had blown across the yard. Whitney shivered and flinched as something banged against the church door.

"What the hell was that?" Sandra gasped.

The thing banged again; this time, the door bulged outward. Little clouds of dust puffed into the air around the door frame. Many of the fighters had stopped and were staring at the church.

"We need to go!" Rami thundered. He grabbed the girls around their waists and hauled them to their feet, but it was too late.

The church door splintered as the thing inside burst through. The stones of the threshold crashed and thudded to the ground as a huge serpent reared up, glaring down at them. It towered fifteen feet above them. Whitney could only imagine how big the rest of it was that still lay out of sight in the church. Its tongue flicked in and out as its head swayed back and forth. Its eyes glinted with malice as it hissed at those gathered in the churchyard.

"How are we supposed to fight that?" Whitney gaped.

TERRIBLE PLAN

For the briefest breath, Apep hovered above them before he surged forward, slashing and striking. Vampire or werewolf, witch or demon, Cecelia's or Madraeus' people, it didn't matter. The snake plowed through them, his fangs piercing and ripping. One after another went down like snowflakes falling in a fire.

Whitney, Sandra, and Rami stood frozen, watching the massacre. Screams filled the night as Apep killed everything in his path. It wasn't like the nature shows. This was no animal killing for food. This was pure evil bent on destruction.

A few of the Hares that had survived the initial attack ran forward trying to stop the snake. Whitney caught sight of Madraeus amongst them. She watched as they hacked and stabbed at the snake's body, but it was all in vain. Their weapons bounced off the monster's scales, giving off little sparks of light. Their efforts only made Apep angrier, and then more people died.

Out of the corner of her eye, Whitney saw Cecelia emerge from the Warren. Anger surged up, coalescing into one thought: *This is all Cecelia's fault.*

Whitney lunged forward out of Rami's lax grip and charged Cecelia. The tall blonde was so intent on watching the snake that she never saw Whitney coming. Whitney pulled out her best football skills and tackled Cecelia. They went down hard. Dew soaked into their clothes as they rolled across the grass.

Whitney came out on top and punched Cecelia in the face. She managed to get in two more hits before Cecelia recovered from her surprise and bashed Whitney in the jaw. Whitney toppled over, holding her head. Cecelia was on top of her in an instant. Whitney felt the jarring impact of another blow to her face. Her vision swam. When it cleared, the first thing she saw was Cecelia's fangs about two inches from her face.

Whitney bucked and thrashed, trying to stay away from her bite, when suddenly, Cecelia was ripped away. The sudden force of Rami yanking Cecelia off her lifted Whitney from the ground. As Cecelia let go, Whitney fell backward again. Her head hit the ground hard. Stars swam through her vision as Sandra appeared beside her.

"Are you crazy?" Sandra shrieked, pulling Whitney to her feet. "Who the hell runs up and punches a vampire?"

Whitney had no answer for that as Sandra grabbed her by the arm and pulled her away from the church.

"Where's Rami?" Whitney looked around.

He was grappling with Cecelia, each struggling to get a hold on the other. She looked toward the battle, hoping someone could help Rami. That's when she realized her mistake. Attacking Cecelia had gotten the attention of the snake.

Terror froze her veins. Apep stared down at her with his tongue flicking in and out. He took no notice of the men hacking at him with swords and axes. Apep's full attention was on Whitney. The serpentine body rolled and coiled as it slithered toward her.

"Whitney!" Madraeus shouted.

Cecelia cackled with joy. "He's going to rip her to shreds!"

"Sandra! Run!" Whitney screamed.

Whitney and Sandra dashed across the cemetery toward the trees. Apep slithered through the grass in pursuit.

"Stay away from her!" Madraeus roared as he chased after Apep.

Behind them, the sound of fighting surged as Cecelia's army rallied. Somewhere beyond the churchyard, sirens began to wail.

They kept running. The rock wall loomed ahead. Whitney jumped over it and dashed into the trees. Stumbling and tripping, she splashed through the edge of the pond. She could hear Sandra off to her left. Behind her, she could hear the snake. Apep was almost in the grove. She knew she couldn't outrun him. She had to hide. Sandra must have thought the same thing because Whitney couldn't hear her running anymore.

The snake reached the grove. Whitney could hear scales scraping against the stones as they slid over the top of the wall. Apep hissed as he slithered through the trees. Whitney could hear twigs snapping under his weight. Whitney dodged behind a tree and stood still. She clamped her hand over her mouth to quiet her breathing. Light from the street lamps on the far side of the trees showed her a possible exit, but she was afraid to try for it in case Apep spotted her.

From behind her, she heard Madraeus snarl, followed by a crash. The snake roared and hissed. Whitney peeked out from behind the tree. She could see their silhouettes against the light from the churchyard. Madraeus had his arms wrapped around the snake's torso just behind its head. Apep tossed his head back and forth, trying to dislodge Madraeus, but he held on. The snake began to twist and roll. Apep coiled himself around Madraeus and squeezed. Madraeus screamed as the snake constricted.

"No!" Whitney dashed out of her hiding place. She didn't know how she could help, but she wasn't going to just sit and watch him die.

She ran toward them. Something slammed into her chest. The air whooshed out of her lungs. She fell, landing on her back. She gasped for air as John stepped out from behind the tree, holding a tree branch the size of a baseball bat. Her hands covered her chest, trying to stop the pain. It felt like her ribs had caved in. She coughed and tasted blood.

John dropped the branch, reached down, and pulled her to her feet. He quickly hauled her away from the snake and Madraeus. He muttered under his breath, but she couldn't distinguish the words past the pain burning in her chest. John half-carried, half-dragged Whitney to the edge of the trees. He pushed her through the gap in the rock wall that served as an entrance gate to the lane. She collapsed, holding her chest.

Whitney gasped and flailed. All she could think about was getting away from John. She didn't know what he was trying to do, but starting out by trying to kill her was a good indication that she should run. She squeezed her eyes shut against the pain and rolled to her knees. As the wave of pain subsided, the sound of John speaking penetrated her brain. She raised her head. He stood over her, chanting in some kind of foreign language, but like nothing she'd ever heard before. She tried to stand but fell back to her knees. She was having trouble breathing. She tried again, but she was too slow.

John grabbed her by the forearm. With his other hand, he reached down and pulled a knife from his belt. He brought it down in a quick slash. Whitney yelped as the blade cut into her arm. Blood flowed freely from the wound. John yanked her forward so that the blood would fall onto the rock wall. He began walking forward, dragging her with him, dribbling her blood along the entire length of the wall as he kept chanting.

Inside the grove, they could still hear the snake thrashing while Madraeus cursed and snarled. Time seemed to slow down as they circled the grove. With every passing second, it became harder and harder for Whitney to stay upright. Her chest burned, and weakness seeped into her limbs. John dragged her around the perimeter of the grove with single-minded zeal. He hurried her along, glancing toward the wrestling match between Madraeus and Apep.

Whitney had lost the strength to fight him by the time they'd come full circle. She felt like a rag doll. Her head lolled to one side, and her feet wouldn't cooperate at all. As they neared the little gate again, Whitney realized someone was shouting at them.

"Hey! Hey!" Sandra dashed out of the trees and skidded to a stop. "What are you doing? Stop!"

John ignored her and continued to spread Whitney's blood along the wall. They had only a few feet to go before they made it back to where they'd started.

"I said stop!" Sandra picked up a tree branch and swung it at John. She hit him hard in the shoulder.

He dropped Whitney and spun around to threaten Sandra with the knife. "Back off!"

Whitney's eyes were rolling around in her head, but she managed to catch a glimpse of them. They stood, facing off, him with the knife and her with the tree branch. Inside the grove, Madraeus was still locked in battle with the snake. They were closer to this end of the grove now.

"What the hell do you think you're doing?" Sandra edged forward.

"I told you." John snapped. "Apep must be stopped!"

Sandra looked at the bloody wall behind him, "You're setting a new trap." She looked down at Whitney's bleeding arm. "And you're making her the Key?"

Key? Whitney's brain didn't seem to want to follow along.

"No! I won't let you!" Sandra lunged forward, raising her branch, but John was ready for it. He stepped to the side and slammed his fist into her stomach. Sandra doubled over, gasping.

Behind them, they could hear the snake rushing forward. Its hissing grew louder as it crashed through the grove. John wasted no time. He spun around and grabbed Whitney, yanking her up by the arm. She couldn't summon the strength to struggle as he dragged her arm along the wall, closing the gap in the blood circle.

Noooo! Apep hissed as he emerged from the trees and realized that John had nearly finished the locking spell. His body flipped and coiled, contracting in preparation to strike at John before the circle was complete, but before he could lunge forward, Madraeus appeared out of the darkness behind him. Once again, he locked his arms around the snake just behind its head and threw all of his weight to the side. Together they slammed into a huge oak tree near the gate. Madraeus' grip broke. He bounced off the tree and landed against the wall.

John glanced up in surprise, but it didn't stop him from finishing his task. The little stone wall around the grove began to glow with a purple light.

Inside the wall, the grove changed. The trees turned black, and the sky shifted from midnight to a deep purple color. Purple light glimmered around Whitney. It grew brighter and brighter.

Noooo! Noooo! Apep roared in impotent anger as his prison reformed around him.

The air surrounding the grove sizzled. Whitney's eyes shot open as a spark of light raced around the perimeter of the wall, burning the blood off. She gasped as power surged through her. She looked toward the grove and saw Madraeus scramble to his feet, spinning toward the wall.

He started forward, but then Apep was there, racing for the gap and his last chance to escape. For a second, Madraeus' eyes locked with Whitney's. In his eyes, she could see every bit of love he had for her, regret for every missed opportunity, and grief for every unfulfilled wish he had for their future. Everything seemed to freeze in that moment. Tears flooded her eyes as she realized he was saying goodbye. A second later, he turned away and locked his arms around Apep, wrestling the snake away from the gap.

The snake bucked and raged, trying to break loose, but it was too late. The spark completed its circuit. The circle closed. The trap snapped shut, and the purple light winked out. The grove was empty. They were gone.

UNFINISHED BUSINESS

Unkhabami ripped and slashed at her enemies, knowing that each and every vampire and werewolf she fought was responsible for the deaths of her people. Her heart burned with vengeance as she pounced on another victim, and yet, as she sank her claws into the man's back, she felt cheated. The one she wanted had disappeared. After Cecelia had ordered her army to attack, she had disappeared into the chaos.

Just as Unkhabami was about to rip into another of Cecelia's vampires, she froze. Deep inside her, she felt a tremor pulsate through the astral plane. She spun toward the church just as the ground started to shake, knocking everyone to the ground. The windows of the church shattered, and the night was filled with purple light.

Unkhabami's eyes grew wide. *Madraeus' vision! Apep is coming!*

She started back toward the church but had only made it a few steps before Apep burst through the front of the church. Stone debris blasted outward. A stone the size of a baseball caught Unkhabami in the shoulder, knocking her backwards. She curled into a ball and rolled. Pain spread across her shoulder and chest. She looked down to see her fur turning red. She bared her teeth and snarled in frustration.

"Whitney!" Madraeus shouted, drawing Unkhabami's attention back to the fight.

Across the yard, the serpent rose higher and higher. Whitney and Sandra stared up at it in terror. Beyond them, Rami grappled with Cecelia.

The priestess watched in horror as Cecelia twisted and lashed out at Rami with her nails and teeth. He outweighed her, but she fought with crazed enthusiasm, smiling with glee as she tried to kill him.

Cecelia cackled with joy. "He's going to rip her to shreds!"

"Sandra! Run!" Whitney screamed.

Unkhabami watched the girls run toward the grove. The snake shot after them. Its undulating body crashed through the debris from the church, knocking a large chunk of stone through the air. Time seemed to slow as Unkhabami watched it fly straight toward Rami and Cecelia.

Rami! She screamed, but she was in leopard form, and her warning came out as just a hiss. Unkhabami surged forward.

The stone crashed into Rami and Cecelia, knocking them apart. Rami hit the ground hard, rolled across the grass, and lay still.

Unkhabami reached his side a moment later. Relief flooded her as she realized he was just dazed. Quickly, she glanced around. No enemies were close by, so she shifted from leopard into woman. Rami stirred and stared up at her.

"Are you all right?"

"Yes," he groaned, reaching for his head, "I am seeing double, though." He shook his head and noticed her shoulder. "You are injured."

"There is no time for that." Unkhabami shook her head dismissively as she looked to where Cecelia had landed. "Come on, we have her!"

Rami sat up and saw Cecelia stirring in the grass a few feet away. Unkhabami surged to her feet only to be stopped by Rami. He was looking toward the grove where the snake had disappeared after Whitney and Sandra. They could hear the sounds of Madraeus battling Apep echoing through the trees.

"We must help Madraeus and the girls!"

"No." Unkhabami shook her head. "Their fate is already sealed. We must stop Cecelia!"

She started toward Cecelia again, but Rami pulled her back again.

"What do you mean? What fate?"

"I have seen it. Whitney is the key!" Unkhabami shook her head. "There is nothing we can do. But we can kill her!" She pointed to where Cecelia lay, only to find her gone. "No!"

Unkhabami's eyes searched the area and caught a glimpse of white as Cecelia disappeared into the church. The priestess ripped her wrist from Rami's grip and dashed toward the church.

"Bami! Wait!" Rami shouted as he staggered to his feet.

Unkhabami saw her discarded dress lying crumpled in the grass. She snatched it up as she sprinted after her nemesis. The priestess pulled her dress over her head and felt it settle around her as she scrambled over the jumble of stones that used to be the entrance to the church. She slowed as she stepped over the threshold.

The night outside seemed bright compared to the shadowy interior. As her eyes adjusted, she picked her way forward past pieces of the broken pipe organ and splintered benches. The ornately carved baptismal font had been knocked over onto its side. The priestess stepped around it to find a large hole in the floor where Apep had burst through. She edged up to the break in the stones and looked down. She could just make out the broken corridor in the Warren below, where they had recently walked through to see the Key. Unkhabami shuddered at the memory and looked away. She couldn't afford to get caught up in the past. Cecelia was in here somewhere, and she wasn't going to let her get away.

"I know you are in here," Unkhabami said to the shadows as she stepped away from the precipice. "I saw you come in, but you will never leave."

"That's what you think," Cecelia's voice echoed out of the darkness.

Unkhabami turned slowly, listening.

"You destroyed my village."

"Too bad I missed you," Cecelia laughed.

"Too bad indeed." Unkhabami squinted toward the altar at the far end of the church, unsure if she had seen one of the shadows move. She cautiously moved forward up the aisle. On either side of her, white pillars rose up to the vaulted ceiling. Unkhabami eyed each column, expecting Cecelia to jump out.

Outside, the sound of sirens grew louder.

"Bami?"

Unkhabami spun around to see Rami standing in the crumbling entrance, silhouetted against the night.

"Stay there!" she called. "Do not let her get past you!"

"Rami. Rami." Cecelia's sing-song voice taunted from the shadows. "I almost killed you before. This time I'll succeed."

"You will not!" Unkhabami hissed, spinning toward the corner on her left.

"Bami, we must go!" Rami called. "The police will be here any moment!"

"I will not lose this chance!" Unkhabami rushed toward the corner but found only statues.

Cecelia's laugh echoed again, mocking her.

"Show yourself, bitch!"

"Tsk. Tsk." Cecelia laughed. "Such a temper."

"Bami!" Rami called again.

Purple light flashed across the night, illuminating the inside of the church. "No!" Cecelia screamed, "No! Father!"

In that moment, Unkhabami saw Cecelia. She snarled and rushed forward, yanking her dress over her head and shifting into a leopard in mid-air. She leaped onto the altar and pounced on Cecelia. Snarling and clawing, they fought, knocking over candelabras and scattering books across the flagstones. Unkhabami tore deep gouges in Cecelia's face and chest as they fought. Cecelia screeched and slashed at the priestess with her nails. Unkhabami sank her teeth into Cecelia's forearm as they rolled across the floor, toppling benches. The vampire grabbed a broken piece of bench and smashed it against the priestess' head. Staggering sideways from the blow, Unkhabami lost her hold on Cecelia.

"Bami! We must go now!" Rami shouted, glancing over his shoulder. The inside of the church lit up with flashing blue lights as police cars filled the parking lot. Uniformed officers moved through the scattered debris, shining their flashlights at the rubble.

Cecelia lurched to her feet and sprinted back toward the entrance.

Unkhabami wanted to scream, "Stop her!" but she was still in leopard form and couldn't.

Rami turned back in time to see Cecelia running straight at him, but the giant never had the chance to do anything about it as several police officers rushed up to Rami. Cecelia saw them and changed direction at the last minute.

Unkhabami yowled in frustration as she watched her quarry disappear down the hole to the Warren. The priestess knew that she had to make a decision: Rami or Cecelia.

She hissed once and then dashed back down the aisle. She burst out of the church, knocking the police away from Rami. The men shouted in surprise as she bared her teeth and hissed at them.

"Bami?" Rami froze, torn between escaping and fighting alongside her.

"Sir, step away from the animal!" The officer motioned to Rami. "Come this way, we can help you."

Unkhabami turned and hissed at him. She glanced back at Rami, urging him to run. Rami shot her a desperate look, shaking his head. She growled and turned back to face the police.

Unkhabami surveyed the churchyard, weighing their options. Bodies of werewolves, vampires, and Hares were scattered amongst the rubble, and the area was quickly filling with emergency services personnel. Their window for escape was closing fast. Their only chance was to go back through the church.

The police officers formed a circle in front of her. She looked from one to the next as they closed in. She took a step back. Rami was behind her, and she sensed him moving with her.

"Sir, don't go into the building!" The officer held his hand out in warning. "Just stay there, and we'll get the leopard away from you."

Unkhabami took another step back and another. Rami continued to move with her, staying right behind her.

"Sir, please," the officer pleaded. "Come back this way."

Another step brought them just inside the threshold. She hoped that Rami understood what she was planning. She couldn't take her eyes from the men in front of her.

"Get its attention," whispered one officer.

Unkhabami glared at him, wondering what he was planning. The man to her left suddenly jumped and shouted, drawing her focus. She didn't see the first officer pull out a taser, but Rami did.

"Watch out!" Rami shouted, but it was too late.

The officer's hand shot out, activating the taser. Unkhabami's world exploded. Her body seized as every muscle contracted. Lightning shot across her nerves, followed by an impossible level of pain. The world tilted and spun. She collapsed. She couldn't see if Rami got away because the police had thrown something over her face. She tried to struggle as her paws were tied together, but her muscles wouldn't cooperate. A feeling of powerlessness flooded her, followed quickly by terror.

What are they going to do to me?

WOLF ON A ROOF

Philtzer and Sophia ran back through the town, coming in behind Cecelia's army as they converged on the church. They joined up with Cody, Hamilton, Regina, Vivian, Malcolm, and others to swoop in fast and quiet, creating chaos amongst Cecelia's army. It was hard to tell who was on whose side. There were too many wolves, Hares, and vampires in a small space. Philtzer had seen Madraeus fighting with a sword and Thomas tangling with Spark, but then he had lost track of them.

The battle had pushed Sophia and Philtzer to the far side of the church. Sophia snarled as she removed the throat of a vampire while Philtzer tangled with an enemy wolf. The ground rumbled, distracting Philtzer just long enough for his adversary to slash his face open with his claws. Philtzer howled in surprise and lunged. The enemy wolf lost an eye and then his life.

The ground shook as the windows of the church shattered. Purple light blazed out.

Philtzer turned away from the dead wolf to see what was happening at the church, but a vampire tackled him like a runaway train. His breath whooshed out. As they landed and rolled, the vampire wrapped his arms around Philtzer's torso and squeezed. He heard a crack and then another crack. Pain blazed through his chest. Philtzer squirmed and kicked with all four paws, but he couldn't break loose. The vampire squeezed harder. Philtzer yelped.

Sophia, momentarily blinded by the blazing purple light, shook her head to clear her vision and saw Philtzer struggling for his life. With a snarl, she lunged forward and ripped out the vampire's hamstring. He went down fast, dropping Philtzer.

Philtzer landed hard, yelping again.

Sophia pounced on the vampire and made sure he didn't get back up. She looked at Philtzer but didn't have time to see if he was okay because Apep burst from the church, attacking everything in its path. The snake didn't seem to care who was on what side. Apep just wanted to kill.

Pandemonium erupted. The Hares and Madraeus' people ran forward, hacking and stabbing, but Cecelia's people were running hard and fast in the other direction. Philtzer wondered if any of them actually knew that Cecelia had wanted that thing set loose, or if they were just following along with the 'fun revolution'. Either way, they didn't seem too keen on dealing with a giant snake and were making a run for it.

Unfortunately, their path took them straight toward Philtzer and Sophia. He staggered to his feet, gritting his teeth against the pain in his ribs. The next few moments seemed like years as they fought hard not to join the ranks of the dead already littering the churchyard.

Philtzer had joked with Sandra about being around at Christmas, but now he wasn't sure if he would still be around by morning. The thought that this might be his last night filled him with anger. Adrenaline rushed through him, giving him the boost he needed to fight on.

Suddenly, Cody and Vivian were there. Cody fought like a rabid wolf, biting, snapping, and ripping. Vivian had a sword and slashed and stabbed anything that came near her. Unfortunately, Cecelia's vampires had also come armed. As Philtzer fought yet another wolf, he caught a glimpse of Vivian just as an enemy vampire skewered her on his sword.

Sophia leaped onto the vampire's back and tore out a section of his neck. Vivian landed on her knees, trying to pull the sword free. Sophia shifted into human form and grabbed the handle of the sword. She pulled hard, yanking it out of Vivian's midsection. Vivian's scream of pain mingled with the screech of police sirens as they surrounded the church.

Philtzer fought with renewed urgency. If the police were coming, they needed to be gone. He twisted and lunged, fighting both the enemy wolf and the pain in his chest. Suddenly, the wolf he was fighting fell over. He looked up to find Sophia, naked and holding the bloody sword with both hands, having plunged it into the wolf.

Philtzer panted as he looked around. What was left of Cecelia's army was gone. Blue light flashed on the far side of the buildings. There was no sign of the snake or the Hares. He looked to where Vivian had fallen, but she was gone. He looked around for Cody and saw his tail sticking out from behind a tombstone.

Wincing, Philtzer got to his feet and ran over to him. As he rounded the headstone, he stopped. Bile rose in his throat. Cody's body was in two pieces. Anguish washed over him, and he sank down into the grass, whining.

Sophia ran up beside him but froze when she saw Cody. She glanced at the police flooding the yard and then back at Philtzer. She ducked down behind the headstone.

"I'm sorry, but we have to go." She tugged on his ruff. "We can't be caught by the police."

Philtzer knew she was right; they didn't have time for grief. He pushed to his feet and led her back toward the stone wall that bordered the church's land. He looked up at the wall. It was nearly eight feet tall. He was going to have to shift back to human in order to climb over it.

This is gonna hurt.

Philtzer swallowed. He took a deep breath and shifted. The pain of changing from one shape to another with broken ribs was too much. He let out a howl that changed to a scream as he completed the transformation. He dropped to his knees, panting.

Sophia appeared at his elbow, holding a pair of pants. He blinked at the clothes, trying to figure out where she had gotten them.

She pointed over her shoulder at one of the dead bodies. "Donation."

Philtzer grinned as he struggled to his feet and pulled on the pants. "I taught you well."

She snorted as she pulled on the dead man's shirt.

He automatically glanced down at her bare legs. He took a moment to appreciate the fact that she wasn't wearing any pants. He grinned at her but flinched as the movement opened up the claw marks that ran the length of his cheek. Hot blood dripped down onto his bare chest, making him realize how chilly it was. It was nearing dawn. They needed to get out of sight before the police noticed them.

"All right," he sighed. "Up and over the wall, sugar."

"Fine and dandy," Sophia snorted, "but how are we going to get up there?"

"Have some faith, girl!" Philtzer gave her a hurt expression.

Philtzer took a deep breath, then took a run at the wall. He scrambled up the brick and grabbed the lip of the wall. Pain blazed through his chest, and he almost fell back again. Fighting against the pain, he heaved himself up and onto the top. It wasn't a wall at all. He had ended up on the top of someone's shed.

For a moment, he stayed still, gritting his teeth against the pain. His face throbbed with the beat of his heart, and his whole body ached. He wrapped a hand around his chest and closed his eyes. He'd heard a lot of cracking before he'd gotten free from that vampire. He was pretty sure he had more than a few broken ribs. He hoped his body would heal fast. He didn't want Sophia to know how badly he'd been injured.

When he thought he'd gotten his expression under control, he sat up and glanced around. He was on the lowest section of an L-shaped building.

He held a hand down to Sophia. She gave him a resistant but resigned look and took a run at the wall like he had. She didn't make it up as easily. She got up high enough to grab his hand, but her momentum wasn't enough to reach the roof edge. Philtzer winced as she slipped, jarring his shoulder as he caught her full weight. He clenched his teeth as he tried to haul her up. Her feet scrabbled against the wall as she tried to climb.

Together, they finally got her to the top. He rolled backward, pulling her the last few feet. She sprawled across his legs. For a long minute, they lay panting and struggling to keep their pain silent. Finally, Philtzer pushed himself up onto his elbows and looked down at Sophia. He opened his mouth to say something but stopped when he saw tears on her face.

"Soph..." he began, but she cut him off.

"Where to now, Spiderman?" Her voice sounded strained, and she kept her face averted.

He knew pride when he saw it and let her have her privacy.

Just then, he heard a policeman shouting, "Hey! Stay where you are!"

They both glanced back at the church. Officers were fanned out in front of where the entrance used to be.

"Who is that?" Sophia asked, squinting at the figure standing in front of the police.

Philtzer shook his head, but then recognition dawned. "That's Rami!"

"And Unkhabami!" Sophia's hands shot up to cover her mouth. "Did they just taser her?"

"Oh shit!" Philtzer muttered. "We gotta go!" He staggered to his feet and reached down to help her up. "Come on."

Sophia stared toward the church. "What about Rami and Unkhabami?"

"Later." Philtzer glanced back. "We can't fight the whole police force."

He led her across the roof, grumbling, "Damn, these tiles are cold!"

"That's what you're going to complain about?" Sophia muttered as she followed him.

Philtzer crept along the roof and poked his head out over the edge. They had the choice between going down into a walled garden or jumping down onto the driveway and making a run for the trees.

"Alright, follow me," he said over his shoulder, then slipped around the corner.

He hopped off the edge of the roof where it connected to a shorter wall, turned, and slid down to the ground. He ducked behind the shrubbery. A moment later, Sophia landed beside him with a grunt.

"You okay?" Philtzer puffed, trying not to whine out loud.

"No," Sophia whimpered.

"Me neither." Philtzer groaned and staggered to his feet.

Their moment of self-pity was interrupted by the door of the house opening. Philtzer grabbed Sophia and pulled her back into the shadows behind the shrubs. He could see someone through the branches. The person took a couple of steps toward the church, moving left and right, obviously trying to see what the noise was about. Philtzer winced as Sophia elbowed him. When he looked at her, she pointed to the person and made a 'let's whack him' gesture with her fist.

Philtzer shook his head, thinking, *I can barely stand up straight! How am I supposed to sneak up on this guy?*

Luckily, he didn't have to try. The man turned and went back into the house.

Philtzer sighed in relief. Sophia tugged at his arm, and he nodded. Quickly and quietly, they ran for the shadowed lane and disappeared into the night.

SACRILEGE

"No!" Whitney's voice was barely a whisper as she flung her hand out toward where Madraeus had disappeared. Her eyelids fluttered closed.

"Whitney?" Sandra crawled forward and wrapped her arms around Whitney, pulling her into her lap.

Whitney groaned and went limp in Sandra's arms.

"What did you do to her?" Sandra hissed.

John came closer and grabbed Whitney's bloody arm. He felt for her pulse. "She's still losing blood."

"No thanks to you, psycho!"

"She can't die now." John dropped her wrist and wiped his hand on his pant leg, leaving a smear of red behind. "We need to find one of the vampires."

"What?" Sandra's grip on Whitney tightened protectively. "Why?"

John didn't answer. He was busy peering over the rock wall toward the churchyard.

"She needs a hospital!" Sandra gasped.

Whitney stirred, trying to open her eyes.

"Stay here!" John commanded.

"Whitney, hold on." Sandra brushed the hair from Whitney's forehead, and her eyes fluttered. She looked around for anything to wrap around Whitney's wound, but there was nothing but grass, leaves, and rocks.

"Damn it!" she snarled. Sandra eased her down into the wet grass and stripped off her jacket. She yanked her T-shirt over her head and then pulled her jacket back on. Moving quickly, she tore her shirt in half and wrapped one part around Whitney's arm. She used the other half as a make-shift tourniquet.

As Sandra felt for Whitney's pulse, John came back with a man she'd never seen before.

"How could you do such a thing?" accused the stranger.

"Apep had to be stopped!" John snarled. "She is the new Key. If she dies, the spell is broken. Apep will be free again!"

"But this is sacrilege, John!" the stranger hissed.

"No." John's voice shook with enthusiasm. "Don't you see, Willie? With a vampire as the Key, she'll never die! We can keep Apep locked up forever!"

"Don't you dare!" Sandra jumped to her feet. In the distance, they could hear sirens approaching. "Take her to a hospital!"

"There's no time!" John looked toward the churchyard again. "We need to find one of Madraeus' bloodsuckers."

"No!" Sandra screeched.

"Sandra?" called a voice from the direction of the main gate.

It took Sandra a second to recognize the voice because she had only just met him at the hotel that morning. "Malcolm! Get over here! Whitney needs help!"

John and Willie spun around as Malcolm came sprinting down the side path.

Malcolm skidded to a halt next to the little group. He looked at Whitney and then at the blood soaking through Sandra's t-shirt bandage. "Shit!" Malcolm muttered, "Why does this keep happening to me?"

"Help me!" Sandra shouted. "She needs a hospital!"

"No!" John stepped over Whitney. "You must turn her!"

"What?" Malcolm looked from Whitney to John to Whitney and back again.

"There's no time." John's eyes blazed. "If you don't turn her, she'll die and the snake will be free again!"

Sandra grabbed John's wrist. "You can't use her like that!"

John shook her off. "You'd let her die instead?"

"I don't think she wants to be a vampire," Malcolm protested.

John's hand sliced through the air. "I don't care what she wants!"

"You don't care about anything!" Sandra snapped.

Malcolm shook his head. "We gotta take her to a doctor."

John glared at Malcolm, pointing at Whitney. "Turn her before it's too late!"

Willie knelt beside Sandra and felt for Whitney's pulse. "He's right, she's dying," he muttered. "She'll never make it to Exeter."

"I can't make that choice for her."

"It's not a choice!" John grabbed the front of Malcolm's jacket and hauled him closer. "Do you want to fight that damn snake demon again? Half your people are dead!" John flung a hand toward the devastation that littered the churchyard. "You think you can take it on alone?"

Malcolm gaped at him.

"Turn her, damn it!" John shouted as Malcolm jerked free from his grip.

"Don't do it!" Sandra stared up at Malcolm.

"Whitney?" Malcolm knelt and shook her shoulders. "Whitney?"

Whitney didn't respond. He tapped her cheek, trying to wake her. Her head lolled to the side, and her eyes rolled back, showing only the whites.

Malcolm looked around desperately. "Madraeus—"

"Madraeus isn't here!" John pressed. "Make your decision!"

"You know he doesn't want her turned!" Sandra braced her hand against Malcolm's chest. "She doesn't want turned!"

"It's now or never!" John hissed. "You want more people to die?"

The sirens grew louder as the local police converged on the churchyard.

"Do it!" John snapped.

Malcolm's voice cracked as he said, "Forgive me, Whitney."

"Malcolm! No!" Sandra yelped, but it was too late.

Malcolm lifted her bleeding arm, leaned forward, and drank. It wasn't more than a few seconds before he sat up. He lifted her onto his lap. He tipped her head back. Her jaw hung slack. Working quickly, he bit his own arm and then dripped some of his blood into Whitney's mouth.

Sandra stared at Malcolm in horror. "I can't believe you did that."

Malcolm glanced at Sandra. "I'm sorry." He looked back at Whitney, watching closely for any sign that the transformation had been successful.

Sandra slowly stood. Her knees were soaked from the wet grass, but she didn't notice. She gazed at Whitney and swallowed hard. All that time in the mine, they had stood strong. Her and Whitney, together, mortals amongst the monsters. Now she was one of *them*. The next time Whitney opened her eyes, she'd be a bloodsucking nightmare. Her best friend, the only human connection she had left in the world, was gone. Sandra's chest constricted. She didn't know if she was going to faint or throw up.

"Apep will never be free again!"

John's enthusiastic exclamation snapped her control. Sandra spun around and lunged at him, catching him in the jaw with a right hook. She was like a wild thing, attacking him with fists and feet.

"Get her off me!" John cowered away from her, covering his face. The other Hare, Willie, tried to get a hold on Sandra to pull her off of John, but he couldn't get a grip.

Sirens echoed off the stone buildings as the police pulled up outside the gate. Blue lights from their vehicles flashed, casting misshapen shadows through the trees.

"Sandra!" Malcolm reached for her but couldn't get close enough with Whitney on his lap. "Sandra!" Malcolm quickly, but gently, shifted Whitney off his lap, lowering her to the grass.

Sandra took no notice of Malcolm or the police flooding through the gate. She wanted only one thing, and that was to kill John. She kicked and punched him over and over.

"Bitch!" John spun sideways and backhanded her across the face. As she reeled from the blow, he rammed his fist into her solar plexus.

"Hey!" Malcolm rushed John and tackled him as Sandra doubled over, coughing and puking.

Willie wasted no time in grabbing the thick branch that Sandra had used earlier and brought it down on Malcolm's head. Although it didn't knock Malcolm out, it dazed him enough for John to get out from under him. Sandra gasped, trying to get her breath back. She watched in horror as John and Willie picked up Whitney and carried her away into the shadows.

Malcolm groaned and looked around, trying to focus his eyes. Sandra was alternating between throwing up and gasping for air. Tears streamed down her anguished face as she pointed to where Whitney and the Hares had disappeared. Beyond the rock wall, the police were shouting and coming closer.

"Sandra?" Malcolm crawled over to her. "We have to get out of here."

"Whi..." Sandra gasped. "Whit..."

"I know." Malcolm staggered to his feet and reached for her. She shoved his hand away. "Sandra. We can't help her if the police pick us up. Now, come on!"

He reached for her again, and this time, Sandra let him help her to her feet. She leaned heavily against him as he looked around, trying to find a way out. The police cars blocked the gate, and the churchyard wasn't an option. He looked down the little path leading away from the church and then glanced at the sky. It was getting lighter.

"Shit." He started down the little path through the trees. It took them past a larger cemetery and down a tree-covered lane. "Where the hell are we?" he muttered.

Dawn was getting closer. They had to find a place to hide.

"Mill." Sandra pointed to a sign next to the path. She was breathing a little easier. "Tourist."

"Tourist spot?" Malcolm glanced at her, and she nodded. "Good enough for me."

They staggered forward through the darkness until he found a wooden door set in a brick wall. Malcolm broke the latch and followed the path. On one side was someone's garage and yard, and on the other was a wooden walkway that led around the back of the mill. He followed the walkway until they reached the waterwheels. He glanced around for a way in. Down under the overhang that sheltered the wheels, he could see an access panel.

"There." He pointed. "It'll be cramped, but we won't run into any tourists."

Sandra and Malcolm crawled into the lower level of the mill and found a spot out of the way.

"Now what?" Sandra was getting some control over her stomach and lungs.

"Now, we wait."

FATHER

Madraeus groaned as he crawled back to awareness. He blinked, squeezed his eyes shut hard, and blinked again. Everything looked purple. Everything hurt. Everything was shaking.

The ground trembled and vibrated as if from repeated impacts. He raised his head and blinked a few more times, trying to get his eyes to adjust to the strange hues. Slowly, the world came into focus. He was surrounded by black trees, not just trees in shadow, but trees with trunks that were shades of black. The air shimmered, creating caustic patterns of light and dark. It was like staring at the sun through purple water. The strange air dampened all sound. And it was cold.

The ground shuddered again.

Madraeus sat up and froze. The snake demon was not more than ten feet from him.

Apep reared up and struck at the shimmering purple air above the low stone wall. The snake contracted its coils like an evil slinky and slammed into the sizzling purple barrier again and again. Each time the barrier rippled on impact but otherwise remained unchanged.

Madraeus' eyes darted from the snake to the trees to the shimmering purple barrier. *I'm trapped in Apep's prison.* Squashing down the panic that followed that revelation, he shook his head; now wasn't the time for emotional reactions.

Madraeus scrambled to his feet and slipped behind the nearest tree. Pain burned across his shoulders and spine as the cuts on his back opened up. Once he was out of the snake's range of vision, he made a quick survey of the area.

They were in a grove of trees. The low wall seemed to circle the grove, and in the center, a statue stood in a small pool. Madraeus remembered seeing the grove when they'd first arrived at the churchyard. That brief glimpse had given the impression that it wasn't very big, but now it seemed a lot larger. Apep was the size of a bus and still had plenty of room to move around.

His brain couldn't process that observation. Madraeus peeked around the other side of the tree. He wanted to put some space between himself and the demon so he could think. The far side of the grove was nothing but shadow; however, it was better than staying where he was.

He glanced back at Apep. The snake continued to furiously strike the same spot above the gap in the wall. Madraeus slipped out from behind the tree and sprinted toward the other end of the grove. It took several minutes before he reached the opposite wall. He frowned. *How big is this grove?* He looked back. There was no sign of Apep, although he could still feel the vibrations coming from Apep's single-minded attack. He tried to puzzle out how a grove that wasn't more than twenty or thirty feet across could suddenly be the size of a small town but couldn't come up with an explanation.

"I hate magic," he muttered and turned to study the shimmering barrier. It was opaque but not a solid color; instead, distorted reflections of the grove danced across the surface. There was a rhythm of power pulsing through it, as if the barrier was breathing. He reached out and touched it. He gasped as his fingers tingled. It was warm to the touch, like living flesh. The spell that had imprisoned Apep before had required the blood of a living person, a Key. Grace, if you could call that monstrosity a person, had been near death when they'd arrived. A vision flashed through his mind, his last glimpse of Whitney, sprawled in the grass with her arm bleeding.

Madraeus' eyes widened. *No!* Anguish twisted his gut. *She can't be the Key!*

The Key? an all too familiar voice hissed in his head.

The ground no longer shook. Apep had ceased his attack on the prison wall.

Madraeus spun around and stared back toward where he had left the crazed snake. Through the strange, muffled air, he could hear the scraping sound of Apep's approach.

Madraeus looked around and quickly picked a solid-looking tree to hide behind. He would fight, but he didn't have to stand out in the open as an easy target.

Come out, come out. Apep hissed.

Madraeus tried to blank his mind.

I know you are here. Traitorousss child. Apep slithered closer.

Madraeus listened, trying to discern where Apep was as he glanced around for a weapon. He remembered dropping his sword as he chased after the snake, but he couldn't remember if it was before or after they had entered the grove.

We could have desstroyed thessse missserable creaturesss, Apep hissed, *but you chossse to fight againssst me.*

Madraeus could hear the snake coming around the tree on his left. He slowly eased around to the right. Near the wall, about twenty feet away, purple light glinted off of something in the grass. He hoped it was his discarded sword.

I could have been free!

He glanced to his left. He could just see the tip of the snake's tongue flicking out past the trunk.

I can sssmell your blood.

Apep eased back out of view. Madraeus took his chance and dashed across the grass toward what he hoped was a weapon. Apep whipped around, alerted by the sudden movement.

I sssee you.

Apep lunged, but his strike missed its mark as Madraeus slid across the grass like a baseball player reaching home. As Madraeus landed, Apep slammed into the barrier above him. Madraeus scrambled forward. Relief flooded him as his hand clasped the sword. He flipped onto his back and plunged the sword upward, hoping to slice open Apep's belly.

Unfortunately, Apep had already retreated, ready to strike again.

Madraeus came to his feet and settled into a fighting stance with his sword held at the ready.

Fool! Apep's voice shrieked in Madraeus' mind. *You could have had everything! You could have ruled the darknesss! Ssspread chaosss acrosss the world!*

"You think I want that?" Madraeus snarled.

Don't you? Apep curled and swayed, watching Madraeus. *Your sssoul sssingsss in the darknesss! Look what you did to that little village. The power! You reveled in it!*

The reflection of purple light flickered oddly in the snake's eyes.

Madraeus blinked and shook his head. He had taken a step closer without realizing it.

"No!" Madraeus tightened his grip on the sword. "That was you. Not me!"

It wasss you! Apep seemed to smile. *You cannot help it! I am in you. You are mine. You can never be free of me!*

As Apep spoke, he slipped to the side, coming a little closer. Madraeus countered, sidestepping the opposite way.

"I've blocked you out before." Madraeus clung to hope, absently wishing that he really did have some kind of armor from God.

The demon laughed. *It never lassstsss. Thessse little rebellionsss of yoursss. It isss a fleeting thing.*

Out of the shadows, Apep's coils rolled and surged around. Madraeus dodged to the side. Apep's tail smacked into the tree behind where Madraeus had been standing just seconds before.

Madraeus' lip curled as he glared at Apep, berating himself for not paying more attention. He hadn't seen the snake's tail moving closer through the shadows. He had no idea how he was going to fight this demon alone. He was outmatched, and he knew it. He was one man with one sword fighting a primordial demon. He had no chance of winning. Despite that, Madraeus had no intention of giving in, so he continued to look for any advantage.

"If you want me to join you so badly, then why attack me?" Madraeus moved parallel to the snake, hoping that if he kept moving, it wouldn't give Apep time to strike.

Apep reared up, towering over Madraeus. *Becaussse you need a lessson in obedienccce!*

With that, Apep surged forward again. Madraeus dodged and brought the sword down on the back of Apep's head. Sparks flew as the metal raked against his scales. The snake roared in anger and twisted around. He lashed out at Madraeus again and again, each time Madraeus dodged, cut, parried, and slashed. Round and round in a brutal dance, each tried to get the upper hand.

The more they fought, the more the wounds in Madraeus' back opened. As his blood oozed out, weakness began to set in, and in turn, his movements began to slow. He knew it was only a matter of time before he couldn't continue, but at least he had the satisfaction of knowing that he'd put up a helluva fight. Apep's blood flowed freely from dozens of lesions and gouges zigzagging across the demon's scales.

Apep coiled, flicking his tongue. Then suddenly, he flashed forward. Madraeus wasn't quick enough. Apep's fangs pierced his right forearm and retreated just as quickly. Fire raced down his arm. His grip on the sword loosened. Apep lashed out, striking Madraeus again and again, beating him down, biting his shoulder, his arm, his leg.

Madraeus dropped the sword and fell to his knees. His entire body was on fire.

You are mine! Apep hissed and surged forward. His fangs sank into Madraeus' chest.

Madraeus screamed and fell to the ground. Pain burned through him. He couldn't think beyond the agony. The world pulsated with purple light. His vision blurred. He was dimly aware of Apep slithering away as he faded into nothingness.

AWAKENING

WHITNEY FELT SOMETHING HOT against the cold skin of her neck. Someone lifted her arm.

"She should be awake by now."

"Maybe she's lost too much blood."

Whitney tried to claw her way up from the darkness.

"If she dies, this has all been for nothing."

"She won't die."

Am I dying again? she wondered as she drifted into oblivion.

"Vampires don't just die."

Jolted back from the darkness, Whitney gasped, *Vampire?*

I don't want to be a vampire! She tried to open her eyes, but she couldn't seem to get control of her muscles. Something cold touched her lips. She flinched at the bitter metallic flavor that filled her mouth. She spit out the liquid and fought to get away.

"Hold her!"

Screaming and spitting, Whitney bucked against their restraining hands.

"John, this isn't going to work!"

John? Memories burned through her mind. The snake, the woods, John, and Madraeus…

She screamed.

"We have to try something else!"

"Give me that!"

She felt a prick in her arm. Numbness seeped into her as she sank back into the abyss. She couldn't move her body anymore. Once again, she felt something cold touching her lips. She tried to close her mouth, but they forced it open. A cold, thick liquid poured into her mouth. She had to swallow or choke.

Panic burned through the sedative they had given her. Whitney thrashed back and forth. Something cold and wet spilled down the sides of her face. Hands held her head still as they forced her to drink. Instinct that wasn't hers took over, and she swallowed greedily.

"All right, that's enough." They snatched the bottle away. "We don't want her too strong. Just not dead."

That was blood! Revulsion filled her. *I don't want to be a vampire!*

She hated them. She wanted to rip their throats out. She wanted to sink her teeth in and…

Whitney lunged.

"Sedate her again!"

Once again, Whitney felt a sharp prick. A fog crept over her mind. Her body felt like lead. Whitney shuddered and moaned.

Everything went black.

Drip.

Drip.

Drip.

Drip.

Whitney stirred as the sound invaded her consciousness. It was so loud. She listened, trying to identify it. It sounded like a dripping water tap. It echoed inside her head. It hurt.

It's so loud!

Whitney rolled to her side and covered her ears with her hands. She froze. Her fingers touched something sticky. She opened her eyes to see what it was. For a second, the light was blinding. She shut her eyes again and then opened them just a slit. She squinted at her hands, fearing what she would see. They were covered in blood.

Whose blood is this?

Burning need blazed through her. Every fiber of her being wanted to lick off every drop of the life-giving liquid. She could taste it already. Whitney gagged.

She scrambled to her feet. She started to shake. Emotions flooded her one after another in rapid succession. Fear. Hunger. Self-loathing. Need. Panic.

Need to get it off!

She looked around, trying to think. The furnishings looked like a bedroom, but the walls were stone. No pictures decorated the room, but there was a bed, a dresser, two wooden chairs, and a table. There were two doors and no windows.

She ran to the first door and pulled on the handle. It was locked. She turned to the second door and opened it to find a small bathroom. A toilet stood against one wall across from a sink with no mirror. The tap was dripping. She quickly turned the faucet on, leaving a smear of blood on the handle. She plunged her hands under the water and frantically scrubbed.

When her hands were as clean as she could get them, she looked at the rest of the room. In the back corner, a shower head stuck out of the wall. There was no curtain. In the center of the floor was a drain. It reminded her of a prison. She closed her eyes, knowing that's exactly what it was. Her prison for all eternity. She was the new Key.

She moaned out loud. She didn't want to be the new Key. She shuddered as she remembered the monstrosity they called Grace. She didn't want to be like that, a prisoner forever tied to the trap holding Apep.

And Madraeus... He's gone! Despair and grief washed over her. It had happened so fast that her foggy brain couldn't process it. He had been caught in the trap. The look in his eyes right before the trap closed haunted her. She couldn't shake the memory. Frustration bloomed in her chest. He had sacrificed himself. He could have jumped free of the trap, but he hadn't.

It's all John's fault, she thought bitterly. *When I find him, I'm gonna rip—* She broke off the thought before it was fully formed. *I don't want to rip anything! I don't want to be a vampire!*

She could still smell blood. Her stomach growled. She felt like she was starving. Whitney turned her head and smelled it again. *Where is it?* Reaching up, she felt her hair. It was thick and sticky. She pulled some of it around to look at it. It was covered in blood. A frustrating cry of disgust and hunger escaped her lips as she dove for the shower. She didn't even bother to get undressed. Whitney scrubbed and ripped at her hair, trying to get it clean. Finally, the smell of blood faded.

Soaking wet, Whitney backed out of the bathroom. She began to pace and cry. Around and around the little bedroom, over and over again, she paced and cried. There was no escape. No exit. No future.

"No!" she screamed.

Picking up one of the chairs, she threw it at the door. The backrest snapped off and skidded across the floor. Whitney stared at it. Desperation pushed her forward. She picked up the backrest and gazed at it. In one swift movement, she lifted it up and then smashed it into the wall. Chunks of wood bounced across the stone floor.

Whitney looked at the splintered mess and picked up one of the spindles. The tip was jagged. She flipped it over and set the point against her chest, right over her heart. She held the stake with both hands. Her breath came in short gasps as she gathered her courage. She closed her eyes, ready to thrust the stake into her heart.

Time stopped. Regrets tumbled through her mind. She wished she'd done so many things differently. Her friends, her grandmother... Madraeus...

Tears streaked down her face as her courage failed. "I can't!"

Whitney sank to the floor. She stared at the piece of wood in her hand.

What am I going to do?

Someone knocked on the door.

Whitney scrambled to her feet and shouted, "Go away!"

"I fear I can't do that, Whitney," a voice said through the door.

She backed across the room, slipping in the blood pool she had woken up in.

"I can help you," the voice called again.

"No one can help me!" Whitney wailed. Even to her own ears, she sounded hysterical.

She stared at the blood on the floor. Pain twisted in her gut, catching her by surprise. She doubled over and sank to her knees. It was like hunger pain, but so much more intense. She couldn't bring herself to even think about what her body was craving. She hated the very idea.

The Hares. They did this to me! She hated them. Rage hotter than she had ever felt flared up.

She glared at the door, holding the chair spindle up like a knife and snarled, "If you come in here, I'll kill you!"

BETRAYED

Sandra sank to the floor, holding her stomach, and watched Malcolm dash around. The small room under the mill's waterwheel was not exactly built for accommodating vampires. In fact, it was the opposite. It had been built to let in as much natural light as possible. With dawn creeping in through every crack, Malcolm rushed to block every opening he found, pulling shut ancient shutters and covering every other opening with grain sacks from the historical displays.

Moments later, Malcolm curled up in the darkest corner with his jacket pulled up over his head to protect him from any stray sunlight and fell asleep. Sandra, however, couldn't sleep. There was just too much... too much everything.

Her mind replayed the fight with John, seeing Whitney bleeding in the grass, and then... Whitney was gone.

Something broke loose inside her.

Whitney is gone!

Sandra tried to stifle the sob but couldn't. She covered her mouth, trying to muffle the sounds. The tears wouldn't stop.

She pushed back into the corner and turned her face to the wall. Her body convulsed with each heaving sob. Anguish seized her lungs, suffocating her. She gasped and shook. It was hours before the tears stopped.

As her body finally stilled, she blinked the tears from her lashes and stared. Not far from her toes, rays of sunlight, which had managed to find a way past Malcolm's hasty blockades, striped the floor. A strange calm filled her as she watched the dust motes dancing in those sunbeams.

With only the faintest flicker of surprise, Sandra realized that this was the first time she had cried since the mine. Losing Whitney had opened the dam. Sandra let out a little laugh at the synchronicity of having finally let loose the flood of emotion while sitting next to a floodgate.

Sandra sniffled and swiped the rest of the moisture from her face. She shifted and pulled her jacket closer. The stone floor of the mill was freezing cold, and it was slowly seeping into her bones. But that was nothing compared to the ice that surrounded her heart.

When Sandra and her friends had been abducted during their camping trip, she had thought it was the worst thing that could happen. But then she became food for an army of vampires and watched her friends die one by one. Her death had been certain and imminent. As the time stretched, Sandra had become more and more apathetic. It was just a matter of enduring. She expected to die, wanted to die.

Everything changed when Whitney showed up. She brought hope into the cell with her. Sandra's time in the mine with Whitney had been short, but shared trauma had created a strong bond between them. Madraeus had even spared Sandra's life because of Whitney. He could have easily included Sandra in the body count, but he hadn't, because of Whitney.

After the Council had declared Sandra legally dead, she had nowhere to go. She couldn't go to her family; she couldn't reenter her life. The Council had made it very clear that she wasn't to have any contact with her former life, or the consequence would be death. She didn't officially exist anymore, but she didn't know how to start over. Whitney was the only human connection Sandra had left, so it made sense to stay with Whitney despite her continued association with monsters. Sandra had told herself that they weren't so bad, but she had been lying to herself.

Betrayal burned in her chest. Sandra looked across the small storage area to where Malcolm slept. The monsters had taken everything from her. Not just the Races, but the Hares too. Her mind flickered back to the monstrosity the Hares had called Grace.

They used her as a tool to be discarded when she had fulfilled her purpose. Grace should have had a life, but it was stolen and warped by the Hares' misguided attempt to save the world. Just like Whitney's! Hate filled Sandra. *They all deserve to die!*

A sudden thump made her jump. Her eyes flicked to the ceiling.

Malcolm rolled over, instantly awake. He looked at her and then followed her gaze.

Another thump followed by muffled voices sounded above them. Dust drifted down from the ceiling. Someone was walking around upstairs.

Malcolm quietly moved into a crouch, watching the ceiling.

In the center of the room stood a spoked wheel mounted on a column. It was part of the mechanism that transferred power from the waterwheel to the grinding stones. Malcolm moved so the wheel was between him and the stairs. Sandra mimicked his movements. She wanted to be ready to run. She didn't know where she would run to, but she wanted the option. Sandra glanced at the sun spots. As a vampire, Malcolm couldn't go out until dusk, but Sandra could.

For a moment, she toyed with the idea of running upstairs and yelling for help. She could get away from this crazy world of death and monsters, but then logic returned. No matter where she ran to, there would be questions and trouble.

More bangs and thumps sounded. Dust rained down on Malcolm and Sandra as the intruders moved around above them. They both jumped as someone rattled the latch on the door at the top of the stairs. Malcolm had checked the door when they'd arrived and found it locked. Thankfully, whoever was up there didn't have the key. The floor creaked again as they moved on.

Another thump echoed dully and then silence settled.

Sandra looked at Malcolm. He watched the ceiling, waiting. He looked toward the windows, listening.

When nothing happened for a few minutes, he looked at Sandra. "I think they're gone."

"Who do you think it was? Cecelia?"

"Nah, probably police." He settled down onto the floor, pulled his knees up, and rested his arms across them.

"Will they be back?"

"I doubt it. They probably found the latch I broke. Then figured the door was on the path coming from the church where all hell just broke loose, so they better check it out."

Sandra sank down to sit cross-legged. "How do you know that?"

Malcolm gave her a self-deprecating shrug. "Not my first run-in with the Old Bill."

"Old Bill?" Sandra shook her head in confusion.

"Coppers, British police," he said, slipping into a British accent.

"You're British?" He looked Korean.

"Was." His tone turned bitter. He looked like he was going to say more, but then he blew out a long breath and said, "They're gonna be crawling all over the church and everything around it for days."

"We can't wait days!" Sandra looked at him sharply. "We have to get Whitney back!"

"I know," Malcolm nodded, "but she's gonna be safer where she is for a while."

"What?" Sandra spluttered. "The Hares took her! They took her away from us! From me!" Sandra beat on her chest with her fist. "She didn't deserve to be used like that!"

"Sandra," Malcolm held out his hands in a placating gesture, "calm down!" He glanced at the ceiling.

"No!" Sandra glared at him. "This is your fault! You turned her into a vampire! You're no different than the Hares! Using people and destroying lives! You're all monsters!"

"Yes, we're all monsters! Nobody can deny that, but you better get your head on straight about what's going on here. Monsters or not, we were trying to stop a chaos demon from destroying the world. That takes priority over all our lives."

"So, what? We're just collateral damage?"

Malcolm's lips twitched as he tried to keep his temper. "What did you want me to do? Let her die? Let the snake out again?"

"You could have taken her to a hospital!"

"Oh, yeah?" Malcolm scoffed, looking around the room for his patience. "Let's think about this." Malcolm glared at Sandra. "We jump up and take Whitney to a hospital. She has heart failure due to blood loss on the way. Uh-oh, Whitney's dead. Here comes the bloody snake. Now, I don't know about you, but I'm not strong enough to kill it. Great! I'm dead, you're dead, everyone's dead! So, yeah, I made a decision. I didn't want to, but I did."

Sandra glared at him silently. Deep down, she knew he was right, but she wasn't ready to accept it yet.

Malcolm scrubbed at his hair with both hands, sending dust flying. He sighed. "Doesn't matter. What's done is done, and Madraeus is gonna kill me for it."

"No, he won't." Sandra picked at the seam on her jeans.

"Yes, he will." Malcolm shook his head. "He never wanted her to become a vampire."

"He'll probably never know." Sandra shifted against the cold stones.

"Why?" Malcolm asked warily.

"He's locked in with Apep." Sandra pulled her knees up and hugged them. "He stopped Apep from getting out at the very last second, but he didn't get out either."

Malcolm froze, staring at her. "Oh shit, what have I done?"

WOLF HUDDLE

"FINALLY!" PHILTZER GROANED AS they stopped just inside the trees across from the hotel.

Coming back to Exeter from Broadclyst on foot had taken most of the morning. It would have been faster to change and run as wolves, but Philtzer couldn't face the pain of shifting again. As it was, he could barely take a full breath. He swayed slightly, leaning against Sophia.

"Almost there." Sophia steadied him.

He nodded, but then groaned, "Crap."

Sophia grabbed his elbow just in case he fell. "What's the matter?"

He looked at her. "Do you have a keycard?"

"Seriously?" She gestured to her pantless legs.

"Oh," Philtzer sighed, "right."

"Give me your pants," Sophia held her hand out, "and I'll go get another key."

"I'm not gonna sit in the bushes naked!"

"Why not? I thought you didn't care about being naked."

"I don't when I can run away and disappear as a wolf." Philtzer held his ribs and winced. "Right now, I can't even shift. Why don't you give me your shirt, and I'll get the key?"

Sophia glared at him, gave him a disgruntled snarl, and started unbuttoning her shirt. She ripped it off, shoved it at his chest, and shifted to wolf before he could catch it.

Philtzer pulled the shirt on much slower than she had removed it and walked toward the hotel's office. It didn't take long to spin a sob story to the desk clerk. His bleeding face validated his tale of woe. He got a new keycard and met up with Sophia at the back door. But his strength was failing. If he didn't rest soon, he was going to pass out. He braced against the wall for support as they walked down the long hallway to their room. Sophia trotted at his side, looking anxiously at him every few steps.

By the time they reached the room, Philtzer was seeing double. He leaned against the door frame, fumbling with the keycard. Sophia looked around. Seeing no one, she shifted and grabbed the card from Philtzer. In seconds, the door was open. Sophia stepped in first, pulling Philtzer in behind her. He only managed two steps before collapsing face-first onto the floor.

"Philtzer!" Sophia landed on her knees beside him.

"I'm okay," he whimpered.

"Yeah, sure." Sophia shook her head and shoved to her feet.

Philtzer heard her banging around and swearing quietly. He stared at a piece of lint stuck on the carpet about six inches from his nose. He was too tired to move, too tired to care. Pain seemed to be the only thing he could feel at the moment.

Someone rattled the door handle.

Gritting his teeth against the pain, he rolled onto his back. The door swung open. Regina, supporting a bleeding Thomas, stood in the doorway. She hauled Thomas forward and kicked the door shut with her heel.

Regina looked down at Philtzer. "What are you doing on the floor?"

Philtzer blinked up at her. "Didn't feel like using the bed."

"We just got here." Sophia glared at her mother as she got dressed.

"You need to get up and start treating those wounds." Regina groused as she helped Thomas to the bed. "The last thing we need is blood on the carpet." Regina retrieved the bag of medical supplies they'd prepared.

"Here," Regina pressed a square of gauze to the gaping hole in Thomas' shoulder, "hold this." She glanced back at Philtzer. "Those aren't your clothes. What the hell you been doing, boy?"

"Oh, you know," Philtzer tried to sit up, groaned, and fell back again. "Got in a fight, lost my clothes, lost the keycard..."

"Philtzer, I thought I taught you better." Regina shook her head. "You don't take your key with you. You hide it outside the hotel and come back for it."

Sophia came over and helped him to his feet.

Doing his best not to wince, Philtzer hobbled over and sat down beside Thomas. "Sorry, mom."

"If I was your mom, I'd kick your ass," Regina snorted and handed Sophia an antiseptic wipe, gesturing to Philtzer's face. "You don't have to be gentle."

Sophia dabbed at the claw marks on Philtzer's face.

"Ow!"

"Sorry."

"No worries." Philtzer gave her a lopsided smile, but the movement split open the cuts again, soaking the wipe.

Sophia grabbed Philtzer's hand and made him hold a towel to his face while she dug through the medical kit for something to hold his cheek together.

"You two are a mess," Regina said under her breath as she wrapped a bandage around Thomas' shoulder.

"At least," Thomas growled, "we took out a good portion of Cecelia's army."

"Not nearly as many as we wanted to," Philtzer sighed.

"But we won, right?" Sophia asked, tearing open another package of gauze.

"I don't call that fiasco a win," Thomas muttered.

"Neither do I." Regina shook her head. She turned to Philtzer and gently pulled the towel away from his face but immediately pressed it back. "No sense bandaging that until the bleeding slows."

"But I'm assuming since we're here and there isn't a huge snake loose, that at least Apep is gone?"

"I don't know," Thomas looked up at her. "Last I saw, Madraeus was tangling with Apep, but they just disappeared into the trees."

"And then there was that freaky purple light," Philtzer added.

"Well, it's daylight now." Regina stepped back from Thomas and gathered up the empty packages. "We won't know anything for sure until dark, unless they call. Who's got the check-in phone?"

"Hamilton."

"Last I saw him, he was fighting near the gate. I didn't see where he went after that." Regina threw the empty packages into the trash can by the desk and turned to Sophia. "Come with me, kiddo."

"Why?"

Regina gestured toward the bathroom. "I know you're hiding a few wounds too. Let's get you sorted."

"You don't have to leave for that." Philtzer grinned around the towel.

"Hush, you." Regina glared at him. "She doesn't need to be ogled by the likes of you."

"Too late." Philtzer snickered to Thomas and earned a kick in the shin from Regina.

"Ow!"

"Serves you right," she said over her shoulder as she led Sophia into the bathroom.

Philtzer sobered after they were out of sight. "Thomas?"

"What?"

"Will you wrap my ribs? I'm pretty sure at least three of them are broken," Philtzer muttered. "I don't want Soph to know."

"Why not?" Thomas stretched and winced. "You usually use any excuse to get sympathy from a girl. Why the sudden change?"

"No reason." Philtzer pulled the towel away, but seeing the amount of blood, pressed it back against his cheek.

"You really like her," Thomas accused as he dug out some bandages.

"What's not to like?" Philtzer sighed dreamily. "She's smart, brave, adorable."

"You must like her if you listed her brain first," Thomas snorted.

"Shut up." Philtzer raised his arms so Thomas could reach around him.

Philtzer closed his eyes against the pain as Thomas bound his chest.

"Doesn't matter. Pretty sure she knows you're a mess." Thomas stepped back and eyed him. "You might need an actual doctor this time."

Philtzer lowered his arms. It hurt to breathe, but the support helped a little. "Nah," Philtzer said through his teeth. I'm good."

Thomas began working on Philtzer's face. He carefully pulled the towel back and watched the cuts. Satisfied that they were only oozing a little, Thomas wiped away the excess blood and then pasted butterfly band-aids across the claw marks. "If you don't move your face, this should keep them closed long enough to heal."

"Right," Philtzer snorted, trying to keep his face still, "that shouldn't be too hard."

"Maybe you should tape his mouth shut." Regina's voice rang out from the other room.

"I love you too, Reggie," Philtzer called, but then winced and held his cheek.

"You see Cody?" Thomas asked as he tossed a shirt at Philtzer's head.

Philtzer struggled into the shirt, gritting his teeth. He glanced at Thomas. He was dreading this moment. There was no good way to tell someone that their foster brother was dead. "Cody went down."

Thomas froze. He swallowed before asking, "Did he get back up?"

Philtzer couldn't bring himself to answer. Seeing Cody in two pieces was too fresh in his mind.

Thomas snarled and threw the bag he was holding across the room, knocking over a chair as it passed.

"Hey!" Regina snapped as she came back out into the main room. "Settle down!" She walked over and set the chair back on its feet. "Getting us kicked out ain't gonna help anyone."

Thomas threw himself into the chair and held his head in his hands, clenching fistfuls of hair. His body shook, and he started to rock. Even from across the room, Philtzer could tell that every muscle in Thomas' body had tightened as he tried to deal with his grief in silence. Cody had been the best of them. He had been gentle, moral, and good. Philtzer closed his eyes, sinking into his own grief.

"Now's not the time, son." Regina's voice pulled him back. "We gotta look to the living."

Cody used to say that, thought Philtzer as he opened his eyes. Sophia was kneeling in front of him, watching him.

She whispered, "Like Unkhabami."

"What about Unkhabami?" Thomas asked without looking up.

"We saw the police taser her," Sophia said.

"What?" Thomas shot to his feet.

Sophia flinched. "She was by the church with Rami when the police showed up."

"So, they've been arrested?"

"Not exactly." Philtzer shook his head. "They tried to grab Rami. She jumped in to free him, but she was in leopard form. They tasered her and tied her up."

"Well, that's a new one," Regina muttered as she picked up the medical bag and jammed the spare bandages inside.

"So, what? We gotta spring her from cat jail?" Thomas let out a bark of incredulous laughter. "What about Rami?"

"I don't know," Sophia said. "We didn't see."

Thomas let out a snarl. Philtzer glanced at him. His eyes were wild, and his hair stuck out in all directions. Losing Cody had pushed him to the edge.

"Thomas!" Philtzer stared at Thomas until he had his friend's full attention. "We're gonna get through this. We're gonna sort it out."

"How?" Thomas shook. "We're on our own! Normally, this is all Madraeus' problem or the Council's, and they just tell us what to do. But the Council has turned genocidal, and even if Madraeus shows up, he's off his rocker!"

"Thomas!" Philtzer stood up, wincing as his ribs protested. Sophia scooted back out of his way. Slowly, he approached Thomas. "This is the job. You know that, man. This is just another Tuesday."

"No!" Thomas' lip curled. "Not like this."

Philtzer paused, remembering that Thomas and Cody hadn't been with Madraeus as long as he or Regina had. They hadn't been through nearly as much, hadn't buried nearly as many friends. Thomas had lost people before, but this was his brother. Philtzer tried again. "Look, Thomas, I am sorry about Cody, but he's not the only one we've lost. And if we don't keep our heads, we're gonna lose a lot more."

Philtzer watched him closely. Thomas was still breathing heavy, but some of the tension had begun to drain out of him.

"Now, we're gonna calm down, huddle up, and make a plan. We're gonna find our friends. And we're gonna get out of here."

Thomas closed his eyes and nodded.

Philtzer turned away and caught Sophia watching him with a thoughtful expression.

He wasn't sure if she was impressed or disappointed, so he said the only thing he could think of. "What's for lunch?"

LUCKY ME

Hamilton propped his head up with one hand, leaning his elbow on the van's driver's side window frame. When they'd arrived last night, they'd parked the van in the far corner of the parking lot the church shared with an old inn. The van was supposed to be a rallying point in case anything went wrong. It wasn't ideal for a getaway since there was only one road in or out, but it had been the best option at the time.

After the battle, as the police arrived, Hamilton had crept back to the van, slipped inside, and settled down to wait. He had hoped the others would come back, but that hope had died pretty quickly as the hours stretched on. When it was apparent that no one was coming, he traded the idea of escape for disaster mitigation.

Since the early hours of the morning, police and other emergency responders had been crawling all over the churchyard. This was the Races' worst nightmare, worse than Madraeus' meltdown in Germany. At least that could have been explained away as a serial killer or a terrorist attack, but this? The front half of the church getting blown off might be written off as a terrorist attack, but the bodies left behind were a whole different problem. All around the church, bodies of werewolves and vampires littered the ground. There was no easy way to explain a bunch of dead wolves. There hadn't been wolves in Britain since the 1700s. The vampires at least looked human, but when the sun came out...

Hamilton knew the exact moment the sun reached the church grounds. The industrious activity of the crime scene investigators turned into a terrified panic as the bodies of the vampires burned. There was no way to hide the fact that multiple victims of this disaster had just turned to ashes. There was too much evidence to sweep under the rug.

And I'm the lucky one who has to figure out what to do about it, Hamilton snorted.

So, he waited and hoped for some kind of inspiration, some crazy plan to snatch the evidence out of the hands of the authorities.

"Where's Philtzer when you need him?" Hamilton muttered.

Philtzer always had the best crazy plans. Hamilton gave a little laugh. *Philtzer would probably saunter in there, give some bullshit story about how a circus dog act had gone wrong, flash some counterfeit paperwork, and waltz out with the bodies in tow.*

He glanced down at the pile of clothing on the passenger-side floor. He tried not to let the fact that Philtzer's clothes were still there bother him. It wasn't all that unusual that Philtzer might be gallivanting around naked somewhere, but this time... everything had gone too wrong.

Hamilton wondered how many had made it through the battle. He didn't want to think about how many friends he might have lost last night. *Calls should start trickling in soon. Then we'll know who made it.*

He had been with Madraeus for a couple of decades, so this wasn't the first time he'd seen battle. He'd been out several times with Madraeus when he'd gone to manage the unruly actions of the Races, taking Philtzer, Thomas, or various others along as backup. Normally, it had been a small group in an isolated area. But this time...

Hamilton sighed, thinking, *This whole thing was done wrong. We should have had a better plan. We should have had an exit strategy. We should never have trusted the Hares.*

They had seen the Hares as a tool, a means to an end, but they should have known better. The Hares were the enemy. They always had been. Teaming up had been a strategic move, and at the time, it had seemed viable. But there were too many enemies on too many sides: Cecelia, the FBI, Apep, the Hares, even the Council. Hamilton snorted as he thought about Lady Douglas and her genocidal vendetta against anyone supporting Cecelia.

His cell phone buzzed. Pulling it out of his jacket pocket, he grimaced. "Speak of the devil. Hello, Lady Douglas."

"Report."

Hamilton had to hand it to her; she was direct. He debated on how much to tell her. "We are in Devon. There has been an incident—"

"An incident?"

Hamilton sighed. He hated being the messenger. "We met with the Hares. Cecelia showed up. Apep was set free. There was a battle. I don't know what happened to Apep exactly, but he is nowhere to be seen. The police showed up—"

"Before or after the battle was cleaned up?"

"Before."

Silence stretched.

"That is a concern."

Hamilton cringed. "I understand."

"Where is Madraeus?"

"I don't know. There hasn't been time to regroup."

"Where are you?"

"I'm outside the churchyard, monitoring the situation with the police."

"Very well. You know what to do."

"Yes, I'll take care of it." Hamilton started to hang up, but Lady Douglas stopped him.

"And, Hamilton? Don't make me come down there to do it myself."

He already knew it was his responsibility to take care of the evidence, but now he would have to answer to Lady Douglas if anything went wrong. Hamilton shivered as he slipped his phone back into his pocket. That woman scared him like no other.

Hamilton blew out a long breath and focused his attention back to the police. Not more than ten minutes later, two black SUVs pulled into the parking area. Three men and two women got out and looked around.

"Ah, crap." Hamilton knew by their suits that someone had called in the 'big guns' and that didn't bode well. If the FBI had files on the Races, it was a good bet that whoever these suits were, they did too.

Hamilton groaned. *Time for some eavesdropping.*

Unfortunately, three of them continued on to the church-yard, but two stayed behind. Hamilton slid a little lower in the seat to avoid being seen. One of the agents pointed to the inn and then gestured to the parking lot. The second agent nodded and headed for the inn. The first agent looked around again and then moved on to the churchyard.

"Crap." Hamilton had seen enough cop shows to know that those agents would begin searching the surrounding area, start-ing with the vehicles. If he was going to get close enough to find out what was going on, now was the time before they found him sitting here. If the van was locked with no one inside, maybe they would just discount it and move on. Maybe.

Hamilton pushed those thoughts aside, opting to worry about things he could control. He waited until the lot was de-serted before quietly slipping out. He hurried around the back of the van, eyed the bushes, and plunged through. He found a tidy little yard with a garden shed at the back. He stepped inside. Quickly, he stripped down and hid his clothes behind some tools. It wasn't so much that he worried about his clothes, but it was important not to lose the van keys and his cell phone. He shifted to a wolf and crept back out of the shed.

This was one of the few times that he was glad he was smaller than most men. It meant that he was smaller than most werewolves too. He could pass as a large dog if he put in the effort to appear a bit more domesticated. Hugging the trees, Hamilton ran back toward the church. It took longer than he wanted to get to a position where he could hear the agents talking to the officers in charge. He had to take the long way around cars and buildings. As he got closer, he could hear bits of conversation between the officers and the forensic teams.

"...something evil..."

You don't know the half of it, Hamilton thought as he looked for the command tent.

"...telling the press it was a gas leak..."

Hamilton slipped behind a large chunk of stone, crouching down as two men in protective suits walked by.

"...did you see those bodies burn up..."

As soon as they were looking the other way, Hamilton dashed toward the trees.

"...dangerous..."

"...that leopard..."

Leopard? Hamilton's blood froze. *Unkhabami?*

"...fugitives wanted for questioning..."

Fugitives? Hamilton wondered who they had seen.

"...Germany..."

"...got a call in to the FBI..."

Hamilton grimaced. *This is just getting better and better.*

He could see the group of agents standing together, talking to the officer in charge. There was no way he could get any closer to them; there were too many people in the way. Hamilton strained to hear what they were saying but only caught snippets.

"...moving the bodies..."

"...truck's here, start loading..."

"...barn at the edge of town..."

If they were going to start loading bodies, Hamilton knew he had to get back to the van and be ready to follow that truck. He dodged back into the trees and began the long process of backtracking through the churchyard. When he was on the other side of the hedge from the van, he heard the gravel crunch in the parking lot.

Hamilton peeked through the bushes. Two officers were circling the van, looking in the windows and checking the doors. One moved to the front and wrote down the license plate number.

Gonna have to ditch the van now. Damn! He would have to find somewhere to stash the coffins first.

Finally, the cops moved on, and Hamilton rushed to get his clothes. When the coast was clear, he slipped back into the cab of the van and slid down low. He watched the officers as they wandered around the parking lot, writing down all the cars' plate numbers. Once they had finished, they returned to the churchyard.

Hamilton let out a sigh of relief and sat up straighter. Knowing he might not get another chance, he fired up the van and drove out of the parking lot. He picked out a place down the street where he could park and wait for the truck carrying the bodies.

Follow the truck, trash the evidence, stay on Lady Douglas' good side. Hamilton nodded. *It's good to have a plan.*

NOT A DAMSEL IN DISTRESS

Unkhabami woke inside something meant for an animal a lot smaller than a leopard. Terror seized her.

No! Not a cage!

Blurry memories of men and flashlights merged with the sounds of metal clanking. She wanted to run, to fight, anything, but her limbs were as confused as her mind.

Her paws shot out, bracing against the metal walls. Visions from her past flashed through her mind of the cage she had been kept in as a child, sold to the highest bidder. The marble room where she had been put on display, the pain as the guards shocked her with cattle prods until she shifted from woman to cat and back again. All for the pleasure of a warlord and his elite sycophants. Years of torture and shame washed over her.

No. We killed them. Rami and I. They are dead. Focus!

She forced her breathing to slow. She used her nose and ears to orient herself. The sound of yowling cats and whining dogs, coupled with the smell of chemicals, told her that she had been brought to a veterinary clinic. She looked down at her shoulder. Someone had stitched her wound.

She looked toward the cage door and inched forward until her muzzle was pressed against the bars. They had confined her in the far back corner of the kennel, away from the regular pets. That was fine by her. She had no desire to be the cause of upset for the animals.

Glancing around, she couldn't see anyone. If she was quick, she could shift from leopard to human, open the cage, and be gone before anyone noticed. Knowing that she would have very little room once she shifted, Unkhabami turned onto her side. Just before she started to shift, she heard voices. She froze.

The employees were arriving for their day. News of their unusual guest spread quickly, and they all gathered to gawk at her.

Unkhabami was on her feet immediately.

They pointed, oohing and aahing.

All the fear and shame from her childhood roared to life. Unkhabami lunged at the cage door, hissing and clawing. Most of them retreated pretty quickly, except for an older woman who merely leaned back against the wall and watched Unkhabami.

The priestess lunged at the cage door again, but the woman didn't move. Unkhabami backed away and studied her. She wore scrubs, and her hair was nearly all silver. She had kind eyes.

"I know you don't want to be here." The woman spoke softly. "I'm sorry there isn't room for you in there. We aren't equipped to handle large animals." She smiled. "Well, we are, just not ones that would try and climb the walls to get out."

Unkhabami bared her fangs in defiance.

The woman cocked her head. "What were you doing in that church?"

Unkhabami hissed.

She watched Unkhabami for a few moments and then shook her head. "You won't be here long. They're coming to take you to the zoo in London tomorrow." She sounded a little disappointed. "I just wish I knew what you were doing there." With that, she pushed away from the wall and left.

A zoo! Having no desire to be on display again, she wanted to tear open the door and rip them all to shreds. She flexed her claws and growled, knowing full well that wouldn't help the situation. Unkhabami curled her tail over her nose and glared out the door of the cage. She had a spectacular view of a cream colored wall. She fought against the suffocating feelings of helplessness by nursing her anger and making a plan.

She would wait until closing time, and when everyone left for the night, she would let herself out and return to the church. She had to find out what had happened to Rami. And then... Cecelia would die screaming. Her lip curled as she thought about getting Cecelia under her claws.

Unkhabami waited, listening to the sounds of the clinic and trying to shut out the smells of antiseptic and pet urine. The hours passed slowly, giving her plenty of time to agonize over Rami's fate.

She had thrown herself between Rami and the police in an effort to save him. She prayed that it hadn't been in vain.

Why didn't he run? She lamented his honorable tendency to stay and fight. *What if they caught him? Where would he be?*

Her mind sifted through all the possibilities, terrified that they had arrested him and confined him somewhere that the sun could reach him. She shook her head to dispel unhelpful thoughts. Although a cage was not the ideal place for peaceful meditation, she needed to get calm. Unkhabami took a deep breath and centered her soul. She let her mind drift in the deep, moving river of the cosmos.

Images flickered through her mind: a flash of purple light, screaming, the world on fire, Apep slithering over the bodies of—

Unkhabami's eyes sprang open.

No! This could not be! Her heart split in two. *So many deaths!*

She had to get out of here. She had to stop this from happening. She reached out and pawed the lock, but it was no use. She needed thumbs. Unkhabami hissed in frustration. She could do nothing but sit and stew. She wanted to pace, but the cage wasn't big enough for her to even stand up straight, much less move around.

Just about the time that her fears had reached the point where she was willing to escape, whether anyone saw her or not, the lights clicked off. Unkhabami froze, listening. She could hear the faint sound of doors closing and the muffled voices of the employees as they left the building. She waited only a few seconds before shifting into her human form. If the cage had been cramped for a leopard, it was claustrophobic for a six-foot-tall human. Unkhabami reached out and fumbled with the lock. She was bent in such an awkward position that she couldn't see the latch. After a moment of frustrated fiddling, she heard a click and the door swung open. Unkhabami launched herself out onto the floor, landing with a grunt.

For a moment, she spread out, stretching her cramped muscles. Being out of the cage calmed her. She rolled onto her knees and looked around. Jumping up, she headed for the exit.

As soon as she was outside, she shifted back into a leopard and escaped into the twilight. It may have been more conspicuous, but she was faster on four feet.

This wasn't Broadclyst. The police had brought her to Exeter. She followed the signs that led back to the motorway, knowing that it was near the hotel. She had decided to try there first on the off chance that everyone had made it back safely. It would save her a long trip back to Broadclyst.

Nearly an hour later, she stopped in the trees across the road from the hotel and pulled out her stash of clothing and keycard. She dressed quickly and went inside. It was still early evening, and the hotel was busy with arriving guests. Ignoring them all, she returned to their rooms. Before she opened the door, she smelled pizza.

A good sign. Maybe they've all returned.

She opened the door, and her heart sank. The room was empty. She ran to the door leading to the adjacent room, but it was also empty. Fighting against the fear, she shifted into her cat form and sniffed the air.

Blood?

Her nostrils flared as she identified the individual scents of Philtzer, Thomas, Regina, and Sophia. Unkhabami shifted back into her human form and picked up an abandoned slice of pizza.

Taking a bite, she thought, *The wolves had come back. They must have tended their wounds and left again. But to where?*

She looked around the room, scanning for any clue. Finding nothing, she called for a taxi. She knew that it was dangerous to leave a traceable trail, but she was pressed for time. Grabbing the last piece of pizza, she returned to the lobby to wait.

The taxi ride gave her a little time to think about her vision. *A flash of purple light, screaming, the world on fire, Apep slithering over the bodies of— It was so much like what had already happened. Could it be the past? No. The world is not on fire. It has to be the future.*

Unkhabami stared out at the lights of the city. In her previous visions, she had seen Whitney as the key. She hadn't completely understood what that meant until they had spoken with the Hares. If that was true, then Apep's freedom had been short-lived.

But what of this new vision? Will he be released again?

The taxi dropped her off outside a small Indian restaurant, but she didn't go inside. Instead, she turned and made her way toward the church, planning to look for Rami first. She was convinced that if Rami had escaped the police, he was probably in the Warren. Caution tape barred every gate into the churchyard, and the police had set up floodlights so the forensic teams could continue working through the night. Several police officers patrolled the grounds. Unkhabami scowled at this development. There was no way that she could get into the church from the front. She would have to find an alternate route. She circled the churchyard looking for a way in. She had reached the side that was the farthest from the town, facing the mill, when she heard someone whispering as they approached down a tree-covered lane. Unsure if it was a police officer, an enemy, or a friend, she stepped behind a tree to wait.

WOLF HUNT

HAMILTON CROUCHED DOWN IN the bushes and watched the barn. After following the truck carrying the bodies from the churchyard, he had stored the coffins and ditched the van. He spent the rest of the day sitting in the bushes trying to decide on a plan of action. The police had appropriated a local farmer's barn to use as a kind of forensics base camp. They had been hauling in crates all day. The place was swarming with technicians, and the black SUVs from the churchyard had arrived mid-afternoon and hadn't left.

This is getting out of hand. Hamilton picked up a small stick and started to break it into tiny segments. Lady Douglas expected him to take care of a few bodies from the battle, but this was going up against a specialized task force. *How am I supposed to take on an army? I need Philtzer.*

Mid-morning, he had received a check-in call from Regina. After explaining the situation, Regina had promised to bring everyone a sundown. First, they needed time to heal and recover. Hamilton glanced at the sky. It was almost dusk.

He picked up another small stick and began breaking it. His hopes for a sneak attack were dwindling fast. The big double doors at the front of the barn stood open, spilling light out into the yard. The level of activity inside had not diminished in the slightest, but he still hoped that at least some of the people working in the barn would knock off for the night and go home, leaving a skeleton crew. Or better yet, just shut down for the night. Unfortunately, it looked like they were setting up for an all-nighter.

They're working on dead bodies. It's not like they would just get up and walk away. Hamilton smiled, thinking that if any of the vampires had survived the day, they might jump up and take off. *Wouldn't that be a nice surprise for the suits?*

Something rustled in the trees behind him. Hamilton froze, listening. The sound grew louder. Hamilton turned to find Thomas, Philtzer, Sophia, and Regina stepping through the foliage. Hamilton relaxed as they crouched down next to him.

"Am I glad to see you guys!"

"Same." Philtzer grinned at him, but it was a little lopsided as the skin pulled against the adhesive strips on his face.

Hamilton glanced around at his friends. There were plenty of cuts, bruises, and bandages. "Are you guys up for this?"

"You know us, we're always up for shenanigans," Thomas said.

Hamilton glanced at him. Thomas' usual smile was missing. It was worrisome.

"Are you sure all the evidence is in there?" Regina asked, nodding toward the barn.

"No." Hamilton sighed and picked up another stick. "I watched them haul the bodies here, but who knows what other evidence they have." He picked the stick apart as he spoke.

Philtzer looked down at the pile of tiny wood chunks in front of Hamilton. "You making kindling for winter?"

Hamilton glanced at him and then looked down at the rather large pile. "I can't help it. Lady Douglas freaks me out, and this has gotten bigger than just a few bodies."

"What do you mean?" Sophia asked.

"She warned me to take care of this so she didn't have to. I do not want to tell her that I accidentally missed something."

Thomas nodded. "Valid."

"But if it's just a few bodies, let's just burn it down," Regina said.

"We can't!" Hamilton shook his head.

"Why not? It's wood," she gestured to the barn, "it'll burn just fine."

"Look who likes fire, now," Sophia snorted, earning a quelling look from her mother.

"It's not about the fire. It's about not knowing what else they have." Hamilton sighed. "I've been watching them all day. They've been hauling stuff in there. Not just the bodies, but plastic crates and stuff."

"Stuff." Thomas nodded.

Hamilton frowned at him. He was not acting like himself. "You okay?"

Thomas grunted but didn't take his eyes off the barn.

"Right." Philtzer tried to take a deep breath but winced. "So, let's go look."

"What do you mean?" Sophia glanced at Philtzer. "You can't just wander in there."

"Why not? We sneak in, look at what they got going on, and then make a decision."

Regina shrugged. "Seems like a plan to me."

"Well, you can go," Sophia looked at her mother and then turned to Philtzer, "but you're not. You can barely move."

Philtzer gave her a sheepish look and finally nodded. "All right, I'll sit here like a good boy. But someone has to go in there."

Philtzer flicked a worried glance at Thomas. Hamilton sent him a questioning look, but Philtzer shook his head, as if to say, *Not now.*

"Regina, you and Hamilton can go scout it out."

Thomas sent Philtzer a pointed look, but he shook his head. "You and I are going to find something to set that place on fire."

Thomas didn't look happy, but he nodded.

"How are you gonna set a fire?" Sophia looked at Philtzer. "Raid someone's garage?"

"Sure." Philtzer gave her another lopsided grin.

"What am I supposed to do?" Sophia asked.

"You, my dear, get to be lookout."

"And exactly what am I looking out for?" Sophia glared at him.

"Anything that will get us killed," Philtzer muttered under his breath, but then said, "Give us thirty minutes, and then send up a howl. Make it loud and then get ready to run." Philtzer turned to Hamilton and Regina. "You got thirty, then we're setting it ablaze."

"Right." Regina nodded and began to strip, handing each piece of clothing to Sophia as she took it off.

Hamilton handed his cell phone to Sophia. "Whatever you do, don't lose it."

Sophia looked at the phone. "Why? I thought they were all burner phones."

"Not that one," Hamilton said as he shucked out of his jacket and handed it to Sophia. "That is the number that everyone has."

"Hamilton is the emergency coordinator," Philtzer said.

"I'm the check-in guy." Hamilton rolled his eyes. "It's kinda my position at InfiniCorp."

"Wow." Sophia looked from Hamilton to the phone. "So, how many have you heard from since last night's insanity?"

Hamilton sighed. "Not enough."

Sophia glanced at Thomas, but he pretended not to notice.

As Hamilton finished undressing, he thought, *At least if we are going in, we can see how many of the dead are ours and how many are Cecelia's.*

Sophia rearranged the stack of clothes over her arm and then looked up to find her mother staring at her intently. "Stay alert. Stay safe."

Sophia nodded as Regina shifted.

"Keys," Philtzer said as he handed them over to Sophia. "As soon as you let out that howl," Philtzer's hand closed around her fingers, "you get to the car. Meet us where this road meets the one going back to Exeter."

Sophia nodded.

"I mean it," Philtzer held her gaze, "don't wait. No matter what you see or hear."

"I will." She looked down at the time on Hamilton's phone. "Okay, thirty minutes. Starting now."

Philtzer winced as he stood. "Tally-ho," he said wearily and disappeared into the trees with Thomas.

Regina braced her feet, shook her whole body from nose to tail, looked expectantly at Hamilton, and bounded away through the trees. Hamilton shifted quickly and followed her.

Hamilton and Regina dashed across the pasture behind the barn and ran along the side of the corrals. Coming around the backside of a small haystack, they paused and looked up at the building. Light glowed in every window.

Can they get any more lights on in there? Regina spoke wolf, glancing at Hamilton.

Too easy to get noticed. Hamilton laid his ears back. He let his gaze roam over the building. *Up there. Hay loft.*

Right Regina crouched low and moved forward, hugging the haystack.

They silently worked their way closer. On the back side of the barn, about ten feet off the ground, a small door stood open. The door was used to pitch hay down from the loft to the animals below. Directly below it, nailed to the wall, was a wooden ladder that looked like it had been built about a hundred years ago when the barn was new. Hamilton and Regina stepped carefully through the straw that littered the ground below the door, conscious of any sound that could give them away. Once they were under the ladder, they quickly shifted. Hamilton went first, climbing quickly. He stopped just below the door and peeked in. The loft was empty except for the hay. He motioned to Regina and ducked in through the door. He shifted and crept across the loft and peered over the edge. Regina quietly joined him.

Below them, it looked like a scene from an alien invasion movie. Halogen work lights flooded the room with bright, glaring light. Plastic storage crates created a false wall along the far side of the barn. Forensic scientists in clean suits swarmed the room like ants, moving amongst tables covered in metal trays with piles of ashes in them. Lab equipment covered two long tables. Machines whirled and buzzed.

Regina nudged Hamilton. *They're doing chemical analysis of the ashes.*

Hamilton laid his ears back and looked away from the makeshift laboratory. On the other side of the barn, the bodies of wolves were laid out in lines on top of black plastic sheets that covered the floor, along with five black body bags. Two autopsy tables had been set up and were in use.

Cody's body lay on one of the autopsy tables. Hamilton's guts twisted and turned to water. His hackles rose as hot anger burned through him.

Regina followed his gaze. *Whoever these people are, they know way too much already.*

Hamilton flattened his ears again and looked down at the lab table. A laptop sat open at the far end. As he watched, one of the scientists came over and entered their data, and a few minutes later, another one did the same.

We need that laptop. Hamilton glanced at Regina.

DOGNAPPED

Regina looked down at the laptop and then back at Hamilton. *How you gonna get it?*

Hamilton looked around. In the corner of the loft, there was a set of stairs that led down to the main floor. He crept across the loft and looked down the stairs. If he was quiet, he could sneak along the storage crates and grab it.

You're going to be seen. Regina said.

You got a better idea? Hamilton looked back at her.

At that moment, voices at the bottom of the stairs caught his attention. It was the 'suits' from the church. They had been at the back of the barn and were walking along the lines of bodies. There was someone with them. The newcomer was tall and thin with icy blue eyes. He looked more intense than the others. He moved through the room as if he knew exactly what he was looking at.

"At last count, we've found eighty-four distinctive remains," the lead suit said as they walked back toward the front of the barn.

How many are ours? Hamilton glanced at Regina. She crept along the edge of the loft and craned her neck, trying to see.

"I want you to double security," the newcomer said.

"Agent Milner," the lead suit began.

Hamilton's attention shot back to the men below. *Milner? The FBI agent? Cross-agency cooperation is bad!*

"I understand that you have been pulled in as some kind of expert, but I assure you we have this handled."

Not so cooperative, Hamilton thought. *That's good.*

The newcomer crossed his arms. "Really? Because the leopard has already disappeared."

Unkhabami? Hamilton and Regina exchanged a loaded glance.

The 'lead suit' didn't seem too happy to be reminded of that. "I was just informed."

"We don't need any more evidence going missing."

"They're dead." One of the 'suits' laughed. "They're not going anywhere."

Agent Milner slowly turned and stared at the man, but before he could speak, an officer called out, "Sir?"

Sophia! Regina gasped.

Hamilton hurried to the front of the loft again. Two officers escorted Sophia into the barn. Her hands were cuffed behind her.

"We found her in the bushes across the road." They stopped just inside the doorway.

Sophia glanced up and saw Hamilton and Regina in the loft, but her expression stayed blank. Her gaze returned to Milner as he approached.

The officer handed Milner keys and a cell phone. "She had these."

Shit! Hamilton almost yelped out loud.

"What were you doing in the bushes, miss?" Milner asked.

Sophia glared at him.

Hamilton... Regina growled.

Don't do anything dumb! A million things ran through his mind. The plan was shot to hell. The getaway car wasn't going to be waiting. Sophia couldn't give the signal for Philtzer and Thomas to set the place on fire. And they had no way to tell them! *What are we going to do? Gotta save Sophia. Gotta get the laptop. Gotta get the phone! Gotta get the keys!* Hamilton looked around desperately trying to find something, anything that would help.

A howl pierced the night.

Thomas! Regina's head shot up. *They don't know she's down there!*

Milner spun around, trying to decide which direction the sound came from.

Sophia looked up at them.

Hamilton glanced at her but then wrinkled his nose as he suddenly smelled diesel fuel. He looked down. The floor slowly turned dark as the liquid flowed down the center aisle from the back of the barn. It looked like someone had tipped over a fifty-five-gallon drum.

"Get your men ready," Milner said over his shoulder. "We're about to have company."

"What are you talking about?" the 'lead suit' asked.

Milner stared straight at Sophia. "That was a warning call."

"The howl?" One of the other agents laughed. "It was just some dog."

"That wasn't a dog." Milner turned toward the door, but then suddenly spun back. He looked at the liquid covering the floor, but he was slow to comprehend what he was seeing until flames raced across the liquid.

"Fire!"

Chaos erupted as agents and scientists dashed for the exit.

Out of time! Regina shot past Hamilton as she ran toward the stairs. *I'll get Sophia!*

Hamilton glanced back at the laptop, knowing he couldn't leave without it. He sprinted across the loft to the stairs. He stopped about halfway down. The fire had spread quickly. He was going to have to go through it to get to the tables. Closing his eyes and praying, Hamilton jumped.

The smell of singed fur burned in his nose as he landed, but he didn't dare stop. He dashed forward, dimly aware that Regina was knocking over tables and equipment, trying to cause as much damage as possible. Hamilton rammed against the table holding Cody's remains. The smell of burnt fur flared as Cody's body was engulfed in flames. Just as Hamilton reached the table where the laptop had been, he came face to face with Agent Milner. The FBI agent had the same idea as he had: get the laptop.

For a second, they both froze, staring at one another. Hamilton recovered first. He lunged forward and snatched the computer from Milner's hands. Carrying it in his teeth, he sprinted for the front door. Milner raced after him.

"Get that dog!" Milner tried to shout, but he inhaled smoke and started to cough.

Outside, the refugees from the fire were slowly getting organized and starting to move their cars away from the burning barn. Unfortunately, there were a lot of cars and only one small gate out of the yard. Waves of heat and smoke added to the confusion as Hamilton dodged through the jumbled traffic jam. Milner staggered after him, bumping into cars as he coughed and blinked away smoky tears.

Hamilton's nose burned, and his jaw ached from trying to keep a tight hold on the laptop. He nearly dropped it twice as he darted around the cars competing to get out of the farmer's yard. He could see the road. All he had to do was get through the gate, turn right, and run. He dashed out the gate. Out of the corner of his eye, he caught sight of a police van coming straight toward him. He stopped just in time, nearly losing his nose as it shot by. He felt something grab his tail.

Hamilton spun around to find Milner reaching for a second handful of his fur. With the laptop still in his jaws, he couldn't bite Milner, and he didn't dare drop the laptop. He twisted and lunged, but Milner held tight.

"Get me a rope!" Milner shouted.

Hamilton dug his claws into the road, trying to get traction as Milner pulled him backward. Pain shot through his tail.

Let go! Hamilton snarled as he tried to get away. He stared longingly down the road.

Behind him, he could hear footsteps getting closer. He was out of time. Suddenly, Milner let go of his tail. Hamilton stumbled forward. He glanced back to see if Milner was coming after him again but froze as he realized why Milner had let go of his tail.

Regina had the agent in a headlock. Milner coughed and struggled, but she held tight. Sophia stood beside her, struggling against her handcuffs. Regina backed them closer to the street.

Regina tightened her hold on Milner while growling in his ear, "Unlock her!"

Milner fumbled for his keys and unlocked one of Sophia's wrists. Sophia let the cuffs dangle from her other wrist as she dug through Milner's pockets. She found the keys and Hamilton's cell phone, then turned and ran toward Hamilton.

"Get to the car!" Sophia shouted as she ran past.

Hamilton spun around and sprinted after her. So far, the smoke and chaos of the fire had kept anyone from noticing Milner's plight, but their luck wasn't going to last forever. By the time Sophia and Hamilton had gotten to the car, Regina and Milner were halfway across the street. Sophia yanked open the back door so Hamilton could get in. She jumped into the driver's seat and started the car. He dropped the laptop onto the seat and shifted into his human form, pulling the door shut just as she pulled out.

Hamilton suddenly wondered if she'd ever driven in England before. But after they skidded around and shot back toward the farm, he wondered if she'd ever learned to drive at all. He braced against the ceiling and grabbed the armrest on the door. Through the windshield, he could see Regina still holding Milner captive. Sophia skidded the car to a halt next to her mother. Regina yanked the back door open and shoved Milner inside. She wasted no time crawling in after him.

Milner shouted for help, but Regina punched him, knocking him sideways into Hamilton. Sophia floored it and sped off down the road.

"What the hell did you bring him along for?" Sophia shouted.

"Insurance!" Regina growled.

"Who the hell are you people?" Milner sat up and took in his surroundings. "Why are you naked?" He started to lunge for Sophia, but Regina yanked him back against the seat.

"Don't even try it," she snarled. "Cuffs!"

Sophia fumbled with the keys as she drove but managed to get the handcuff off her wrist. She tossed them over her shoulder. Hamilton caught them before they hit Milner in the face. Regina grabbed them out of his hands and cuffed Milner.

"Sit there and be quiet," she snapped.

Hamilton glanced at Milner. He was surprised to see that the man seemed more curious than worried.

"Your stuff is up here," Sophia nodded toward the passenger seat. "I'm sorry I got caught. That cop saw me as I came back from the car."

Regina leaned forward and grabbed their clothes off the front seat, handing Hamilton his. "It's all right, kiddo. This kind of thing takes practice."

They were already dressed by the time that Sophia pulled over where they were supposed to meet up with Philtzer and Thomas. She glanced in the rear-view mirror. "This car isn't built for six."

"We'll make do." Regina shoved Milner closer to Hamilton.

Anxious seconds ticked away as they waited.

"What's taking so long?" Hamilton's gaze shifted from window to window.

"You think they got caught?" Sophia kept glancing in the mirror.

Just then, Thomas dashed up to her side of the car. He opened the driver's door and gestured with his thumb, "Out. I'm driving."

Sophia scrambled out and ran around the other side just as Philtzer appeared down the street. "Hurry up, old man!" she shouted.

Philtzer doubled his pace, but it was obvious he was in pain. He sank gratefully into the front seat. Sophia squeezed into the back next to her mother. Hamilton tried to make enough room for them all to fit as Thomas got them back on the road.

Philtzer glanced back at Milner. "Reggie, what'd I tell you about bringing home strays?"

Hamilton groaned, thinking, *Lady Douglas is gonna kill me.*

DOWN THE RABBIT HOLE

"I KNOW!" MALCOLM HISSED. "But if you don't zip it, we'll have more than the Hares to deal with!"

Sandra clamped her lips together and glared at his back, secretly hoping that he would trip and fall in the dark. They had left the safety of the mill after sunset; however, they had not yet come to an agreement about where to go. Malcolm wanted to go back to the hotel to regroup and reevaluate the situation. Sandra wanted to find Whitney. Neither was willing to back down. Either way, they had to backtrack along the tree-lined path past the church.

Malcolm stopped suddenly, thrusting his hand out to stop Sandra from passing him. She watched him slowly scan the trees. She looked around but couldn't see anything. Cautiously, he took a step forward. Out of the darkness, a figure stepped into their path.

Sandra gasped, stumbling backward, but her feet weren't as fast as her fear. She tripped and fell onto her backside.

Malcolm took a step toward the figure. "Unkhabami?"

"Malcolm." The priestess looked past him. "Sandra."

Sandra scrambled to her feet and dusted off her rear. "You scared us."

"My apologies." The priestess looked over her shoulder. "The guard is coming," she whispered as she slipped back into the shadows.

Malcolm spun around and grabbed Sandra, pulling her behind the closest tree. Sandra stayed as still as she could, watching Malcolm as he watched the lane. Behind her, she could hear footsteps and then saw flashes of light as the night guard came down the path. Malcolm moved slightly, keeping the tree between them and the officer. Sandra couldn't see Unkhabami anywhere. Sandra bit her lip and closed her eyes. The bark of the tree was digging into her back, but she didn't dare move. Finally, the guard moved away, returning to the church.

"What are you doing here?" Unkhabami said in her ear.

Sandra flinched. She hadn't heard the priestess approach.

Sandra said, "Looking for Whitney," just as Malcolm said, "Going back to the hotel."

"There is no one at the hotel," Unkhabami whispered. "Some of the wolves have been there, but they have gone."

Sandra poked Malcolm. "I win. We look for Whitney."

"You were separated?" Unkhabami glared at Sandra.

Sandra nodded. "That Hare, John, made her the new Key." When Unkhabami didn't react, Sandra peered at her. "You knew that, didn't you?"

"I suspected."

"Did you also *suspect* that he," she pointed to Malcolm, "turned her into a vampire?"

"What?" Unkhabami looked sharply at Malcolm.

"Oh," Sandra threw up her hands, "that got your attention!"

"I had no choice." Malcolm sighed. "She was near death, and there was no way we could have fought that snake off a second time."

Unkhabami stared at him for a long moment. "Madraeus—"

"—is in the trap with Apep!" Sandra flung her hand out in the direction of the grove.

"But that cannot be!" Unkhabami turned away and stared toward the church.

"Believe it. I saw it." Sandra crossed her arms. "After that, the Hares took Whitney."

When Unkhabami turned back, her expression was filled with fear. "Show me where Apep's prison is."

"Not 'til you tell me why you're so freaked out!" Sandra grabbed the priestess' arm. "What do you know?"

Unkhabami glared at Sandra, shaking off her hand. "There is no time! I must see!"

"This way." Malcolm walked off into the night with Unkhabami right on his heels.

Sandra huffed but had no choice but to follow.

Malcolm led them through the trees to the little grove. He stopped just inside the edge of the trees. His gaze wandered across the floodlit churchyard. Here and there, forensic specialists worked, and a few police officers milled around. When they were looking the other way, he crouched low and ran to the little stone wall that surrounded the grove and sank down beside the gap that served as a gate. Seconds later, Unkhabami and Sandra joined him.

Sandra watched the priestess rise up enough so that she could peek over the wall. It looked like she was sniffing the air. She sank back down. Unkhabami closed her eyes and stretched out her hand toward the space that formed the gate. She opened her eyes and frowned at the gap.

Unkhabami turned to the vampire. "Malcolm, reach through."

He looked at her in confusion. "Reach through what?"

The priestess pointed toward the gap. Malcolm shrugged and thrust his hand through the gap. He immediately snatched his hand back.

"What's the matter?" Sandra asked in a hushed voice.

Malcolm flexed his hand. "It tingles."

Sandra looked at him and then reached out. She couldn't feel anything. She waved her hand around in the space but still felt nothing. She dropped her hand and looked at Unkhabami and Malcolm, shaking her head and shrugging.

Unkhabami's frown deepened. She gestured to Malcolm. "Try again."

Sandra and Unkhabami watched intently as he reached out again, this time slower.

"Is that glowing purple?" Sandra whispered.

They all leaned forward, staring at his hand. His fingers faded slightly, almost like they were translucent. He snatched his hand back again and rubbed it.

"What the hell was that?"

Unkhabami sighed. "That is a very large problem. We must find Whitney."

"How?" Malcolm peeked over the wall and ducked back down. "The only entrance to the Warren that we knew about was the side door of the church, and the police are crawling all over it."

"We can go through the church." Unkhabami glanced over the wall. "Apep left a hole in the floor that led to the Warren."

"Same problem." Malcolm shook his head. "Police."

"So, we find another entrance." Sandra peeked over the wall. "Barbie said there were tunnels all over town."

"And how do we find secret entrances in a town that we know nothing about?" Malcolm snorted. "Ask around?"

"Can the wolves track their scent?"

"We don't have a wolf handy."

"I can," Unkhabami said as she started to undress.

"No," Malcolm stopped her, "you're a giant cat! May as well wear a sign saying, 'arrest me now!'"

"I can help," said a quiet voice from behind them.

They all spun around to find Barbie lurking in the shadowy trees. She stepped out just enough that the light from the church illuminated her pale hair and ashen face. Her arm hung in a sling and her neck was covered in dark purple bruises. A white bandage covered her forehead and her eyes looked a little glassy. She looked like a ghost.

"What happened to you?" Sandra gasped.

"I was guarding the Key..." her voice trailed off. "I don't know... It was all so fast. I was outside the door..." Her eyes glazed over. "Something hit me... this blur of white..." tears filled her eyes and her voice wobbled, "someone grabbed me by the throat..." Barbie blinked and refocused. "I can't believe he actually..." Barbie sank down into the grass.

"What?" Sandra crawled over to her.

"John." Barbie shook her head. "He talked about a permanent solution to the Key problem. That an immortal would be the best replacement, but I never thought he'd go through with it. It's sacrilege to all we believe."

"I guess they had a change of heart," Malcolm snorted.

"This is not right." Barbie shook her head. Sandra watched the expressions on her face as she fought a war of loyalty versus morality, until finally Barbie straightened and looked at them. "I will help you find Whitney."

"You?" Unkhabami curled her lip. "Why would you help?"

"I know you have no reason to trust me—"

Malcolm scoffed, "Damn Skippy!"

"—but I want to help Whitney." She looked desperate. "She didn't deserve what John did."

"So, you're gonna help the enemy?" Malcolm peeked over the wall again.

"No." Barbie shook her head. "I'm going to fix a mistake."

"You can't fix this." Sandra glared at her. "Whitney's a vampire now. There's no fixing that."

Barbie grimaced and hung her head. "You're right, but I can at least try to free her from John."

"Where is she?" Malcolm asked.

"In the Warren," Barbie looked up, "but not here, not under the church. It's not secure."

Unkhabami stood. "Take us."

Malcolm took a quick look over the wall to make sure she hadn't been seen.

Barbie nodded, got to her feet, and disappeared into the trees.

Malcolm, Unkhabami, and Sandra followed her quickly so they wouldn't lose her in the dark. She led them in a circuitous route around behind the church and down a long house-lined road.

"Malcolm." Sandra tugged on his sleeve, motioning him to slow down. When there was some space between them and Barbie, she whispered, "What if there are a bunch of Hares waiting for us?"

Malcolm shrugged as they continued walking. "We'll just have to take care of them."

"You're a trained fighter," Sandra gestured toward Unkhabami, "and I'm sure she can hold her own, but not me. Shouldn't we get some help?"

"Now you want to find the others?" Malcolm chuckled.

"I just don't want to fail a rescue attempt," Sandra said.

Malcolm glanced at her. Sandra could tell that he was considering the situation, but he ran out of time. Barbie had stopped across from an Indian restaurant. The smell of curry floated out through the open door.

Barbie turned to address them. "It's been pretty busy tonight. There's a lot of customers, just follow me through to the kitchen."

Without waiting for them, she turned and walked across the street. Barbie led the way through the cluster of people standing just inside the door, waiting to be seated. They passed rows of white, cloth-covered tables filled with customers. The earthy scents of saffron, ginger, turmeric, and cloves spiced the air. Sandra gazed at the steaming dishes with envy.

Entering the kitchen, the sound of organized chaos dropped off slightly as the staff stopped and watched them curiously. The air was thick with the smells of chicken and lamb, setting Sandra's stomach growling. Malcolm glanced at her and frowned.

Sandra glared at him, thinking, *It's not my fault I haven't eaten since yesterday afternoon.*

Sidestepping cooks and servers with trays, Malcolm reached out and snatched a piece of naan bread from a basket sitting under the warming lights and handed it to Sandra. Surprised, she took it from him slowly. She knew that he had heard her stomach growling, but after the things she'd said to him in the mill, she didn't expect him to care.

Barbie opened a door near the back of the kitchen and led them down into the basement. Sandra looked around as she ate. Crates of beer and wine were stacked against one wall, and storage shelves filled with dry goods covered the opposite wall. Filing cabinets stood along the back. In the middle of the room was a desk with a computer and phone on it. There were no other doors or exits besides the stairs behind them. Sandra glanced at Unkhabami and then at Malcolm, but neither seemed worried.

Barbie went around the desk and reached under it. They heard a soft click. She reached down and pulled open a hatch in the floor, revealing another stairway.

"This way," Barbie said and descended into the darkness.

Unkhabami and Malcolm exchanged a loaded look. Malcolm gestured for Sandra to go first. She had the sneaking suspicion that they were using her as cannon fodder, but she stepped forward anyway. Sandra stared down into the dark hole, reluctant to go into yet another dark cave. A light flared at the base of the stairs, and Barbie stepped into view.

"Come on. We don't have much time."

Down the rabbit hole, Sandra thought and started down the stairs.

A STOLEN LIFE

As they moved through the Warren, Unkhabami and Malcolm checked the rooms on one side of the corridor, while Sandra and Barbie checked the doors on the other side. They found nothing.

"Are you sure she's down here?" Sandra asked, opening a door and peeking inside. It was empty.

"Yes." Barbie checked another room. "They had to move her away from the church. Apep's escape caused a lot of damage, exposing that section to the outside world."

"What if the police get in?"

"There are precautions in place."

"What does that mean?" Malcolm asked as he tried the knob on another door. He flung it open, but the room was empty, so he started up the passage again.

"It means that if anyone gets in, it'll look like an old access stair to the church basement, and then they'll find it dead ends."

Barbie led them down corridor after corridor, twisting and turning through the maze that made up the Warren. They checked every room they came to, but there was no Whitney.

"How are we ever going to find her in this?" Sandra muttered. "This thing must run under the whole town."

"It is pretty extensive," Malcolm agreed, checking another door.

Barbie glanced over her shoulder. "This was the largest Warren."

"Was?"

Barbie used her keys to open one of the doors, but she shut it quickly and locked it again. "Cecelia decimated our numbers. There were only a handful of us left before the battle. Even less now."

They continued on, checking room after room.

"How are we going to get out of here once we find her?" Sandra looked back the way they'd come. She glanced at Malcolm. "Do we have a plan?"

"Find Whitney and leave," Malcolm growled as he pulled a door shut.

"What about the sun?" Sandra asked. "What about the police?"

"The sun isn't up yet, and we have avoided the police before."

"I can't believe that Willie would be a part of this," Barbie muttered as they searched.

"Why? Who is he?"

"He's the head of our Warren."

Sandra glared at Barbie. "So, it's his fault that John tried to kill Whitney?"

"No." Barbie shook her head. "He would never!"

"You expect us to believe that?" Sandra scoffed.

"Sandra." Malcolm gave her a warning look.

"You're thinking the same thing," Sandra muttered.

Barbie stopped when they came to a junction in the passageway where three tunnels carved from rock and braced with thick timbers fanned out. Barbie looked down each, deciding which way.

Sandra slipped around Barbie and looked at the three choices. They all looked the same, old and creepy.

"Which way now?"

At that moment, a loud crash, followed by shouting, echoed up the corridor to the left. Exchanging glances, they rushed toward the commotion. They rounded a corner and found a group of five Hares gathered just outside a heavily reinforced door. Debris from broken chairs and shards of glass littered the floor. One Hare was fiddling with the lock on the door. The others stood behind him, armed with knives and wooden stakes. John stood off to the side, hefting an axe.

Malcolm growled and started forward.

One of the Hares turned and caught sight of them. His eyes grew huge. His hair stuck out from under his tweed flat cap in gray tufts. He pointed toward Malcolm and the others. "Lads!"

The Hares turned and quickly spread out across the wide hallway, brandishing their weapons.

"How did you get in here?" The gray Hare shouted.

John saw Barbie. "Traitor!"

"John!" Barbie stepped forward. "This isn't right! Willie, please!"

Willie glanced at John before saying, "You need to leave!"

Malcolm took another step forward. "Where is Whitney?"

"She's ours now!" John gripped his axe tighter. "She's the Key!"

"She has a name, asshole." Sandra pushed past Malcolm, but Barbie grabbed her and pulled her back.

"She belongs to no one!" Barbie shouted.

"You begged for our help," Malcolm flung a hand out, "and now you pull this?"

"We aren't pulling anything!" John glanced at his fellow Hares. "We are the guardians. She is the Key. We will keep her safe."

"Like the last Key?" Unkhabami stepped forward.

"That's different!" John spluttered. "That was centuries of damage. Whitney is a vampire now; she will never age. We'll never need a replacement!"

"Was that your plan all along?" Barbie looked at the other Hares, settling on their leader. "Willie, it's sacrilege!"

Willie glanced at John again and shook his head. "What's done is done, Barbie."

John puffed up his chest. "It was the most viable solution!"

"You're messed up!" Sandra shook off Barbie's hand. "I'm sorry I ever met you!"

"Without the Key," John flicked a glance at Sandra, "Apep will escape. We are here to make sure the Key stays in good health."

"She isn't just a Key." Sandra started forward again, but this time, Malcolm blocked her. "She's our friend."

"You no longer have a claim on her." John hefted the axe in his hand.

"Claim?" Malcolm snapped. "She's not a coat! She's a woman!"

"She is the responsibility of the Hares now," Willie said.

"You have no rights here," said the Hare behind John, holding his knife out in front of him.

"You are no longer welcome here, demons! You will leave the Warren!" John spat. He pointed at Barbie. "And take that traitor with you!"

"You expect us to just walk away?" Unkhabami scoffed.

John shook his head. "We have no problem fighting you."

Malcolm let out a short, malicious laugh. "Go ahead and try it."

"You're in our territory," the gray Hare added.

"You think that matters?" Rami said from behind them.

Unkhabami's face lit up with joy. "Rami!"

His sudden appearance sent an uneasy ripple through the Hares. They quickly shifted their positions so they could watch both Rami and the others simultaneously.

"You're outnumbered." Malcolm crossed his arms. "But honestly, I'm gonna wipe out every one of you without even breaking a sweat."

John eyed Malcolm. "You're a cocky bastard."

"Not really." Malcolm smiled slowly, showing his fangs. "I'm giving you fair warning. You have one chance. Turn Whitney over to us."

John glared at Malcolm. "How about you turn around and walk away."

Malcolm's lip curled. "Not happening."

John's eyes narrowed as he looked from Rami to Malcolm and Unkhabami. Tense silence stretched between them. He hefted the axe again, shifting it restlessly in his hand. "She is not leaving the Warren. Her place is here now."

An inhuman snarl erupted from the door behind the Hares, making them jump. The Hares shifted their attention nervously between the vampires, Unkhabami, and the door behind them.

The door rattled.

"Not again," one of the Hares muttered, jumping forward to hold the door closed.

Whatever was in the room screamed again, sending a shiver down Sandra's spine.

"What is that?" Barbie took a step backward.

Sandra looked at Rami and then Unkhabami. Their expressions answered her question, but she didn't want to accept it.

"No! No!" Sandra shook her head. "That is not Whitney."

Malcolm rushed forward, grabbing John by the shirt front and slamming him against the wall. His axe fell to the floor. "What did you do to her?"

John kicked at Malcolm as Willie jumped forward, trying to loosen Malcolm's hold on John. Unkhabami dashed toward the men as two of the Hares lunged at Malcolm. The gray Hare raised his hand, ready to plunge a stake into Malcolm's heart. In that moment, Unkhabami grasped the hand that held the stake and wrenched it backward, knocking the gray Hare to the ground. At the same time, the second Hare jabbed his knife into Malcolm's lower back.

Malcolm roared in pain but didn't let go of John. Rami sprang forward and grabbed the one who had stabbed Malcolm and yanked him backward, throwing him across the corridor. The Hare's head hit the rock wall and slid to the floor in a limp heap. Rami spun around to grab Willie, but the leader of the Hares had let go of Malcolm and was cowering against the wall. Unkhabami pulled Willie to his feet and held him against the wall by his throat.

Malcolm reached back and pulled the knife out of his back. He brought it around and held it to John's throat as his fist curled tighter into John's shirt. "Start talking. What did you do to her?"

John lifted his chin as he tried to put some distance between himself and the blade. "She... she hasn't eaten—"

"You are starving her?" Rami roared.

"What the hell is wrong with you people?" Sandra shouted as she ran forward. She knocked the Hare, who was bracing against the door, out of the way.

"No!" John protested.

"Sandra!" Rami turned to stop her, but it was too late.

Sandra yanked the door open. She could see Whitney in the shadows, sliding along the wall like a trapped animal.

"Get out!" Whitney hissed at her from the darkness.

"Whitney?" Sandra whispered.

"Sandra!" Whitney's voice shook. "Please! Leave now! I..." Whitney clung to the wall with her back to the door, then turned suddenly. Light from the hall glinted off her fangs just before she lurched forward.

Sandra staggered backward and landed hard on the floor. Whitney was on her in a flash.

"Get her!" John shouted.

The remaining Hares rushed forward to grab Whitney, hauling her off Sandra.

Sandra scrambled backward like a crab, trying to get out of the way.

Whitney kicked and thrashed, trying to break free.

Malcolm let go of John and lunged at the Hares holding Whitney. He tackled one, ripping him away from Whitney and driving the knife into the man's chest as they fell to the floor.

"No!" John shouted.

Whitney's black-eyed gaze focused on John. "You! You stole my life from me!" Her nostrils flared as she bared her fangs. "You took everything from me!" With a scream that encompassed all the pain and anger she had suffered, Whitney tore loose from the remaining Hare and tackled John, sinking her teeth into his throat.

Everyone froze in shock.

She's killing him! Sandra watched in horror as Whitney ripped away from John. She was covered in blood.

The remaining Hare cried out and rushed Whitney again. She spun around. Her eyes were dark orbs of hatred as she attacked the second Hare.

"Whitney! Stop!" Rami shouted.

Whitney let go of the man and turned on Rami. She snarled at him. She looked ready to attack the giant.

Sandra stared down at Whitney's second victim. He lay gasping and bleeding. He would be dead in seconds. Sandra tore her gaze away and looked at John. He was dead. His vacant eyes stared up at the roof. Sandra looked over at Willie, the supposed leader of the Hares. He hadn't even tried to break away from Unkhabami to help. His bulging eyes flicked from Whitney to Unkhabami.

The priestess' eyes focused on Whitney, watching, waiting. Sandra kept watching too, not knowing what to do.

"Whitney, please!" Rami held out his hands in a placating gesture as he stepped forward.

Malcolm slowly came to his feet. Whitney didn't notice him; she was focused on Rami.

Rami shook his head as he took another step. "We will not hurt you, Fair Maiden."

Crouched and panting, Whitney watched him.

Malcolm inched closer. In a flash, he wrapped his arms around her from behind, pinning her arms to her sides. Whitney struggled to get free, but he held tight.

"Whitney," Malcolm spoke quietly into her ear, "I'm sorry for this. I didn't want to." Whitney thrashed and snarled. Malcolm grunted as her head smacked into his jaw. "You have to calm down before you hurt anyone else."

His words finally registered. She stopped struggling and looked around. Her eyes returned to their normal green as she looked at John's bloody neck and empty eyes. She looked at the other Hare that she had attacked and then down at her blood-soaked shirt.

"What have I done?" Whitney whispered and started to shake.

WEAKENING

Malcolm hugged Whitney to his chest. "It's gonna be okay."

"Nothing's okay!" she wailed. "How can anything be okay? I just killed two people!" She struggled against his embrace as she cried.

"I know you didn't want this, but—" Malcolm winced as her struggles pulled the wound in his back.

"I killed them!" Whitney ripped away from him. Turning away from the dead, she ran back into her prison room.

If I stay locked away, I can't hurt anyone.

She spun around, intent on closing the door and barricading herself in, but Malcolm stood silhouetted on the threshold. Beyond him, she could see Unkhabami still holding Willie against the wall.

"Whitney?" Malcolm peered at her through the darkness.

"Please, stay away!" Whitney sobbed as she retreated to the other side of the room.

"Leave her," Unkhabami said softly.

"She needs help. She's freaked out!" Whitney heard Sandra gasp.

"And we will help her," Unkhabami said, glancing toward Whitney's prison room, "but she must be calm."

Whitney felt like the priestess was looking straight at her, talking directly to her. Whitney tried to breathe. Unkhabami was right; she needed to calm down.

"First, we must deal with this lot." Unkhabami turned back to Willie. "How many more Hares are here?"

Willie's voice shook. "N...none."

"None?" Rami asked.

Barbie's answer was barely a whisper. "The six of us were the last."

Whitney froze. *The last? There were only six Hares left, and I killed two of them?*

She looked down at her chest and hands. They were covered in blood. She ran for the bathroom again. She ripped off her clothes and frantically fumbled with the shower knobs. Water blasted out, nearly scalding her skin. If she scrubbed hard enough, maybe the guilt would wash away with the blood.

Desperately, she scrubbed and scrubbed and scrubbed, finally sliding to the floor as the water rained down on her. Whitney pulled her knees up, wrapping her arms around them, hugging herself tightly. She felt like she was shattering. Too much had happened in too little time. Too many things to think about. The self-loathing. The hunger. The guilt. Relief that Apep was gone. Relief that she wasn't dead. Despair that she was forever imprisoned. Heartache swooped in as she remembered Madraeus. She would never see him again. It was emotional overload. All she could do was stare as the water pounded down on her.

Then it stopped.

Whitney turned to find Unkhabami standing above her. She had turned off the shower and was holding a towel.

"Please!" Whitney pleaded hoarsely, "Make it stop."

"Come, little one. There is a time to break, but it is not now." She reached down and helped Whitney to stand.

"No," Whitney tried to back away, "I don't want to hurt you!"

"You will not hurt me, child." Unkhabami chuckled as she toweled Whitney dry.

Whitney stared up at her. "I won't?"

A glint twinkled in the priestess' eyes. "I am a priestess of the Paka-Watu. You couldn't hurt me if you tried."

"But I killed those men." For a moment, the smell of blood was with her again. Whitney's gut twisted.

"They deserved it," Unkhabami hissed.

Anger flashed through Whitney. "John did!" Her anger died away. "But the other one? I didn't even know his name."

"Would that have made a difference?" Unkhabami began to dry Whitney's hair.

"Yes. No." Whitney buried her face in her hands. "I don't know."

Without another word, Unkhabami turned and left the bathroom. For lack of a better plan, Whitney wrapped the towel around herself and followed her out. Whitney blinked at the brightness. Unkhabami had turned on the lights, making the room seem less like a tomb. The priestess glided across the room to the bed and picked up a stack of clothing.

"Barbie found some clothes for you. Get dressed. We have urgent problems that we need to discuss."

Whitney shook her head. "I can't."

Unkhabami raised her eyebrows. "I have known you for a very short time. However, in that time, I have never known you to sit by as events unfolded. Now is not the time to start. You are the Key. Our immediate problem concerns you."

Whitney paled.

"You must come to terms with the truth." Unkhabami's eyes glowed. "You are a vampire, whether you like it or not. There is no going back."

Whitney clutched the clothing to her chest. It felt real, but she didn't. Despite that, Unkhabami's matter-of-fact attitude was somehow soothing.

"Get dressed." Unkhabami walked toward the door. "I will get the others."

Not wanting to get caught naked, Whitney dropped the towel and pulled on the sweatpants and hoodie. She crawled onto the bed and hugged her knees.

As soon as Unkhabami left the room, Sandra slipped in but stopped just inside the door. Whitney could tell that she was torn between fearing the monster her friend had become and fearing for her friend.

"You doin' okay?" Sandra asked without looking her in the eye.

"Is that even possible?" Whitney muttered.

Sandra watched her for a moment. "I don't know anymore."

"Thanks." Whitney scoffed. "Nothing like optimism."

Sandra let out a bark of bitter laughter. "What is there to be optimistic about? You're one of *them* now."

Anger flared up in Whitney's chest. "It's not like I had a choice!"

"Yes, you did! After the mine, they moved on. You could have stayed with your grandmother and had a normal life, but you chose to stay with them! What did you think was going to happen? Did you think that it would be a picnic?"

"No, but—"

"We are in the world of monsters." There was a razor-sharp edge to Sandra's tone. This wasn't just scary, practical Sandra. This was viciously honest Sandra. "From the moment we stepped into their world, willingly or not, we became part of it, with all of its death and blood. We were human. There was never a way for us to survive it!"

Whitney stared at Sandra. Every word felt like a nail in the coffin of her hope.

"I thought you'd be different. That our time in the mine, tortured by those monsters, would stop you from becoming like them." Sandra shook her head. "But I was wrong."

"I'm not like that!" Whitney pleaded. "I'm still me!"

"Are you?" Sandra stared her down. "Because I just saw you kill two people."

"Even *you* wanted to kill John!"

"Because he tried to kill you!"

"He did kill me!"

"No." Sandra shook her head. "Malcolm did that."

Whitney shivered. She had never heard Sandra sound so malicious, so dangerous. Something had gone terribly wrong in Sandra. Whitney could see it in her face. All this time, she'd joked about Sandra being unhinged. Whitney had thought all that dark humor and stark practicality was just her way of coping with what had happened to her. But now, it was clear. Sandra was broken, more than anyone had suspected.

Before Whitney could gather her thoughts, Rami and Unkhabami came into the room.

"Are you better, Fair Maiden?" Rami stepped forward cautiously, reminiscent of that moment after Mrs. Myers' party when Rami had been forced to show her his fangs to prove that vampires were real. He had been so reluctant, so sensitive. Rami, the gentle giant. He had never been a monster. He had been a vampire for hundreds of years, but he had always been kind. Yes, he had a temper and a dangerous side, but no more than any other man. Some of the fear about being a vampire eased in Whitney's chest.

"I don't know yet," Whitney said honestly, glancing at Sandra.

"The transition can be jarring." Rami neared the bed and sat.

Whitney leaned into his shoulder. She felt better just being next to him, but she could feel Sandra glaring at her. Just then, Malcolm herded Willie and Barbie into the room and stayed in the doorway, blocking the exit. The Hares stayed close together, their eyes constantly moving from one person to another.

Malcolm clapped his hands and rubbed them together. "Down to business?"

"Just like that?" Sandra glared at him. "Back to normal?"

Malcolm returned her glare. "Times are getting desperate, and we need to focus on the big picture for a while."

"You're all psychopaths," Sandra muttered and moved away, closer to the bathroom.

Malcolm turned on her. "No. This is the world we live in."

"Children!" Unkhabami held up a hand. "We are short on time."

"What is it?" Rami stiffened at her urgent tone.

Unkhabami looked at each of them. "Apep will be free again soon."

"No!" Barbie cried.

"How can that be?" Rami gaped at Unkhabami.

Whitney shot off the bed. "So, what? This," she gestured wildly, taking in the Warren, herself, and everything, "was all for nothing, then?"

"Silence!" Unkhabami snapped. "The trap is weakening."

"What?" Willie gasped. "How do you know this?"

"It's true." Malcolm crossed his arms. "I could almost put my hand through it."

Whitney began to pace, trying to breathe. Barbie and Willie exchanged expressions of terror.

"But I couldn't," Sandra protested. "Nothing happened when I put my hand through."

Unkhabami looked at Sandra. "You are not a vampire."

"Wait, what?" Whitney stopped and looked at the priestess.

Unkhabami explained, "John cast the spell using human blood."

Willie nodded. "And as long as that human is alive, the trap holds."

"But she is no longer human." Unkhabami raised her eyebrows. "She is a vampire. A descendant of the thing you trapped. Apep's blood now runs in her veins. You have corrupted the spell. It is only a matter of time until the trap collapses."

Barbie covered her mouth as understanding blossomed.

Sandra threw her hands up and paced away, muttering, "You've got to be kidding me!"

"This can't be!" Willie rubbed a shaking hand over his face.

Whitney's knees weakened, and she landed hard on the floor. *I died for nothing. I killed for nothing. It's all been for nothing... Madraeus? His sacrifice was for nothing.*

"What can we do?" Malcolm asked.

"We prepare to fight again." Unkhabami's nostrils flared as she looked at the Hares. "We must find a way to kill the snake."

WELL, WELL, WELL

"If we knew how to kill Apep, we would have!"

Malcolm took a menacing step toward Willie. "Oh, come on, you have to know something!"

Unkhabami stalked toward Willie. "All these centuries trapping and killing supernatural creatures, and you know nothing?"

"Apep is a chaos demon!" Barbie shook her head. "How can you kill a demon?"

"Same way you kill anything else," Malcolm smiled wickedly, "cut off its head."

"We tried!" Willie flung a hand toward the door. "You saw it! We barely scratched the bloody thing!"

From the corner, Sandra quietly spoke. "How did Ra kill him?"

"What?" Whitney stopped pacing and looked at her.

"You told me that Apep tried to stop Ra every night so the sun wouldn't rise." Sandra looked at Barbie. "So, how did Ra stop Apep every night?"

Willie stared back at her dumbly. "That's just a story."

"So are they." Sandra hooked a thumb toward Rami and Unkhabami.

Barbie stepped closer. "It makes sense. All myths are based in some truth."

"If we were back at InfiniCorp, we could research this properly." Rami sighed. "There are ancient texts there that could help."

"But it's all packed away," Whitney said.

Sandra shoved away from the wall where she had been leaning. "I can't believe how archaic y'all are."

Malcolm raised his eyebrows. "Meaning?"

"There's a thing called the internet." Sandra shrugged. "I found a ton of info about the Hares before I even met them."

"It is worth a try," Rami looked at the Hares. "Do you have a computer?"

Barbie looked at Willie. "Can we get to the library?"

Willie shook his head. "The roof collapsed when Apep escaped. That whole wing is blocked."

"There's a computer back in that room under the restaurant." Sandra hooked a thumb over her shoulder.

"Right." Malcolm pointed at the Hares. "You two, lead the way."

Barbie and Willie moved toward the door. He followed them out.

Unkhabami gestured for Sandra to follow them. "Well done."

"I didn't do it for you." Sandra shot her a disgusted look. "I did it to save humans."

"Fair Maiden?" Rami offered his arm to Whitney as if they were in an old-fashioned ballroom.

Whitney stared at him. "I can't."

"You must leave this place sometime." Rami smiled and took her hand. "Now is as good a time as any."

He walked toward the door, pulling her along with him. Whitney put on the brakes, but he didn't seem to notice. As they left the room, Whitney closed her eyes, not wanting to see the bodies of the men she'd killed.

"Whitney, open your eyes." Rami's deep voice echoed off the stone walls. "You cannot hide from what you are, even if you do not like it."

Whitney opened one eye just a crack. The corridor was empty. The bodies were gone. Just a bit of blood spotted the floor.

She glanced up at Rami, questioningly.

"Malcolm removed the remains."

She glanced at the blood spots. She could smell it, but it didn't spark the wild hunger as it had earlier. "Why was I crazy before when I smelled blood, but not now?"

"You were starving. Any animal will attack when it is starving."

"I think I have a lot to learn," Whitney muttered.

"Indeed." Rami started down the corridor again. Just ahead, the others disappeared around a corner. "Unfortunately, you have no time. We must deal with this crisis first. Madraeus and I will teach you."

Whitney blanched. *He doesn't know!* "Um, Rami? About Madraeus..." Whitney faltered.

Rami glanced at her. "Do not fear, we will find a way to free him."

"You know?"

"Malcolm told me."

"He did?"

"Yes. Malcolm is quite distraught about it." Rami glanced at her. "And about having to turn you. He regrets what he had to do."

"Me too." Whitney muttered. "Madraeus sacrificed himself to keep Apep from getting free." Tears blurred her vision.

"You will see him again."

"I may not be alive by then," Whitney whispered. "The last trap broke when the Key died."

Rami put an arm around her shoulders. "We will do our best to avoid that path."

It didn't take long to reach the restaurant's basement entrance. As Whitney started up the stairs, Rami turned suddenly and stared down the corridor behind them.

"What's the matter?" Whitney looked past him down the hallway.

"I thought I heard someone."

"More Hares? I thought Barbie and Willie were the last ones."

"Perhaps…" Rami watched for a moment longer before turning back and motioning her up the stairs. "Go ahead. I will be along in a moment."

Barbie and Sandra were bent over the computer already by the time Whitney climbed up through the trap door. The aroma of spicy curries drifted down from the restaurant above. It was enticing, reminding Whitney that she would never eat that kind of food again. She turned away and noticed Unkhabami standing in the corner with Malcolm. He had pulled his shirt up so she could check his wound. Whitney walked over to them.

"What happened?"

Malcolm glanced at her. "Hare got me with a knife earlier."

She didn't remember that. *Was I that far gone?* Whitney shuddered and looked at the wound. The hole was already closed, leaving just a dark red line. "You're healed?"

"Not quite." Malcolm pulled his shirt down. "Need a bit more blood to be back to normal."

Whitney remembered what Madraeus had told her about vampires needing blood to repair injuries. *It's like a superpower, but gross,* she thought, and then an involuntary thrill went through her. *I can do that now too.* Whitney shivered as she realized that she would have to drink blood to do it.

"Will have to wait on a full healing until the kids are in bed," Malcolm nodded toward Sandra and the Hares, "but I'm well enough at the moment."

Whitney glanced at Sandra; she was watching them over the top of the computer. Her eyes held accusation and disgust. Whitney's fears from earlier grew. She wondered if they would be able to trust Sandra now.

Sandra returned her attention to Barbie as they discussed what they had found and where to look for more information. Whitney could hear everything even though they were across the room. *Vampire hearing is amazing.* She flushed as she remembered every time she had muttered something disparaging about Madraeus under her breath. *He must have heard every word. And yet he still likes me...*

"We found something," Barbie looked up, "but we have to go to the British Museum."

"For what?" Malcolm stepped closer.

"There is a papyrus there called *The Books of Overthrowing Apep* that contains spells to use on Apep. Also, they have the Book of the Dead. It explains how to fight him."

"*The Books of Overthrowing Apep*?" Malcolm laughed. "Seriously?" He looked at Willie. "Wow, no idea how to get rid of him, huh?"

Willie squirmed.

"There is no way it's that simple," Whitney snorted. "That seems ridiculously obvious."

"Says it right there." Sandra pointed at the screen. "It's technically called the Bremner-Rhind Papyrus, but same thing."

"Great!" Whitney gave a short laugh. "I guess we'll just pop down to the museum and check it out." Whitney started for the stairs.

"You can't!" Willie rushed forward and caught her arm.

Whitney jumped, making Willie flinch.

"Sorry, but you're the Key."

"So?" Whitney couldn't keep the defensiveness out of her tone.

"It's just..." Willie fidgeted, "...there are some rules."

"Rules?" Whitney jerked her arm out of his grip. "Like never get to have a life?"

"No, not exactly," Willie shook his head, "you can have a life, but... you can't leave the area. You have to stay near the trap."

Whitney's stomach dropped. "How near?"

"A few miles at the most." Willie wrung his hands. "You might be able to go to the edge of Broadclyst, but not much farther."

Whitney's lip quivered. "What happens if I get too far away? Does the trap open?"

"No," Willie laughed nervously, "that would be bad. No, you just can't."

"Can't what?" Malcolm came up behind him.

"You physically can't go any farther," Willie stammered, clearly terrified of Malcolm. "It would feel like you walked into a wall."

Whitney started to shake.

Malcolm shoved Willie from behind. "So, she's just as trapped as Apep?"

"Yes." Willie's response was barely audible, but it was so loud in Whitney's ears.

It echoed and deafened her. *Trapped!*

Rage bubbled up, burning away the fear. She snarled and lunged at Willie.

Malcolm grabbed her, bodily hauling her to the other side of the room.

"I'm sorry!" Willie wailed. "I don't make the rules!"

"No," Unkhabami snarled, "you just use others like a coward."

Malcolm held her against the wall as she struggled. "Whitney! Get a grip!"

Whitney snarled and thrashed, trying to get free. She wanted to kill them all. She wanted to run.

"The trap is gonna break anyway!" Malcolm panted as he wrestled with her. His words sapped the fight from her limbs.

Yes, it'll break. Madraeus will be free. I'll be free. Whitney shuddered. *And Apep will be free.*

She went limp. She looked around. Everyone in the room was watching her. Some of their expressions held fear and some held concern.

Guess I know who my friends are, Whitney thought. Surprisingly, it wasn't the humans. "I guess you all go. I'll wait here."

"We will not leave you alone," Rami said as he came up through the trap door.

"Sandra and I will return to the hotel and find the wolves." Unkhabami walked toward the stairs. "We will send them to the museum and return here." She looked at Rami over her shoulder. "We have unfinished business."

Sandra looked at Unkhabami and then walked over to Whitney. Her eyes held sadness and a lot of pain. "Take care of yourself." She looked like she wanted to say a lot more, but instead, she turned and ran up the stairs.

Whitney watched her go, wondering why that felt like goodbye.

LET'S STEAL A BOOK

"Philtzer, I swear!" Sophia hissed as she pulled him down behind the car. "You have the dumbest ideas!"

"It's not dumb." Philtzer grinned as he watched the side door. "It's inspired."

"By a movie!" Sophia punched him.

"Ow!" Philtzer rubbed his shoulder. "You got a better idea?"

"Yes," Sophia said. "How about we just walk in and look at the damn book?"

"Where's the fun in that?" Philtzer wrinkled his nose.

"This isn't about fun!" Sophia argued. "This is about saving time and energy."

"Spoil sport."

"Look," Sophia took a deep breath, trying for calm, "if we try it my way and it doesn't work, we can try it your way."

"Oh, fine," Philtzer huffed. "But if we can't find what we need. We pull a heist."

Sophia rolled her eyes and growled something under her breath about the maturity of men. "Come on."

She led him around to the main entrance of the British Museum, through the ornate wrought iron gates, up the stairs, and followed the signs to the Egyptian exhibit.

"Well, that was boring," Philtzer grumbled.

"Good!" Sophia snapped. "We've had enough excitement lately. Seriously, between mom kidnapping an FBI agent and you nearly dying—"

"Pfft!" Philtzer waved away her words. "I didn't nearly die."

She stopped and turned to stare at him. He grinned at her. She stared him down.

He crumbled. "I got a little broken, but I didn't nearly die."

"Seriously, I've had enough!" Sophia shook her head. "I mean, what does mom think she's gonna do with an FBI agent locked in the hotel bathroom?"

Philtzer shrugged. "He won't get away by saying he needs to pee."

She snorted and walked away, looking at the exhibits.

Philtzer followed her. "Reggie's right, Soph. If we keep Milner locked up, then at least we know where he is. We won't have to keep looking over our shoulders."

"Yeah, but they're gonna come looking for him and that laptop."

"Yep, and if we're lucky," Philtzer pressed his nose close to a glass display case, "we'll be long gone by the time they find him."

"What about the laptop?"

"Hamilton will get it to Marcus. He'll do his techno voodoo on it and then we'll know what they know." He turned to look at another display. "And hopefully, he can delete anything they have."

"That's a lot of hope and luck," Sophia muttered as they moved on.

"Hey, check this out!" Philtzer pointed to a statue of a large cat. "Remind you of anyone?" When she didn't answer, he pointed again. "It's Unkhabami's twin!"

This time, she didn't scoff. It did actually look like Unkhabami. "She's not that old, is she?"

"Nah, but maybe they had were-cats back then too."

They continued their journey through the exhibit. Sculptures and statues lined the aisles. Along the walls, tablets and artifacts were displayed behind glass. Sophia and Philtzer looked at each one, but neither found anything depicting a snake. Day faded away as they wandered through the gallery.

"There're a million things here. How are we going to find the right one?"

"Attention patrons, the museum will be closing in thirty minutes," announced a voice over the loudspeaker.

"We're running out of time!" Sophia sped up her search.

"Soph!" Philtzer called her over. He pointed to a tablet with rows of what looked like dogs. "Look at this! It says, 'limestone stela depicting Wepwawet, the Opener of Ways. A wolf god known for leading armies into battle and guiding the deceased into the underworld.'" He grinned at her and pointed to himself. "Wolf god!"

She was about to make a snide remark but noticed the tablet next to that one. It had a lot more of the dog-shaped figures. At the bottom was a man with a ram's head and a man with a wolf's head spearing what looked like a reptile that was crawling up from the bottom of the tablet. "Is that...?" She looked at Philtzer.

He pointed to each figure. "Werewolf, reptile, ram..." He laughed. "Rami?"

Sophia rolled her eyes. "Be serious."

"I am!" Philtzer looked at her, and for once, his expression was serious. "If Apep was the origin of all vampires, then what if this Wepwawet is the origin of werewolves?"

Sophia shook her head. "This is getting weird."

"We need to find that papyrus." Philtzer noticed a man coming out of a door tucked in the back corner of the gallery. It was marked 'Staff Only'. He trotted over to him. "Excuse me, you work in this section?"

"Yes, I'm the assistant curator," the man said as he turned, but his voice faded out as he took in Philtzer's bandaged face and Sophia's black eye.

"Could you tell us where to find the Bremner-Rhind Papyrus?"

Pulling himself together, he said, "It's currently not on display."

Philtzer leaned in. "We really need to see it."

"You'll have to wait until we have it out again. Museum is closing soon, best finish your tour." He moved to step around them.

Philtzer reached out to stop the man. "Actually, we need to see it now. It's kinda life or death."

The man laughed. "Is this some kind of joke?"

Philtzer smiled. "I wish! What's your name?"

"John," the man said warily.

Philtzer shot a look of exasperation at Sophia. "Why is everyone in this country named John?"

Sophia rolled her eyes.

"Look, John, we need some information, and you're going to help us get it. We got a snake problem, and we need the Bremner-Rhind Papyrus and the Book of the Dead."

John's gaze shifted from Philtzer to Sophia and back again. "Wouldn't an exterminator be better?"

Philtzer let out a bark of laughter. "I like him," he said to Sophia. He hooked an arm over John's shoulders and started walking him back toward the 'Staff Only' door. "No, John. That's a nice suggestion, but we have a really big snake problem. As in The Snake problem. We need to know how to get rid of Apep."

John gaped in disbelief. "Apep is just a representation of a chaos demon; he isn't real!"

"I beg to differ, friend. He's real and nasty." Philtzer pointed toward his face. "Where can we find the info we need?"

"This is ridiculous." John shook his head.

"Please?" Sophia came up on his other side.

John glanced at her and sighed. "All right. Let's say you're not delusional, just for a moment."

"I'm game!" Philtzer grinned. "Consider me sane."

"You could look it up in our archives, but it won't do you any good unless you read Hieratic or hieroglyphics."

"Can you?" Sophia asked.

"Yes." John looked insulted. "What exactly are you looking for?"

Sophia produced a list and handed it to John. "Bremner-Rhind Papyrus with any spells that can work against Apep. And the chapters that deal with killing Apep in the Book of the Dead."

"And anything else that would help," Philtzer said. "This is the fate of the world we're talking about."

John read the list and then looked at them both. "You're serious!"

"We said that." Philtzer looked at Sophia. "Didn't we say that?"

Sophia nodded. "We did say that."

John looked at them both again. For a moment, he looked like he wanted to believe them but then shook his head. "Look, I'm sorry, but you have to go. Make an appointment with the library, I'm sure they can help you." He started to push past them.

Philtzer grabbed John from behind, locking his arm around the man's neck. As he started to struggle, Philtzer whispered into his ear, "Stay quiet and you'll live."

John froze.

Sophia glanced around to see if anyone had noticed them. Most of the patrons were trickling out of the gallery. The noise level had lessened considerably. No one was looking in their direction.

"Don't try to call for help. I'm faster than them." Philtzer tightened his hold on the man's neck. "Comprende?"

John nodded quickly.

"What's behind that staff door?"

"Maintenance corridor."

"Perfect. Let's chat." Philtzer turned John toward the keypad. "Open it."

John quickly punched in his code with shaking hands. As soon as it unlocked, they slipped inside.

"Here's the deal, John. You help us find what we need, and we let you live. Deal?"

John nodded again.

"All right, where do we go?"

"An...anthropology Library and R...research Centre." He stretched out a hand and pointed. "That way."

Philtzer looked around. "Staff shortcut?"

John nodded.

"Great! But remember, no funny business." Philtzer gave John a little squeeze before letting go of his neck.

John stumbled forward so he didn't see Philtzer grimace and hold his ribs, but Sophia did. She shot him a worried glance, but Philtzer gave her no indication that he'd noticed. They turned and walked with John between them toward the research center.

Inside the center, it felt as if the air pressure and temperature were completely different, and it was much quieter. John led them through the little maze of tables where scientists sat studying artifacts to a private room off to the side. The room contained a table with a swing-arm lamp and two chairs.

John shut the door and turned toward them. "You seem like nice, if not confused, people." He glanced at Philtzer. "You can still leave without getting into trouble."

"We can't." Sophia shook her head. "We weren't kidding about the life or death thing. We need that information."

"You're talking about ancient stories!" John pleaded. "They aren't real!"

Sophia sighed. "What if we could prove it?"

"Soph," Philtzer warned.

"We don't have time." She glanced at him. "Here's the thing, John. You look like someone that once believed in magic, and heroes, and villains." She glanced down at his comic book inspired tie. She gestured, encompassing the whole museum. "You obviously got into this stuff for a reason. What if I told you I could show you something that would rekindle those beliefs?" She started to unbutton her shirt.

John's eyes bulged as he watched her fingers.

"But there's a catch," John looked up at her face, "you have to help us and say nothing about any of this."

John looked back at her half-open shirt and nodded.

"Great." Sophia smiled. A second later she was standing in front of John as a wolf.

John stumbled backward and landed hard in the chair.

Philtzer braced one hand on the table and leaned down close to John's ear. "You see that, John? That's a werewolf."

John stared at Sophia, breathing hard. She sat back on her haunches and tilted her head, watching John.

"So, it's not a real big stretch to think that maybe we're right about the snake problem, is it?" Philtzer patted him on the back.

John swallowed and sat up a little straighter. He stared intently at Sophia as a silly little smile slipped onto his lips. He looked up at Philtzer. "Where's that list?"

Sophia changed back as Philtzer extracted John's solemn promise that he wouldn't breathe a word of this to anyone.

"Follow me," John said as he moved to the door, reading the list.

Philtzer's eyes twinkled as he grinned at Sophia.

She shrugged. "What? I don't get to be rash?"

PREPARE

"This is the weirdest thing I've ever read." Sophia flipped through the information that John had printed out for them at the museum.

After seeing Sophia's wolf, John had become remarkably helpful. He had pulled out books, made notes, looked up digitized artifacts, and printed out translations, all while grinning at Sophia like a teenager on his first date.

"Can't be that bad." Philtzer squinted against the fiery glare of the setting sun as it blazed in through the windshield.

Sophia pointed to the papers. "Seriously, listen to this. Apep is supposed to be speared, cut, decapitated, roasted, and consumed by fire. His heart is supposed to be taken by Mafdet, the first cat goddess."

"A cat goddess?" Philtzer raised his eyebrows.

"Yeah," Sophia flipped through the pages, "she's either an Egyptian lynx, lion, or cheetah war goddess, depending on which translation you're looking at."

"Sound like anyone we know?"

Sophia let her hands fall into her lap. "You don't think..."

"I do think!" Philtzer nodded. "I think that there are way too many similarities happening here."

Sophia shook her head. "No, come on."

"Think about it. We've got a snake demon that creates vampires. You've got all those tablets with wolves on them. Wepwawet, right? The wolf god that leads the army and escorts the dead. That's werewolves. You've got Mafa...Metda..."

"Mafdet."

"Yeah, that one. Cat goddess that looks like a cheetah, that's Unkhabami." Philtzer stopped talking as a grin split his face. "And you've got Madraeus." Philtzer hooted and banged his palm against the steering wheel. "Ha! That's so cool!"

"What's cool?"

"Madraeus!" Philtzer giggled. "Rami always calls him Ray." He glanced at Sophia, disappointed that she wasn't getting it. "Oh, come on! Ray, as in sun rays? Madraeus? As in Ra? The guy that battles the snake?"

"I think you're reaching now." Sophia shook her head. "You're telling me that you think Madraeus is Ra, Unkhabami is this cat goddess, and we are all fated to reenact this epic battle from ancient Egyptian mythology?"

"It's synchronicity, man." Philtzer shrugged. "It's weird!"

"There is no way that all that is actually related." Sophia shuffled the papers. "That's not how real life works!"

"Says who?" Philtzer glanced at her again. "Look, who knows how all this is supposed to play out. Is it fated? I don't know, but

I choose to think of it as all connected because it makes my little wolf brain happy. It's more like a superhero movie, and that's cool."

"It's not cool. It's ridiculous!" Sophia threw the stack of papers up onto the dashboard. "I was in college just a couple weeks ago, getting ready to graduate. I was gonna get a job and enjoy life for a while."

Philtzer shrugged. "You can still do that."

"We're preparing to fight a chaos demon with sketchy magic directions from ancient Egypt!" Sophia scoffed. "I didn't even believe in magic until a couple weeks ago. I'm still not sure I believe in it."

"Yeah, life's weird."

Sophia gaped at him. "Don't you ever get freaked out by all this?"

"Nah, been doing it too long."

"Right." Sophia shook her head and stared out the side window.

They drove for a few miles in silence. Philtzer kept glancing at Sophia, trying to decide what to say. Finally, he tried for 'business as usual' conversation.

"So, what else does it say?"

Sophia turned back from the window and pulled the papers back off the dashboard. "Um, there are spells here to weaken Apep, but we will need some wax, papyrus, and some green ink."

"Ink and wax will be pretty easy, but papyrus?"

"We have to draw a picture of Apep in green ink on it and write his name in green ink on a wax image. And then burn them."

"And that weakens him?"

Sophia nodded. "And there are some spells to create sympathetic magic to do actual damage to him. We'll need an iron spear, knives, and swords."

"That might take a bit of looking." Philtzer frowned. "The police confiscated any weaponry that was left in the churchyard."

"Maybe the Hares have some." Sophia leafed through the papers again. "It also says some of these rituals have to be done in the morning, mid-day, and at night again."

"It's gonna take a whole day to get all this stuff ready?" Philtzer blew out an impatient breath as he changed lanes.

"Basically, yeah."

"We still have a couple hours before we get back to Broadclyst." Reaching into his jacket pocket, he pulled out a burner phone and handed it to Sophia. "Call Hamilton. They can gather supplies. And you can read off all the spell stuff to Unkhabami so she can get started."

"Why the sudden hurry?"

"No sense wasting time." He shrugged. "We gotta get you back. You got a graduation to get to."

Sophia smiled at him.

"What?"

"You try to make everyone believe that you're just a goofy playboy, but you're not."

"Pfft." Philtzer rolled his eyes. "I don't know what you're talking about."

She leaned over and kissed him on the cheek. "You're a good man, Philtzer."

Philtzer's grin became a little lopsided as his face turned red.

"Are you blushing?"

"No!" He pointed at the setting sun. "It's just hot in here."

Sophia laughed as she dialed Hamilton's number. She spent the next hour reading spells to Unkhabami as Philtzer drove.

It was nearly ten by the time Philtzer pulled up outside of the Indian restaurant. He grinned at Sophia. "Best hideout ever!"

Sophia gathered all the papers from the museum. She had stacked some on the floor and some on the dashboard while working with Unkhabami.

Philtzer led the way into the restaurant. "I would love to have seen how they got that FBI agent in without anyone getting suspicious."

"I think I'd rather not know," Sophia said, looking around the dining room.

A few customers still lingered, including Hamilton and Thomas. Philtzer poked Sophia in the back and pointed toward their table.

Hamilton looked up as they approached. "How was the museum?"

"Fun." Philtzer hooked a thumb toward Sophia. "She did a striptease."

"I did not!" Sophia protested when Hamilton's eyebrows shot up.

"Do you want to see my wolf?" Philtzer mimed, taking his jacket off. "Little furry shoulder here, a little tail wagging."

"Philtzer!" Sophia smacked him in the arm and glanced around the restaurant, but no one was paying any attention to them.

Philtzer grinned at her as he sat down across from Thomas, but Thomas didn't even look up. He just kept slowly turning his glass. Philtzer looked at the four empty pint glasses and at the nearly untouched plate of vindaloo sitting in front of Thomas. He glanced at Hamilton.

Hamilton shook his head.

Philtzer nudged Thomas with his toe.

Thomas raised his pain-filled eyes, looking first at Philtzer and then at Sophia. His gaze landed on the stack of papers tucked under Sophia's elbow. "Those the spells?" At her nod, he stood and held out a hand. "I'll take them to Unkhabami."

Sophia handed them over, and Thomas walked away toward the kitchen.

"He doesn't have much of a sense of humor."

"No one does at the moment," Hamilton murmured. "I got a call from Mrs. Myers. She chewed me out for not finding Jeff Monroe yet."

"Isn't that the Weaver-pixie-werewolf guy that Cecelia was after?" Sophia asked and Hamilton nodded.

Philtzer snorted. "Did you tell her we've been a little busy?"

"Yeah, she doesn't see it that way. And Marcus called. Lady Douglas is getting more and more vicious about hunting Cecelia's supporters. He said it's making everyone nervous."

"I am not going to be the one to tell her to stop." Philtzer shook his head. "That's above my pay grade."

"It's above all our pay grades, except Madraeus, and he's stuck in a magic trap," Hamilton said as the waiter came over to take their order. Hamilton waited until the waiter left to say, "And there's more."

"There's more?" Sophia gaped. "Isn't that enough?"

"We have a human problem."

"Human problem?" Sophia asked.

"Agent Milner, Sandra, the Hares, and the police." Hamilton nodded. "Sandra is acting weird. She's snapping at everyone. There are only two Hares left, and the police are still crawling all over the churchyard. I don't know how we're going to get them out of the way for this whole fiasco. And Milner knows way too much. If we let him go, he'll just keep hunting us."

"You can't just kill him!" Sophia gasped. They all glanced toward the other customers. She lowered her voice. "That's murder."

Hamilton and Philtzer said nothing.

One look at their expressions and she started shaking her head. "No. No. Killing someone that's trying to kill you is one thing, but killing someone because they might be a prob-lem? No. That's just plain wrong."

Philtzer rubbed his chin and sighed. "First things first. Where is everyone at on the spell thing?"

"Unkhabami is working on it. She set up her..." Hamilton waved his hands around like a magician, "...thing in one of the rooms downstairs."

"You managed to find papyrus and an iron spear?" Sophia leaned forward.

"Ish." Hamilton shrugged. "We had to improvise. Un-khabami said that parchment would work too. We couldn't find an iron spear, so we had to adapt. Took a piece off a wrought iron gate."

"Hope that doesn't mess anything up," Sophia said as the waiter brought their drinks.

"Me too," Hamilton said as his phone rang. "Hello?"

Philtzer turned to Sophia and spoke quietly. "We still have to figure out how to get the trap open without killing Whitney."

Sophia opened her mouth to speak but Hamilton's excla-mation stopped her.

"Jeff? Where are you?" Hamilton frowned. "What? Slow down."

The three werewolves flinched as they heard gunshots through the phone's speaker.

"Jeff?" Hamilton sat straight up. "Jeff? You all right?" Hamilton looked at Philtzer as he listened. "Yes—" he stopped as Jeff spoke, "but—" Hamilton looked at his phone and then put it back to his ear, but hearing nothing, he flipped it shut.

"Um," Hamilton swallowed, "that was Jeff Munroe." He slipped the phone back into his jacket pocket.

"Guess you can tell Myers to get off your case." Sophia shrugged, taking a drink.

"Not really. He was being hunted." Hamilton blew out a long breath. "I'm gonna have to go find him."

"It'll have to wait until we're done here." Philtzer shook his head. "Why did he call?"

"He had a message." Hamilton gestured helplessly. "He's a Weaver and he had a vision."

"Which said?"

Hamilton shook his head in confusion. "He said keys open doors from both sides."

"What does that mean?" Sophia asked.

Hamilton shrugged.

Philtzer rubbed his face. "I'm pretty sure it has to do with Whitney. She's the Key and we're trying to open the trap."

Sophia groaned. "How many people we got?"

"'Bout a dozen." Hamilton sighed.

"Damn." Philtzer's face fell. "Not much of an army."

"We didn't do too well last time, and we had three times the people," Sophia grumbled.

"Well," Philtzer rallied, "at least we won't have to fight Cecelia at the same time."

Hamilton grimaced. "Um..."

Philtzer slumped back in his chair and stared at Hamilton. "Oh, come on! Can't we ever catch a break?"

BROKEN

Madraeus stood facing the barrier wall. Slowly, he reached out. He could almost feel Whitney's soft skin as he let his fingers skim along the warm surface. "I know that you didn't want to be loved by a monster." Madraeus couldn't hide the bitterness in his voice. "I didn't want this life for you either."

He dropped his hand with a sigh.

The barrier shimmered like ripples on the surface of a pond when a stone is dropped in the water. Madraeus frowned. He reached out again and touched the wall. This time his fingers sank into the shimmering surface.

"What on Earth?" he muttered, pushing his fingers farther through the barrier until most of his hand had disappeared. "That's not..."

He pulled his hand back and looked at it. There was a residual tingling feeling in his fingers. He rubbed his thumb and fingers together, thinking, *Something's changed.*

Bending down, he winced as he picked up his sword. The bites, scratches, and cuts he'd received from the first battle at the church were healing slowly. The bites from his second battle with Apep were healing even slower. He felt drained. Due to the lack of fresh blood, his body had turned on itself for nourishment. If he couldn't replace the blood his body was burning through to heal itself soon, he would die of starvation. He had nearly perished in the mine from the same problem. He had no desire to go through that again.

Perhaps I should carry an emergency pack of blood, he mused, knowing full well that he wasn't leaving this trap alive.

He turned away from the wall and saw Whitney. He remained frozen in place as she ran toward him. Joy washed over him until he saw her raise her hand. She was holding a stake. Her face contorted as she screamed, "Murderer!"

He threw his hand up to ward off the blow, but it never came. Madraeus lowered his hand and stared at the empty space in front of him. She had faded from sight. Disappointment washed over him as he realized that it was just another hallucination of Whitney's futures, his own personal punishment for relying on magic.

"I don't even get spared from that torture?" He shook his head and started walking. He didn't have a destination in mind. There was nowhere to go.

Somewhere in here, Apep still raged against the trap. The snake had left him to bleed and slithered off into the trees. Madraeus hadn't seen him since. He could hear him sometimes, either in his head, hissing and cursing, or through the trees, pounding against the barrier.

The sound of laughter floated through the shadowy trees. Madraeus caught a glimpse of movement. He peered into the darkness. Whitney ran through the trees, laughing. His heart constricted. He looked away. *I'll never hear her laugh again. Or see her smile.*

He hefted the sword, resettling it in his hand. He turned away and started walking again.

He stopped. Just ahead of him, Whitney was slumped in the grass, bloody and torn. Apep rose above her, his fangs dripping with blood.

"No!" A thousand emotions slammed into Madraeus as he roared and ran forward with his sword raised.

Apep hissed and slithered away into the shadows. Dropping his weapon, Madraeus landed on his knees next to her body. As he reached for her, his hand went right through her, grabbing nothing but cold ground. He curled his hands into fists, ripping the blades of grass out of the ground. He sat back, and looking to the sky, roared out in frustration and pain.

A hissing laughter filled his mind as Apep enjoyed his pain.

Madraeus clenched his jaw. He refused to give the snake any satisfaction. He picked up his sword again and staggered to his feet. He surveyed the trees and then set off in a random direction.

The grove seemed even bigger than before, as if it kept growing in size. Madraeus walked for about an hour until his path brought him to the little pond with the statue in the center. He stood for a long time looking up at the statue. It was an angel in full battle armor, his wings arched up behind him. He held a shield, bearing a cross, and his sword was poised to strike. Under his foot, a coiled snake hissed, defiant but defeated.

Michael the Archangel, Madraeus mused. He looked down at the stone snake and then eyed the angel's armor. *I can see why you won. You have actual armor from God.* He glanced down at his own sword. *And I just have this.*

He let out a short bitter laugh and then looked up at the sky. In desperation, he drove the sword into the ground and knelt in the grass in front of it. He clasped the blade with both hands and prayed. "I do not deserve your forgiveness. But, please, I beg you! Let her live free from the taint I have caused."

He closed his eyes and leaned his forehead against the hilt. "Please!" he begged. "Let her have a long and full life, filled with joy."

She will die, Apep hissed inside his head.

Madraeus squeezed his eyes shut, trying to push his voice away.

"Madraeus?" Whitney voice whispered.

He couldn't even turn and look. It was too much to hope that one of her futures could have been with him where they could talk and laugh. But it was just another hallucination.

Why am I having so many visions of her futures? They have never come this often before. Perhaps it's because I am inside a trap made from her blood.

The thought that he would forever be surrounded by her, but never allowed to touch her or see her again, shattered his control.

He sat back and screamed with all the rage and pain ravaging his heart.

Sssuch sssweet torture, Apep laughed.

"Madraeus?" Whitney's shaking voice begged for his attention.

He turned and looked toward her. "Can't you leave me be?"

"Madraeus, please!"

"Stop torturing me!" he shouted. "You're not real!" He shoved to his feet, ripping the sword from the ground. He turned and flung it at the vision.

Whitney gasped and ducked as the sword flew over her head. She glared at him. "What the hell is wrong with you?"

Madraeus froze.

Whitney straightened but didn't come any closer. "I know that I piss you off a lot, but you don't have to try and skewer me!"

Madraeus shook his head. "Whitney?" He took a hesitant step forward. "It's really you?"

He couldn't help but smile as relief and joy flooded through him. He rushed forward but stopped suddenly. His smile faded. *Something's not right.*

"What?" Whitney glanced around, baring her fangs. "What's wrong?"

He took another step closer and peered at her. He didn't want to believe what he was seeing.

"You're not Whitney."

She gave out a snort of incredulous laughter. "Oh, I am. I wish I wasn't, but I am."

"No." Madraeus shook his head. "You can't be. You're a vampire."

"Yeah, um, funny story." Whitney winced. "I kinda died, and—"

"What do you mean you kinda died?" Madraeus marched forward. "I saw you. You were bleeding but alive."

"The cut John gave me was bleeding out too fast." Whitney's hand covered the spot where the Hare had sliced her forearm. "John had me turned into a vampire so the trap wouldn't open again."

Rage burned through him as all the implications ran through his mind. "I'll kill him!"

"You don't have to," Whitney whispered, making Madraeus pause. "I already did."

"What?" Madraeus whispered.

"I killed two people." Her eyes glittered as the purple light reflected off her tears. "John and another Hare."

"No." He shook his head. "No, I should have sent you home! I should have kept you out of this!"

Whitney laughed, but it morphed into a cry. "Well, you didn't!"

In his mind, he heard the low hissing laughter. *The feasst comesss to me!*

Madraeus snapped out of his anguish and looked over his shoulder, remembering the vision of Apep rising over Whitney.

He looked back at Whitney. She was wearing the same clothes that he had seen ripped and bloody just a few moments ago.

Apep laughed again.

"You have to go! Now!" Madraeus lunged forward to grab her, but his hands went right through her.

Madraeus stared at his empty hands, thinking frantically, *That was too real. She dodged the sword! If that was real...? Is she a vampire now? How much of what she said was true?* Madraeus swore in frustration.

You will sssee her die!

Madraeus spun around to see Apep slithering toward the entrance gap in the stone wall.

I will feassst on her corpssse!

"No!" Madraeus roared. He searched the ground, looking for his sword. "You will never have her!" Madraeus found it and sprinted toward the wall. He reached it before the snake, spinning around with his sword raised.

Apep stopped, coiling back on himself. *Traitorousss child! You ssstill haven't learned!*

"I will always stand against you!" Madraeus held his sword at the ready. He backed away from the crazed snake until his heel hit the wall.

Apep rose higher and higher, glaring down at him. *Then you will die!*

Madraeus heard the barrier wall crackle. He glanced back to see it shimmer and ripple like the surface of a pond broken by a stone. Madraeus turned back to face the snake just as Apep roared and lunged.

OPENING DOORS

Whitney jolted awake. Her rapid breathing sounded harsh in the stillness of the Warren.

Her nightmares were different now. Instead of running from the monsters, she was the monster. In her dream, she had been hunting her own grandmother. Whitney wanted to cry. Guilt washed over her.

Grammy was right. I should have stayed home and not come to Europe. If I'd listened to Grammy, I'd be alive right now. I wouldn't be a blood-sucking, murderous monster. She closed her eyes, willing it all away.

How will I ever face her? Whitney moaned. *What if I never see her again?*

Whitney's heart shattered. She curled into a ball and cried. She'd broken her grandmother's heart, lost Madraeus, traumatized Sandra, and become a murderer.

I killed two men! I'm a monster! The weight of that knowledge plunged her deeper into despair. *How do I live with that for the rest of my life?*

Realizing that 'the rest of her life' meant *forever* had her wishing that Malcolm would have let her die. She finally understood how Sandra felt about surviving the mine.

Sometimes it is better to die than to live with the memories and the guilt. Maybe Madraeus had done the right thing by putting them all out of their misery.

Madraeus. She let out a broken sob. From the moment he'd hired her, she'd made his life hell. He'd had to defend her from lecherous businessmen, save her from Justin, even rescue her in the mine. No matter how many stupid decisions she'd made that had gotten her into trouble, he had protected her, saved her again and again, kissed her, killed for her—

Killed for me? Whitney froze. When Justin had ambushed her in her apartment, Madraeus had killed Cecelia's wolves to protect her. In the mine, he had killed to protect the Races. When he'd thought Rami dead...

Whitney's heart stumbled. She held very still. She felt like she was standing on the edge of a deep chasm. Deep below her was the truth if she was willing to jump.

Unbidden, memories of Madraeus floated up into Whitney's mind. His arms wrapped around her, holding her hand to his heart, holding her as she cried. He'd been there every time she'd felt overwhelmed. Tears streamed down her face as she thought, *I'd give anything to have Madraeus here right now.*

She could still see the look on his face as the trap closed. All that regret and longing! *He sacrificed himself to save us all.* Her heart constricted. *How can I live with that?*

She had to do something. She had to find a way to save him.

She swiped at her tears, took a long, deep breath in through her nose, and froze. *Madraeus?*

Her eyes popped open. She could smell his cologne. Whitney sat up and looked around. She was alone in her room in the Warren.

Inhaling again, Whitney tried to open all her senses. She could smell him, his cologne, his sweat. Whitney frowned. There was something else... she inhaled again... something alien. She couldn't identify it. Concentrating, she heard a faint thumping. *A heartbeat?* Suddenly, Whitney felt a caress slide across her cheek. It felt like...

Whitney's eyes shot open. "What the hell?" She clambered out of the bed.

Standing in the middle of the room, she touched her face where she'd felt the phantom caress. It felt like when Madraeus had brushed her cheek with his thumb. She shivered.

Madraeus? How am I feeling this? Whitney tried to think it through. *He's in the trap. He can't be here. He's connected to me, sees my futures, but how does that relate to this? He's in the trap. The trap? I'm the Key to the trap.*

She looked down at the thin line on her arm where John had cut her. It was healing slowly because she refused to drink any more blood. *If my blood made the trap, and I'm connected to it. Can I feel what's in it?* Whitney shivered. *Creepy!*

Whitney perked up. *If I can feel him, he's alive!*

Suddenly, she was filled with a burning desire to go to the grove, to see the trap. She turned and gathered her clothes. The need seemed to grow with every second. Quickly dressing, she ran to the door, yanked it open, and froze.

Cecelia's hate-filled eyes bored into Whitney. "Hello, Whitney."

Snapping out of her paralysis, Whitney tried to slam the door in Cecelia's face. Cecelia snarled and shoved it back open. She grabbed Whitney by the shoulders, spun her around, and slammed her face-first into the door.

Holding her against the wood, Cecelia snarled into Whitney's ear, "That's no way to treat a sister."

"I'm not your sister!" Whitney hissed, struggling.

"Oh, but we are. The blood of my father runs in your veins now."

"You gonna ask me to join you again?" Whitney tried to push away from the door, but Cecelia was too strong.

"Too late for that, little rabbit." Cecelia smiled. "You're the Key. I need your blood to open the trap."

"That's not how it works."

"I didn't say it needed to stay in your body," Cecelia laughed.

Whitney's eyes widened.

"You're going to die today," Cecelia snarled into Whitney's ear. "Personally, I can't wait! Every time I try to kill you, you manage to survive. It's annoying."

Whitney pushed against Cecelia's hold. "What makes you think you'll get it right this time?"

"Oh, I will," Cecelia hissed. "The only way to break the trap is for you to die."

"You're lying."

"The priestess said your blood must be spilled. I'm happy to oblige."

Whitney tried to push away from the door again. "All I have to do is scream and they'll all come running."

"Go ahead. Spark and the others will raid this place. Do you want everyone you know to die?"

Whitney's mind raced. *Is she lying? How many from her army escaped the battle? She could be bluffing. She's tricked me before. But what if she isn't? I can't take that chance.* Whitney's shoulders slumped. "No."

"Look at you being all noble," Cecelia laughed. "Too bad you'll be dead either way." Holding her by the upper arms, Cecelia yanked Whitney away from the door and pushed her forward. As soon as Whitney was through the door, she saw Sandra off to her right, coming up the corridor with an armful of wood. Whitney threw herself against Cecelia so she wouldn't see Sandra. They stumbled backward.

Cecelia grabbed Whitney's wrist and twisted it up behind her back. "Do that again, and I'll break your arm."

Cecelia pushed her forward again. Frantically, Whitney looked for Sandra, but she was nowhere to be seen. She prayed Cecelia hadn't noticed her. Whitney turned left, hoping to take Cecelia past the room Unkhabami was working in, but Cecelia yanked her back to the right.

Whitney looked around as they hurried along. She had never been to this part of the Warren. "You seem to know where you're going."

"I've made good use of my time."

"Have you been down here all this time?"

Cecelia snorted. "What better place to hide than right under your noses? Heard some pretty interesting things too."

"You've been listening?"

Cecelia laughed, "Not just listening. I watched you make your first kill." Her nostrils flared as she smelled the air. "Mmm, tasty."

Whitney couldn't hide her disgust. "You're messed up."

Cecelia's lip curled, but she said nothing and hurried on.

"What's the rush?" Whitney asked, deliberately slowing her pace just to annoy Cecelia.

"Are you that stupid?" Cecelia flicked her a glance. "Can't you feel it?"

"Feel what?"

"Dawn."

Deep down, an awareness that Whitney had never felt before told her that Cecelia was right. It would be dawn soon.

"That bitch is back there performing rituals that will kill Father. She'll be ready by tomorrow. I intend to get Father out tonight. We'll be long gone before she's ready."

"Where're you gonna go? He's a fifty-foot snake! It's not like people won't notice."

"What do I care?" Cecelia snorted. "They'll all be dead."

Cecelia stopped at the bottom of a ladder that stood in the middle of the corridor. She shoved Whitney toward it. "Up."

Whitney rubbed her wrist and looked up. The top of the ladder disappeared into a dark shaft in the ceiling.

"Up!"

Whitney slowly stepped up to the ladder and started to climb. The ladder ended at a trap door. Whitney pushed against the old wood. The door flew open, and Whitney stared up into the sky-blue eyes of Spark, Cecelia's right-hand werewolf. Spark reached down and hauled Whitney up out of the shaft, shoving her to the side. Whitney tripped on some bags of potting soil but caught herself on the workbench. Everything smelled of plants. They were in a gardener's shed.

The trap door banged shut, making Whitney jump as Spark opened the door to the outside. The first thing Whitney saw was the church tower. They had come up on the back side of the church, very near the grove. Cecelia grabbed Whitney's arm again and started walking.

"Take care of the guards," Cecelia said to Spark as they neared the wall of the church.

Spark shifted and loped down the path between the church and the cemetery. Whitney flinched as she heard screaming.

"You're horrid!"

"Oh, don't get so worked up." Cecelia giggled. "They're just humans."

"I was human," Whitney gasped. "And so were you, once."

Cecelia bared her fangs. "I was never human. I have always been superior to those useless cattle!" She smiled proudly. "That's why Father chose me. I could hear him even before he blessed me with his gift."

Whitney gaped at Cecelia. "How is that possible?"

"My soul is of the darkness. A queen born to reign through chaos and destruction. Madraeus will be my king." She giggled. "Father has nearly broken him. Then, the world will fall." Cecelia purred, "And Father will feast on their bones!"

They stopped just outside the stone wall that ringed the grove. Whitney shuddered, realizing, *This is where I died.*

The grove glowed a faint purple. The air above the wall shimmered and pulsed in time with her heartbeat. She glanced down and flinched. Her hands were glowing purple too.

"Looks like this is your stop." Cecelia snarled as her free hand came up holding a stake. Whitney froze, staring up at it. Cecelia drove the stake into Whitney's heart and then sank her teeth into Whitney's neck.

Whitney screamed.

NOT AGAIN

"I would love some sleep," Sophia yawned as she and Philtzer followed Hamilton through the kitchen and into the restaurant's basement.

"We've got some time until Unkhabami is ready. How 'bout a nap?" Philtzer waggled his eyebrows at her.

She laughed and rolled her eyes. Once inside the Warren, Hamilton led them to the room where Unkhabami was working. It smelled like wax, hot metal, and burnt grass. The priestess stood over a small fire pit. She threw something into the flames and dark green smoke curled up, obscuring the priestess momentarily.

Rami watched her with his arms crossed over his chest. He stood next to a folding table in the center of the room. He glanced at them. "We found as many weapons as we could."

Kitchen knives, daggers, swords, and a couple of battle axes were scattered across the table. A long metal rod rested on top of the pile.

"What's that?" Sophia pointed.

"That's supposed to be the spear," Vivian said from the shadows.

"Vivian!" Sophia crossed over to where the vampire lounged on a bench in the corner. "You okay?"

"I am." Vivian moved over so Sophia could sit beside her. "Thank you for helping me before. Sorry I didn't stick around."

"That's okay." Sophia shrugged. "We didn't either."

While Sophia and Vivian caught up, Philtzer poked through the weapons on the table. "These gonna be enough?"

"Once the weapons have been treated," Unkhabami left the fire and stepped up to the table, "they will aid in the destruction of Apep." She picked up a chef's knife and examined the blade. "I will use this to cut out Apep's heart."

Philtzer raised his eyebrows at the malicious tone in the priestess' voice and looked at Rami. "Any idea how we get the trap open without killing Whitney?"

Unkhabami lowered the knife. Her eyes glowed with power. "Whitney's blood must be spilled."

Philtzer glared at the priestess. "I'd like to avoid that."

"As would I," Rami said.

"Hey, guys?" Malcolm appeared in the doorway. "You better come look at this."

Philtzer and Hamilton followed him out.

"Sandra was supposed to get some more wood for Unkhabami's fire pit," he said as he led them down the corridor. "She didn't come back, so I went to check on her and found this."

He pointed to the floor. Small chunks of wood had been laid out on the floor in the shape of an arrow.

"What do you think? It smells of Sandra, but why would she do this?"

Philtzer studied the arrow for a moment. The kindling pointed down a hallway that they, so far, had not used. He looked the opposite direction; the way that led to where the priestess was working, the restaurant entrance, and Whitney's...

Philtzer ran to Whitney's room. It was empty. "Are you freaking kidding me?"

Malcolm dashed in behind him. "Whitney's gone?"

"Did you not remember her tendency to wander off?" Philtzer slammed the door back against the wall as he stormed out of the room. "She's like a toddler, you have to watch her!"

Malcolm hurried after him.

Hamilton was waiting for them in the hallway. "Whitney is a danger magnet. If she's gone, then all hell is about to break loose."

"Where could she have gone?" Malcolm asked.

Philtzer stopped and looked at Hamilton. At the same time the both said, "Keys open doors from both sides."

"What does that mean?" Malcolm asked.

"Trouble," Hamilton said as Philtzer took off at a run, following the arrow's direction. "Go tell the others."

"Where are you going?" Malcolm called after them.

Hamilton threw up his hands in a helpless gesture and then sprinted after Philtzer. By the time Hamilton caught up with him, Philtzer was standing with one hand on the rung of a ladder and one wrapped around his ribs. Philtzer's face was sickly pale.

"You up for this?"

"No," Philtzer flicked him a pained glance before starting to climb, "but it's almost dawn."

"Right," Hamilton huffed and followed him up the ladder.

They scrambled up the ladder and into the shed.

"Guess we found a back door." Philtzer rested his hands on his knees as he waited for Hamilton.

As soon as Hamilton stepped off the ladder, Philtzer closed the trap door.

Hamilton started to strip. "This'll go faster if I track them."

Philtzer nodded and followed his wolf friend out into the night. They sprinted along the path between the church and the cemetery. Hamilton followed Sandra's trail into the trees.

"Wait!" Philtzer froze. "Listen!"

Hamilton turned back with one front paw raised. His ears flicked back and forth. Sirens screamed through the night. Hamilton growled and looked toward the parking area on the other side of the church.

"Shit!" Philtzer hissed. "They're coming here!"

The ground shook and purple light flashed across the pre-dawn sky.

"Not again!" They shared a look of panicked resignation before dashing through the trees toward the grove.

They came out of the trees just in time to see Apep surge out of the dark grove, hissing and snapping. Hamilton and Philtzer dove to the side, barely escaping Apep's first strike. Spark burst out of the shadowy trees and tackled Hamilton. Philtzer caught a glimpse of Cecelia running toward the grove just as a second werewolf dashed out in front of him. Philtzer picked up a tree branch and swung it at the wolf's head but missed. The wolf lunged at him, knocking him backward and sinking his teeth into Philtzer's leg. Philtzer yowled and swung the branch again. This time, he made contact. The wolf yelped.

"Come back here, you bastard!" Madraeus shouted as he vaulted over the rock wall, sword in hand. He ran straight at Apep with his weapon raised.

Apep's body rippled as his tail came rolling out of the darkness, mowing down Madraeus and smashing through the grove's wall. Stones broke loose and sailed through the air. One hit Hamilton in the back, bowling him over. Spark jumped clear to avoid getting hit too.

"Father!" Cecelia shouted. "The sun!"

Apep reared up and hissed at the sky. The snake's head swung to the left and right as if searching for an escape.

"Spark!" Cecelia snapped.

Spark left Hamilton where he lay and sprinted toward the gate. Apep slithered after the white wolf. Shouting and crashing came from the direction of the parking lot as Apep and Spark plowed through the police.

Cecelia raced after them, but Madraeus leapt into her path. Her white dress glowed in the early morning light as she bared her fangs at him.

"Sun's coming," she giggled. "You really want to start this?"

"I don't care as long as you die!" Madraeus snarled and slashed at her with his sword.

Cecelia dodged his swing. "What about dear Whitney?"

Madraeus paused. "Where is she?"

"Her blood made the trap. Her blood destroyed it." Laughing, Cecelia pointed back toward the grove. "Make a choice: fight me or save her."

Madraeus resettled his grip on the sword. His eyes were black orbs.

"Tick. Tock. Better hurry." Cecelia pointed to the sky. "It's nearly breakfast, but don't worry, I already ate."

She licked her lips, and Madraeus got the message. She'd drained Whitney to break the trap. With a frustrated roar, Madraeus turned and ran back toward the grove.

Madraeus found Whitney and Sandra sprawled in the wet grass. Whitney's head rested on Sandra's knees, and Sandra was passed out across Whitney's legs. Madraeus quickly checked Whitney's pulse and then Sandra's. They were both still alive.

Blood covered Whitney's neck and chest. A blood-covered stake lay in the grass beside Whitney's hip. Rage burned through Madraeus as he realized that Cecelia had staked Whitney before ripping open a vein to let her bleed out. Madraeus lifted Sandra's arm from where it lay across Whitney's chest and found a still-bleeding cut across her forearm. He looked from the cut to Whitney's mouth. Sandra had cut her arm and fed Whitney to keep her from dying.

"It seems I owe you again," he muttered to Sandra.

Hearing a commotion, Madraeus glanced over his shoulder. Police were coming through the gate.

"Boss!" Philtzer groaned as he struggled to carry an unconscious Hamilton. Philtzer's leg was bleeding, and his face was gray. "Let's go!"

Madraeus looked back down at Whitney and Sandra. He could only carry one. He muttered a quick apology to Sandra and promised to send someone back for her, then picked up Whitney and hurried after Philtzer. Behind them, the police shouted as they entered the churchyard.

Philtzer limped his way through the trees and back to the gardener's shed. Madraeus chafed at the slow pace but refrained from saying anything because Philtzer's face was becoming grayer by the minute. Once inside the shed, Philtzer fell to his knees, unintentionally dropping Hamilton.

Madraeus lowered Whitney to the floor and checked her pulse again. It was faint, but at least it was there. He secured the door then looked around.

Philtzer pointed. "Trap door."

Madraeus stepped carefully over Whitney and sidled past Philtzer and Hamilton to reach the latch.

"I'll climb down and you can lower her down to me."

"I don't think so, boss." Philtzer panted. "I'm not even sure I can climb down right now."

Madraeus looked at the blood oozing out of Philtzer's calf. "Right."

"Ray?" Rami's voice floated up from the ladder hole.

"Guess the cavalry is here," Philtzer muttered.

"Rami!" Madraeus hung over the hole. "I've got three injured up here!"

"Can they climb?"

Madraeus sat back. "Whitney and Hamilton are out cold."

Rami's head and shoulders emerged through the hole. "Hamilton first."

Madraeus and Philtzer rolled Hamilton until he was close enough for Rami to reach. The giant hefted the wolf over his shoulders and disappeared down the ladder. From below they could hear voices. Madraeus reached over and gathered the pile of Hamilton's clothes. He threw them down the hole.

Philtzer coughed and squeezed his eyes shut.

Madraeus eyed the little spots of blood speckling Philtzer's chest. *He's bleeding internally.* "You next."

Philtzer shook his head. "Whitney next."

Not entirely agreeing, but knowing that arguing would take too much time, Madraeus shifted Whitney closer to the opening in the floor.

"All right, pass her down," Rami's voice floated up.

Madraeus held her by the wrists and lowered her down. Rami climbed halfway up the ladder and caught her.

"Come on." Madraeus helped Philtzer scoot over until his feet were dangling into the hole. Climbing down onto the ladder, Madraeus positioned his body as a safety net. Philtzer slid into the hole until his good foot landed on the nearest rung. Philtzer grunted but made no other sound as they inched their way down rung by rung. Madraeus kept his arms on either side of Philtzer, just in case the werewolf slipped. He had to feel the way slowly, not knowing how far they had to go. His ankle jarred as he reached the floor unexpectedly. Dim light illuminated the passage.

Rami appeared at his side. "Thomas took Hamilton, and Malcolm took Whitney."

As they stepped away from the ladder, Philtzer collapsed. Madraeus caught him before he hit the floor.

Rami lifted the young werewolf into his arms and grinned at Madraeus. "It is good to see you again, my friend."

SACRIFICES

Madraeus stalked down the corridor as Rami carried Philtzer. "Where did they take Whitney?"

"Probably her room."

Madraeus glanced at his friend. "Her room?"

"A lot has happened in a very short time, my friend." Rami explained the plan to kill Apep.

Madraeus snarled, "The sooner the better. I've had it up to here," he held his hand out flat above his head, "with that damn snake."

Sophia ran up the corridor to meet them. "Is he all right?"

Madraeus stopped her from pulling Philtzer out of Rami's arms. "His leg!"

She stopped, glancing down at Philtzer's bloody pant leg and then at the blood droplets on his chest. She looked both worried and livid. "Damn it, Philtzer," she muttered and dashed ahead of them to open a door. "Bring him in here."

Rami ducked inside and laid Philtzer down on the bed. Madraeus lingered in the doorway.

"Whitney?" Madraeus pointed vaguely.

"Two down on the left," Sophia answered as she ripped Philtzer's pant leg open.

Madraeus took off down the corridor. He found Whitney's room but stopped right inside the door. Malcolm sat on the side of Whitney's bed with his back to the door. He held a bottle to Whitney's lips.

She twisted away.

"Come on, Whitney!" Malcolm wrestled with her.

"I know you don't want to drink, but you need to." She rolled to the wall, pushing the bottle away. Malcolm nearly dropped it. "Damn it!"

"How did she become a vampire?"

Malcolm flinched at the sound of his voice, but he didn't stop trying to get Whitney to drink.

Madraeus stepped closer. "Who turned her, Malcolm?"

Malcolm's shoulders slumped. "I did."

"What?" Madraeus could barely speak. Betrayal burned through his chest.

"I'm sorry." Malcolm turned and stood.

Faster than he could react, Madraeus grabbed Malcolm by the shirt front and marched him backward into the wall. Madraeus bared his fangs. "Why?"

"I had no choice." Malcolm didn't even try to fight back. "She was dying. The snake would have gotten out. I didn't know what else to do."

"She didn't want it!" Madraeus jerked him away from the wall and slammed him back again.

"I know! I didn't want to! I am truly sorry, Madraeus."

Madraeus searched his face, seeing the truth, seeing the remorse.

"It was an impossible choice." Malcolm shook his head. "But I couldn't let Apep out."

"Well, he is out again, so it was all for nothing," Madraeus growled and then, with great effort, reined in his anger. He let go of Malcolm's shirt and took the bottle. He jerked his head toward the door. "Get out."

Malcolm nodded and left quickly. Madraeus turned to stare down at Whitney. The wound in her neck was already closing thanks to the blood Sandra had graciously donated, but she still had a pale, sunken look. His eyes slid to her chest. His gut clenched as he thought of the stake piercing her heart.

I almost lost her, again.

Slowly, he approached the bed and sat down. His hip brushed hers, and she groaned. He reached out and brushed the hair from her forehead.

"Whitney," he slipped a hand behind her neck and lifted her head and shoulders, "you need to drink this." He held the bottle to her lips.

She shook her head and twisted away from him, curling into a ball and groaning. He knew from experience that her body was screaming out for blood.

"Whitney?" Madraeus leaned over her.

"It hurts..." Her face contorted in pain.

"You must eat."

"I can't!" Whitney gasped. "I can't drink blood!"

"It's the only thing that'll stop the pains." He laid a hand on her shoulder. "Your body is trying to repair itself from the damage Cecelia inflicted. Your body has a lot of repairing to do. You must eat."

"No!" Whitney shook her head.

Madraeus sighed. "Whitney. If you don't drink on your own, I'll hold you down and pour it down your throat."

Whitney stopped trying to get away. "Madraeus?" She turned and stared up at him through her tears.

He smiled at her. "Hi."

In a flash, she threw herself into his arms. "You're here!"

Madraeus squeezed his eyes shut. It felt so good to hold her, to know that she was still alive after all those visions in the grove.

He hissed as her fingers found the cuts on his back. She gasped and pulled back, searching his face. "Are you okay?"

He let out a disbelieving laugh. "I'm fine, but you need to feed. You had a stake in your heart." His voice cracked. "If you don't feed, you'll die."

Whitney whispered, "I... I don't want to be a vampire," Whitney sniffled, "but I don't want to be dead either."

"I know." He traced her cheek with his thumb.

"I'm scared, Madraeus," Whitney whispered. "What if I bite someone? What if I—"

"Whitney—"

"What if I *want* to hurt someone?"

"You won't. You can control it," Madraeus stared into her eyes, "but you have to drink. You have to give your body what it needs."

Her body convulsed again as the pain took over.

"Drink." He held the bottle out to her, and this time she drank. She gagged a couple of times, but she finished the bottle.

She collapsed back onto the bed. Her body arched as the fresh blood coursed through her, healing her wounds. Madraeus smoothed her sweat-soaked hair back from her face, trying to soothe her, but he knew that until the pain subsided, there was nothing he could do.

"I'm sorry, Whitney."

After a few minutes, her body went limp. Tears ran down her temples.

"Malcolm said there was no time, but they shouldn't have turned you without your permission. I never wanted you to be exposed to any of this. When I almost lost you in that mine, I knew I had to leave. So you would have a choice. So you could go back to a normal life. So you would be safe."

She whispered, "You're always trying to keep me safe."

"And failing miserably," he scoffed.

"That's not true." Weakly, she shook her head, finally opening her eyes. The pain in them matched his own.

"Whitney, I..." he paused, suddenly afraid to speak. Gently, he took her hand and tried to explain. "Whitney, I am old. I've lived for so long, just existing, but when I met you, it was like seeing in color again. You made me crazy and confused me. You brought me back to life and made me feel. You saved me, but I haven't been able to keep you safe."

"There was no keeping me safe." She swiped at the tears on her cheeks. "I was supposed to be the Key all along. Just ask Unkhabami."

Madraeus reared back and stared at her. Snatches of conversations with Unkhabami trailed through his mind, leaving behind gouges in his heart. *The priestess knew all along.* Betrayal deeper than he had ever known burned through him.

"There was nothing you could do to stop all of this." She let out a rueful laugh and waved the empty bottle at him. "I was destined to become a monster."

"You're not a monster."

"Yes, I am." Whitney stared at him through her tears.

"No, you're not. You're an angel compared to me. After everything I've done," Madraeus couldn't hide the bitterness in his voice, "I'm the monst—"

"Don't say that! You're a good man, Madraeus," Whitney whispered, squeezing his hand. "The best I've ever known!"

"Oh, Whitney," Madraeus let out a bone-weary sigh. "You deserve better than to be loved by me."

"Loved?" Whitney whispered, staring sadly at the bottle. "So much has happened. I don't even know what I am now."

"I understand." Madraeus sighed and moved to stand.

"Wait!" She clutched his hand. "That doesn't mean leave! I'm just mixed up right now. I need time. I'm sorry."

"Rest up." He leaned down and kissed her forehead. "This can wait." He found a blanket and tucked it around her. "Sleep." Madraeus turned and walked to the door. "I'll come back in a bit. I need to talk to the priestess."

Madraeus followed his nose to the priestess' workroom. Unkhabami was alone. Through the pungent haze swirling through the air, he could see her bent over the table.

"You knew."

"I know a lot of things." Unkhabami glanced up from where she was forming wax into a snake-like figure. "I am a seer."

"You knew Whitney would become the Key." Madraeus stalked forward.

"Yes." Her hands continued to work the wax.

"And yet, you let her come anyway." Madraeus let out a bark of cold laughter. "Not just let her, but encouraged me to bring her along, to keep her by my side."

"Yes."

At her lack of remorse, he slammed his fists down on the table, making the weapons rattle. "How dare you play with her life!"

"I did not play with her life!" Unkhabami threw the wax figure down. She braced her hands on the table and leaned toward him. "Whitney had to become the Key."

"No!" Madraeus hit the table again. "You could have prevented this! You knew!"

"Yes!" The air crackled. The hair on the back of his neck stood at attention. "Just as I knew Apep would be free again! Just as I know this world will burn unless I act!"

"So, you try to change this future but not hers? Her life didn't have to end!"

Unkhabami glared at him. "It was a sacrifice I was willing to make."

Madraeus glared at her silently, barely controlling his temper. "What else— who else are you willing to sacrifice?"

"Her life as a *mortal* had to be sacrificed to save everyone else!" Her hand sliced through the air. "I have seen Apep slither over your corpses! You and Rami, Whitney. All of you!"

Madraeus slowly straightened, realizing that her amber eyes glowed not with power, but with fear.

"So, yes, I sacrificed Whitney for a chance to save you all!"

"You better not be wrong," Madraeus growled under his breath.

THE RAID

"WAKE UP! WAKE UP! Wake up!" Thomas shouted, jolting Madraeus from sleep.

Madraeus was up and running for the door before he was fully awake. "What is it?"

"Police found the Warren!" Thomas shouted as he threw open door after door, waking the others.

Madraeus ran to Whitney's room. She met him at the door. She looked terrified. "What's happening?"

"Police are coming." Madraeus held out his hand. "We gotta go!"

They ran for Unkhabami's workroom. Vivian helped the priestess gather her magical paraphernalia and stuff it into a duffel bag. Rami was already there too, handing weapons to anyone within reach, including the Hares.

"We're not gonna fight them!" Barbie gasped as she juggled an armful of knives, nearly dropping a knife on her toe.

"No." Rami handed a couple of swords to Madraeus. "These are the enspelled weapons. We cannot leave them."

Thomas, Malcolm, Philtzer, and Sophia crowded through the door. Madraeus ran his eyes over the small group. "Everyone accounted for?"

Thomas nodded. "Regina and Hamilton are out trying to find where Apep went."

"Where're we supposed to go?" Sophia rushed forward and scooped up the papers from the museum. She shoved them into Unkhabami's bag.

"Gardener's shed?" Philtzer leaned against the door.

Madraeus shook his head. "They might be watching that."

Rami picked up the iron bar. "He is right."

"We gotta go now!" Willie appeared at the door.

Philtzer looked at Willie. "You got an escape route?"

"Yes, but hurry!" Willie disappeared.

"We're supposed to trust them now?" Madraeus glared after the Hare.

Thomas' face was grim. "You got a better plan?"

Madraeus reluctantly agreed, and everyone followed the Hare out the door. Willie ran down the corridor that led to the gardener's shed. Behind them, they could hear a rhythmic thudding.

Barbie glanced over her shoulder. "They're trying to break through the restaurant entrance."

"What about Milner?" Sophia shot a worried look at Philtzer.

"Guess the police will find him." Philtzer winced, limping as he tried to keep up with the others. "Nothing we can do about it now."

About halfway to the ladder that led to the gardener's shed, Willie stopped and pushed open a section of wall. He motioned the others through and then pushed it closed again. From inside the wall, they heard a hissing sound followed by a metallic thud. The new corridor was dimly lit and much smaller, only about two feet wide. Willie sidled along the wall until he was in the front of everyone and then took off again. They ran in silence until they came to another ladder.

"What is it with you people and ladders?" Philtzer whined.

Willie ignored him and climbed up into the dark shaft. A moment later, light glowed above them. Madraeus motioned for Thomas to go up first and check it out.

"All clear, boss," Thomas called down.

Vivian and Malcolm both stood on the ladder, one above the other, forming a relay line to hand the weapons up. And then, one by one, they each ascended the ladder.

Whitney leaned her head against Madraeus' shoulder. He looked down at her and squeezed her hand. "You okay?"

"Just tired."

"It's daylight. It drains us whether we're out in it or not." He kissed the top of her head. "Come on, your turn."

He watched her climb and then turned to Philtzer. His breathing came in ragged gasps. "Up you go."

Philtzer rolled his eyes, let out a very fake laugh, and climbed up, slowly hopping from rung to rung on his good leg. Madraeus followed him up, watching closely in case he passed out again. Willie shut the trap door and locked it as soon as Madraeus stepped off the ladder.

"Where are we?" Sophia asked, looking around at the washer and dryer, the shelves stuffed with boxes, and the various stacks of seasonal items. There were no windows.

Willie eyed the shelves with his hands on his hips. "This is my basement."

"Which way is out?" Thomas glared down at the Hare. "I gotta find Hamilton and Regina and warn them."

"Right." Willie nodded. "Follow me."

Unkhabami knelt on the floor and started unpacking her bag. "I must finish." She indicated the floor in front of her. "Stack them here."

The sound of metal hitting concrete filled the basement as everyone piled their weapons next to her.

"Barbie?" Sophia motioned her over. "What happened? How did they find the Warren? I mean, your society has been here forever and no one took any notice."

"I don't know." Barbie shook her head.

"Maybe it was the high traffic through the restaurant's kitchen," Vivian snorted.

"No. The locals have known about us for ages." She glanced at Madraeus with fear in her eyes.

Madraeus nodded and said what she wouldn't. "But that was before people started dying."

Barbie nodded.

"I don't think that's it." Sophia crossed her arms. "They would have raided it days ago."

"Sandra," Philtzer's voice was quiet, but his words shook the room.

"What do you mean?" Whitney squatted down beside him where he sat on the floor.

"She was already in a bad way after what happened to you." Philtzer stretched his legs out and rested his head back against the shelves. "She fed you and we left her."

"She fed me?" Whitney sat down abruptly.

"Cecelia left you to bleed out. She found you before we got there." Philtzer winced and tried to find a way to sit so his ribs wouldn't hurt. "She saved your life."

"But you left her?" Whitney looked at Madraeus.

"I could only carry one person. Dawn was coming, and there was no time. I'm sorry."

Whitney looked down at the floor, absorbing his words. "You think she got mad and told them about the Warren?"

"It's possible." Philtzer reached out and squeezed Whitney's shoulder. "Sorry, Whit."

"That's why we don't tell mortals," Vivian said, glancing at Barbie.

Barbie wrapped her arms around her waist and hugged herself. "What happens now?"

Madraeus glanced at Rami and then to where Unkhabami was working. "We stick to the plan. Find Apep, before night if possible, or we'll lose any chance of catching him."

Whitney raised her eyebrows. "But it's daylight."

"We'll have to get creative." Madraeus took a long deep breath and let it out slowly. "Until then, we rest and wait."

***

"You should rest," Unkhabami purred.

"So should you," Madraeus said as he paced.

He knew he should be sleeping like the others, but he couldn't. He glanced around the room. Along the wall, Malcolm, Rami, and Vivian slept. Barbie had found some blankets earlier, and everyone had settled in to get as much rest as they could. Whitney had curled up next to Philtzer, who hadn't moved from where he'd first sat down.

Madraeus was worried about the young werewolf. It was obvious that his injuries weren't healing like they should. Philtzer needed a proper doctor. He didn't need to be gearing up for another battle. He felt a twinge of guilt that he had sent Sophia on a mission. She hadn't wanted to leave Philtzer, but they needed an escape vehicle.

"I have nearly finished." Unkhabami sat back on her heels. "This is the last ritual."

Madraeus closed his eyes and took a deep breath. "It's almost sunset, and the others haven't returned."

"They will." Unkhabami bent over the weapons once more and began chanting.

Madraeus growled under his breath and resumed pacing but then stopped to listen. "Someone's coming."

Footsteps thumped above them, and then Thomas thundered down the stairs, startling the others awake. "We found him. Time to go."

A moment later, Regina, Hamilton, and Willie came down the stairs carrying jerrycans.

"What are those for?" Madraeus asked as he pulled on his jacket.

"Have to burn the snake, remember?" Regina grinned wickedly and held up one of the canisters. "Gas makes a big fire."

Madraeus raised his eyebrows at her malicious enthusiasm. "Right. Where to then?"

"They're holed up in the leisure center." Willie hooked a thumb over his shoulder.

"How do we get there?" Madraeus gestured toward the stairs. "It's still light out."

Willie opened the trap door again.

"Seriously?" Philtzer groaned.

"Not you." Madraeus looked down at Philtzer.

"I'm fine, boss, really."

Madraeus looked at all of Philtzer's bandages and snorted. "You look like a mummy."

"Yeah?" Philtzer huffed half-heartedly. "You look like Dracula."

Madraeus' lips twitched. "Your injuries will only make you a liability, and you know it."

Philtzer nodded, but his expression said he wasn't happy about it.

"Whitney—" Madraeus said as she stood.

"I wanna help."

"I know, but I need you to stay with him." Madraeus pointed at Philtzer. "When Sophia gets back, help get him out."

"But—"

"Whitney," Madraeus took her by the shoulders, "for once in your life, please, do as I ask. Apep is stronger than anything we've ever fought. I need to be completely focused. I can't be worried about you and do what I need to do."

She huffed out a sigh but nodded. "Okay."

He peered at her. She'd never given in that easily.

She rolled her eyes. "Really. I'll stay here."

Madraeus kissed the top of her head and then turned to Unkhabami. "You finished, Priestess?"

"In a moment."

"Right." Madraeus turned to the others. "We're up against Apep, Cecelia, and Spark for sure. We don't know how many others she has with her. Try to avoid eye contact with Apep. I fell for that, and he almost got me."

"Remember the plan," Rami added. "Speared, cut, decapitated, and consumed by fire."

Unkhabami stood. "And I take his heart."

"There must be no evidence left." Madraeus made eye contact with each of them. "Watch each other's backs and don't get dead."

"Easy-peasy," Philtzer muttered.

Hamilton handed his cell phone to Whitney. "Guard it with your life. If it rings, answer it. It might be us calling for a ride."

Whitney gave him a solemn nod and clutched the phone to her chest.

They gathered their enspelled weapons and followed Willie down into the Warren again. Running in grim silence, Willie led them through a maze of corridors.

This doesn't feel right, Madraeus thought. He hadn't gone into battle without Philtzer in decades. He never realized how much he appreciated Philtzer's inappropriate humor until that moment. It functioned as a natural morale booster. Without it, their prospects seemed less positive.

Hamilton interrupted his dark thoughts by asking, "How much money did you guys spend building all this? And how much more did you spend bribing contractors to make secret entrances to every structure in Broadclyst?"

"It's not like it was done overnight," Barbie panted. "This Warren has been evolving and expanding for centuries."

"Quiet." Willie slowed his pace. "We're here."

"All right," Thomas snarled, "let's kick some snaky ass."

"Snakes don't have asses," Hamilton muttered as he watched Willie climb the ladder.

Thomas slowly turned to stare at him.

"What?" Hamilton shrugged. "Just sayin'."

Madraeus smiled, feeling more confident that they just might survive this.

As soon as Willie gave them the signal, they started to climb.

At Your Leisure

Madraeus paused halfway up the ladder. Thomas, who was just above him, had stopped. Madraeus squinted up into the darkness. The smell of cleaning products and disinfectant burned his nose.

Above him, Thomas hissed, "Move!"

"I can't," Malcolm whispered back. "There's no room."

"Hold on." Madraeus could hear Willie fumbling with the doorknob.

"Let me," Malcolm whispered.

Madraeus winced at the overly loud sound of boxes falling. "Shhh!"

Everyone froze, listening.

"I think we're okay." Willie's voice was barely a whisper.

Madraeus heard the door open, and the line started moving again. At the top, he stepped out of the maintenance closet and into the employee locker room. The room was empty.

"You think anyone's here?" Barbie asked.

Thomas handed his knife to Hamilton, stripped off his clothes, and shifted to wolf. The others watched as he sniffed along the underside of the door. His tail wagged a couple of times, letting the others know it was safe. The other wolves handed their weapons to the vampires, stripped, and shifted. Rami gathered their clothing and dropped it back down the hole into the Warren.

Willie opened the locker room door and led the way into the center's office. "What happened to all the employees?"

Vivian bared her fangs and pointed. "I don't think they made it."

The office was in shambles. Splatters of blood stained the carpets and desks. Broken chairs and papers peppered the floor.

"If anyone made it out, there'll be police soon," Barbie breathed, staring at the blood.

"Keep moving," Madraeus whispered.

Willie led them forward. Large windows spanned the front of the reception area. The vampires hung back. It wasn't sunset yet.

"Is there another way around?"

Barbie tapped Madraeus on the shoulder. "We could go back through the pool."

Madraeus nodded. Barbie led them back through the office and down a short hallway to a second set of locker rooms. Regina and Thomas checked them both but found nothing.

"You sure they're in here?" Vivian looked at Willie.

"Thomas tracked them to the center." Willie shrugged. "He circled the whole place and didn't find any evidence that they left."

"They're here." Madraeus bared his fangs. "I can hear him."

"Are you in control?" Rami looked at him sharply.

Madraeus nodded. "Let's go."

They moved into the main pool room. The air was humid and thick with the smell of chlorine. Spaced out about every five feet along both walls, tall, narrow windows illuminated the room.

Madraeus turned to glare at Barbie. "This doesn't help."

Barbie shook her head and pointed to the ceiling. A balcony circled the room above the pool. There were no windows up there. He nodded, and she led the way to the stairs. Quietly and quickly, they traversed the pool room and came out near a set of double doors that led to the gymnasium.

Thomas shifted and peeked through one door's window. Madraeus edged up and looked through the other window. Basketball hoops were spaced out on each side of the gym. In the far corner, he could see more double doors. Someone had blocked their windows with hastily taped-up cardboard. Sports equipment lay scattered around the room. He could see four people sleeping on a gymnastics mat near the wall. His eyes dropped to the center of the basketball court where the snake slept, coiled in a massive pile.

Apep. Rage boiled up in Madraeus' chest. His eyes turned black, and his fangs slowly extended. His grip on his sword tightened.

"We can use that net," Thomas breathed. "Pin him down."

Madraeus glanced at the roof. Attached to tracks that ran along the ceiling, a large net hung in great swooping swags. He glanced at the others. They nodded their understanding. Carefully, he depressed the latch, but it was all in vain. A loud click echoed through the gym. Cecelia's vampires jumped up from the mat.

"So much for surprise," Thomas hissed, yanking the door open.

Madraeus and the others burst into the gym. Cecelia's vampires ran straight at them with swords raised. At the same time, half a dozen werewolves shot out from the other side of Apep as the snake reared skyward.

Vivian, Malcolm, and the Hares met the vampires halfway across the gym in a clash of swords. Thomas, Hamilton, and Regina turned to tangle with the wolves. Thomas fought like a wild man, bent on taking revenge for Cody from every single one of Cecelia's minions.

Rami and Madraeus ran straight at Apep. Madraeus slashed at the snake's underbelly, leaving a gaping wound.

Apep twisted away, hissing, *I will feassst on your corpssse!*

Madraeus roared, lunging forward to strike again, but Apep flipped around, knocking Madraeus against the far wall. He fell into a pile of sporting equipment. Balls, bats, and pieces from croquet sets shot in every direction.

Across the gym, Rami raised the iron bar, ready to impale the snake. But before he could, Cecelia dashed out from a door to their left and ran straight at Rami. She jumped on his back, stabbing at him with her knife. Rami dropped the iron bar and tried to throw her off.

"Bitch!" Unkhabami dropped her enspelled knife and lunged straight at Cecelia. The priestess shifted into a leopard mid-stride and ripped Cecelia away from Rami. Unkhabami and Cecelia rolled away, snarling and cursing.

Vivian screamed, landing on her knees near Rami. Blood poured from a gash on her leg. The vampire she had been fighting raised her sword to finish Vivian off, but Barbie swung her ax and took off the enemy vampire's arm. Barbie ran to Vivian to help her away from the fight. Apep's tail slammed into them, catapulting them both backward across the room.

Malcolm slashed the vampire he was fighting but didn't wait to see him fall. He dodged in and opened a gash along Apep's side with his enspelled sword. Apep whipped toward him. At the same time, the snake's tail shot forward, aiming for Malcolm.

"Watch out for his tail!" Malcolm shouted as he dodged it.

"Get the bar!" Rami roared as one of Cecelia's wolves pounced on him. He rolled, flipping the wolf through the air.

Apep coiled and flipped over, knocking Malcolm and Rami backward.

Madraeus climbed free from the ball rack and rushed forward with a look of maniacal hatred. Blood ran down his forehead, and his eyes were black orbs. He slashed and stabbed at Apep.

Rami scrambled to his feet and ran toward where he had dropped the iron bar, dodging the snake's undulating coils, but was hit by his tail again. Apep smashed Rami into the gym floor.

Malcolm dodged in from behind Apep and slashed, leaving another gash on the snake's side. One of Cecelia's wolves shot out and grabbed Malcolm by the leg. Malcolm roared in pain as he turned on the wolf. He didn't see Apep rear back to strike.

The snake lunged straight at Malcolm's back. Madraeus threw himself in front of Malcolm with his left arm up to ward off the attack. Apep's fangs pierced his arm. Madraeus roared as he fell to his knees.

For a moment, everything slowed down. All around him, Madraeus could hear the screams of the dying. From the corner of his eye, he saw bodies of wolves and vampires.

Apep reared back for another strike.

Across the gym, Willie threw a dodgeball at Apep. It bounced off with a phtong sound. "Hey! Apep!" he shouted and waved his arms. "Over here!"

Apep reared, swaying from side to side. His tongue flicked out as he glared down at the Hare. Apep shot straight at Willie. He dodged to the side, but the snake was faster. Apep ripped through the Hare.

"Willie!" Barbie screamed.

The Hare's sacrifice had given Rami enough time to grab the bar and thrust it into Apep's side.

The snake rolled away from the pain, lifting Rami into the air. The giant tightened his grip as Apep tried to shake him loose. Madraeus staggered to his feet. Blood poured down his left arm. Madraeus thrust his sword into a gaping hole on Apep's side just as Malcolm sliced at the snake's other side.

Madraeus ducked as Thomas sprang past him, hauling the net down on top of Apep.

The snake rolled and thrashed as he fought on all sides, becoming entangled in the netting. Each wound seemed to slow the snake more and more.

Rami braced his feet and shoved the iron bar farther into the snake. Apep flinched as the bar pierced his heart. The snake tried to strike at Rami but shuddered and missed. Apep crashed downward. The ground shook, and dust billowed upward.

"Hurry! Head off, heart out, and burn it!" Barbie screamed as she ran forward into the haze with her ax raised and began hacking at the scales just behind Apep's head.

Apep twitched and thrashed as Rami, Vivian, Malcolm, and Madraeus stabbed and slashed. As Apep gave his last dying twitch, Thomas picked up Unkhabami's discarded butcher knife and began cutting out Apep's heart.

Rami saw what he was doing and looked around in alarm. "Where is Unkhabami?"

Looking around, the priestess was nowhere to be seen, but the double doors leading to the pool had been smashed. Rami looked at Madraeus.

"I'll go." Madraeus pointed to the snake. "You finish this."

Madraeus ran for the door, stopping only long enough to pick up a broken croquet mallet. The head had been knocked off, leaving a jagged spike.

THEN WE BURN

Madraeus followed the trail of blood and damage left by the brutal fight between the priestess and Cecelia into the pool area. He spotted them on the far side of the room. He flicked his eyes to the windows where light from the setting sun streamed in, reflecting off the water. The stairs were behind him. Cecelia was backed into the corner, cut off from any escape.

Not far from Cecelia, Regina was sprawled at the edge of the pool, unmoving. Madraeus clutched the stake so hard his knuckles glared white. He raised his eyes. Cecelia had Unkhabami in a choke hold, using her as a shield. Unkhabami panted. Her skin was wet with sweat and blood, but her face showed no fear, only anger.

Cecelia's white dress was streaked with blood from gashes and puncture wounds. Her breath came in ragged gasps, and her eyes were wild. She bared her fangs and turned to face him. He could see her knife pressed into the priestess' side.

"You killed father!" Cecelia screeched at him.

Madraeus stepped closer, raising his sword. "And your next."

"You would never kill me," Cecelia giggled. "We're the same!"

Unkhabami caught his eye and stared pointedly at the stake and then at the windows.

"We are not the same," Madraeus growled as he tried to understand what the priestess wanted him to do.

Unkhabami glared at Madraeus, willing him to understand. She flicked her glance at the windows again. Her eyes flashed.

"But we are!" Cecelia snarled. "Father picked you for me! We could have watched this world burn!"

"If you want to burn, I can call the sun for you!" the priestess hissed.

Madraeus' eyebrows twitched as he realized what she was planning.

Cecelia jabbed the knife farther into Unkhabami's side. "If you do, we'll burn together."

"Then we burn!" Madraeus snarled, giving Unkhabami a quick nod.

Unkhabami closed her eyes. Her lips moved as she chanted. The air thickened and crackled as she pulled magic from the elements around her. The pool roiled and sloshed.

"What are you doing?" Cecelia jerked her backward. Unkhabami gasped as Cecelia drove the knife into her ribs, burying it up to the hilt. Unkhabami opened her eyes. They glowed with amber fire.

Cecelia shoved Unkhabami toward the pool. Madraeus dropped his sword as he dashed forward to catch the priestess. Unkhabami twisted in his arms, and at the same time, she snatched the stake from his hand. With a scream of rage, the priestess threw herself at Cecelia, knocking her backwards. She jammed the stake into Cecelia's heart, pinning her to the wall.

"You destroyed my village!" Unkhabami snarled. "Now, I destroy you!" She threw her head back and screamed, "Kule-ta jua!"

The air crackled and sparked as magic coursed through Unkhabami and into the stake. Cecelia screamed. Her eyes became pools of glaring white light. Her skin glowed fiery orange, growing brighter with every second.

Madraeus dove into the pool just as Unkhabami's sunlight blazed outward. The water glowed and boiled around him. Unkhabami's sunlight reached deep into the pool, seeking his life. His skin burned. He dove deeper, trying to escape the heat.

Just as his lungs wanted to burst, everything went dark. Unkhabami's sun winked out. He spun around and squinted up through the churning water. He could see the distorted outline of Cecelia as the flames engulfed her. Madraeus kicked to the surface. He sucked in a deep breath, shook his head, and spat out pool water.

Blinking away droplets of water, he watched Cecelia writhe and thrash as Unkhabami's fire burned away her flesh. Her screams turned to gurgles and finally stopped. He watched until she turned to ash and crumbled to the floor, leaving only a scorched chunk of wall.

"It is over." Unkhabami groaned from where she lay at the edge of the pool. A thin trail of blood ran from her body to the pool's edge and dripped in, turning the water around him red.

He glanced at the window. It was finally getting dark. In the distance, they could hear sirens approaching.

Madraeus coughed out more water. "Not quite."

He swam to the side of the pool and heaved himself up and out of the water. He was suddenly exhausted. His arm throbbed and burned. His skin hurt.

Unkhabami staggered to her feet as Madraeus crawled over to check Regina. She was alive. Unsure that he had enough strength left to lift her, he looked around for something to carry her on. Nothing was readily available. With a sigh, he lifted her onto his shoulders and staggered toward the door. Unkhabami waited for him, propped against the doorframe. She leaned heavily on his sword and held her side. He raised his eyebrows.

She nodded to his unspoken question. "I will live."

Together they stumbled back to the gymnasium. The sirens were closer now.

"Can't we do anything without the police showing up?" Thomas complained as he ran to gather discarded weapons.

Rami rushed over to Unkhabami.

"I am all right." The priestess reassured him as Madraeus lowered Regina to the floor.

Madraeus looked around for the bodies that he had seen earlier. "The others?"

"We only lost Willie. Vivian is wounded. Two of Cecelia's wolves and three of the vampires are dead," Rami answered, pointing.

Madraeus looked at what used to be Apep. His creator was now a pile of bloody chunks. The bodies of Cecelia's wolves and vampires were stacked on top. Madraeus had seen a lot of battles, dealt with a lot of carnage, but for some reason, this turned his stomach.

"Burn it," Madraeus muttered. "Burn it all."

"Already on it, boss." Hamilton sprinted past him with the jerrycans.

Thomas and Hamilton doused the pile of gore with gasoline.

Malcolm came around from the backside of the pile, carrying a croquet mallet wrapped in some sort of cloth. He reached into his pocket and pulled out a lighter. Flicking it open, he lit the makeshift torch on fire. He circled the pile, setting fire to everything that would catch.

Outside, the sirens grew very loud and then cut off.

"Back to the Warren!" Hamilton shouted.

Rami hefted Regina onto his shoulder and hooked his other arm around Unkhabami. The priestess hissed in pain but leaned on him anyway. They hurried into the hallway. Malcolm pulled Vivian's arm over his shoulder and helped her hop toward the door.

As everyone made a run for it, Madraeus stood alone, watching Apep burn. He didn't understand it, but he felt empty. He would not miss that creature hissing in his head, and yet...

everything that he had been, everything that he had done, was because of Apep. For good or for evil, Apep was his father. Sadness washed over him as he watched his creator burn and crumble into ash.

"Never mind!" Thomas shouted as he sprinted back into the gym.

Madraeus snapped out of his thoughts as the others dashed in behind Thomas.

"Police are already in the building!" Thomas ran to the back doors and ripped the cardboard off the windows. He jumped back. "Shit! They're back here too!" He quickly grabbed a base-ball bat and jammed it through the door's push bar.

"We're surrounded." Hamilton looked to Madraeus for di-rection.

Madraeus scanned the room, thinking. "Grab the gas. Torch everything. We'll make a run for it in the confusion."

"On it!" Malcolm grabbed a gas can and ran for the locker room area.

"Hamilton." Madraeus grabbed a burning baseball bat. "Call Whitney. Get us a ride."

Precious seconds ticked by as the others sloshed gasoline on the walls, doors, and anything that wasn't still alive. Madraeus followed along with his burning bat, igniting everything. Mal-colm shot back into the room. Behind him, shouts echoed through the locker rooms as the police fled the fire. All around them, the flames spread. Madraeus glanced around. The fire had grown faster than he had expected.

Rami shouted over the roar of the inferno, "If we do not leave now, we are in danger of joining Apep!"

AFTERMATH

SOPHIA SAT IN THE driver's seat of a panel van, watching the leisure center. She glanced in her mirror when she heard the sirens. She could hear them but couldn't see them yet.

"The police again?" Whitney grumbled from the back of the van.

"Keep your head under that blanket! It's not sunset yet!"

Whitney let out a disgruntled snort that sounded more like a raspberry and pulled the blanket back down. Sophia glanced back at her and then at Philtzer. He was stretched out on the floor behind the passenger seat. His eyes were closed. He didn't look good.

"At least, tell me what's happening!" Whitney's voice was muffled.

Sophia looked back out the window. "Well, four wolves that I've never seen before just high-tailed it."

"Is that good or bad?" Whitney asked.

"I'm assuming bad," Sophia groaned, "because now there's smoke."

"Smoke!" Whitney peeked out from under the blanket.

"Will you stay covered!" Sophia snapped.

"Argh!" Whitney ducked again.

"The sun's almost down. Just be patient."

"I'm not good at being patient," Whitney grumbled.

"I've noticed," Sophia muttered. Her eyes scanned the surrounding area, hoping she'd see any of their friends.

A bright light flashed out from the narrow windows along the side of the center.

Sophia threw a hand up to block the glare. "What is that?"

"What is what? What's the matter?"

"Whatever you do, don't lift that blanket!" Sophia squeezed her eyes shut but could still feel the brightness of the blaze. "It's like looking into the sun!"

Suddenly, the light winked out. Sophia lowered her hand and blinked, trying to get rid of the spots floating across her vision. Outside, the sirens were closer.

"Sun's down. You can come out now."

Whitney popped up beside her like a gopher.

"Come on, guys!" Sophia muttered as they both watched the building.

"Get down!" Sophia ducked down as several police cars shot into the parking lot of the leisure center.

"Crap!" Whitney dove behind the seat.

Sophia slowly eased up and peeked through the window. Two black SUVs screeched into the parking lot. Several agents got out and started shouting orders. Milner was among them. With weapons drawn, the police fanned out around the building. Whitney and Sophia heard the glass of the front doors shatter as the police forced their way inside. Not a moment later, a huge plume of black smoke billowed upward.

"Oh no."

Whitney appeared beside her again. "That's a lot of smoke!"

As the girls watched in horror, police evacuated the building. In the silence of the van, a phone rang. Sophia looked at Whitney as she dug in her pocket for Hamilton's phone.

"We need a ride!" Hamilton yelled.

Whitney's eyes were huge as she spoke. "Can you get out? We're outside. Police are everywhere."

"We're trapped in the gym!"

Sophia grabbed the phone. "Do you have an exit?"

"Kinda..." Hamilton coughed. "Southwest corner!"

Sophia looked around, thinking. She smiled. "Get ready. I got a plan!"

"What plan?" Whitney stared at her.

"Get up here, you're driving," Sophia said as she got out.

"What?" Whitney asked, but at Sophia's glare, she stopped protesting and climbed in the front.

"See that door?" Sophia pointed to the side of the building. Whitney nodded. "I'm gonna create a distraction. You drive right up to it and bang on the door. Be ready because they'll be coming out in a hurry. As soon as you have them, go."

"What about you?" Whitney asked as she started the van.

"I'll catch up," Sophia said and then took off at a run.

Sophia dodged around behind the van and across the road. She ran up to the closest police car. The lights on top were still flashing, and the door was open. They had left the engine running. She peeked over the trunk. All the officers were closer to the building, shouting and trying to gain control. She crept along the car and slipped into the driver's seat. Quickly, she dug around until she found the officer's nightstick. She jammed it against the gas pedal. The engine revved to a dangerous level. She slammed it into gear. The car shot forward. Everything went from zero to sixty way faster than she had anticipated.

"Bad plan! Bad plan! Bad plan!" Sophia plowed through the police closest to the gym door. The officers dove to the side, shouting. Sophia spun the steering wheel. The car fishtailed and shot back toward the front of the center. They chased after her, leaving the gym door unguarded.

The car shot straight at the shattered front windows. Sophia threw the door open and jumped. She shifted in mid-air. Her paws hit the ground running just as the car rammed into the doors of the reception area. Behind her, police shouted as she ducked behind the shrubs that ran along the side of the building. Once the officers coming from the gym side had passed by, she took off at a dead run. Her jeans started to slide off, nearly tripping her. She jumped and shifted again. She straightened her clothes the best she could while running.

By the time she made it to the southwest gym door, the van was already pulling out. Malcolm and Madraeus held the back doors open.

"Run!" Malcolm shouted.

Sophia sprinted as fast as she could. The van slowed ever so slightly. She jumped up into the back. Madraeus caught her as Malcolm pulled the doors shut.

"Go!" Madraeus shouted.

Madraeus and Sophia nearly fell as the van sped up. Wrapping an arm around her waist to keep her from falling, he grabbed for the wall, while Sophia braced against the ceiling. When Whitney's driving felt stable, Sophia nodded her thanks. Madraeus let go of her and sank down against the rear door. He looked haggard. Sophia suppressed a worried frown and carefully worked through the tangle of legs to reach Philtzer. He didn't look much better than Madraeus.

"That was nuts!" Hamilton sat scrunched up against the back of the driver's seat across from Philtzer.

"Not our finest adventure," Rami grumbled.

"Any adventure you can run away from," Philtzer chuckled weakly as Sophia settled in next to him. "What'd I miss?"

"Went to a snake barbecue." Thomas grabbed a blanket and wrapped it around his waist. "Don't recommend. Zero out of ten."

"Apep is gone then?" Whitney asked while she drove.

"Yes, Apep has been destroyed, for now." Unkhabami winced as she twisted, trying to see her knife wound.

"Yeah, but he's a chaos demon. And according to the lore, he'll reform and return one day," Barbie said as she climbed up into the passenger seat.

Whitney glanced at her. "Great."

"It will not be for another few millennia," Rami said as he shifted onto his knees next to Unkhabami to examine her wound.

"Well, that's something at least," Whitney muttered.

"Turn here." Barbie pointed.

"Where are you taking us?" Hamilton peered over the seat.

Barbie glanced back over her shoulder at him. "You need clothes."

Hamilton nodded. "That would be nice."

Barbie guided Whitney to a small house on a corner a few blocks away.

"Just be a minute," Barbie said and hopped out.

"It's amazing how fast we started trusting a Hare," Vivian muttered.

"Desperation makes strange bedfellows." Malcolm stood with his hands braced on his knees, watching out the back window.

Whitney turned in the driver's seat. "Not that I don't love being the get-away driver, but does anyone else want to drive? This whole driving on the left is weirding me out."

Malcolm hooked a thumb toward the passenger seat. "Shift it."

Whitney immediately clambered into the other seat. The van rocked as everyone tried to shift their feet out of the way. Malcolm limped to the front. He plopped into the driver's seat, and Whitney peered down at his calf. She could see a bloody gash through the rip in his pants. She stared at the blood. Her mouth dropped open as she leaned forward. Realizing what she was doing, she shook her head. She pointed to Malcolm's leg. "Can you drive with that?"

"It'll heal soon enough," he said as the back door opened and Barbie handed Madraeus a duffel bag.

"Here. Clothes and a first aid kit." She made eye contact with everyone in the van, stopping at Madraeus. "Thank you. We couldn't have stopped Apep without you and your people."

Madraeus nodded. "I'm sorry for what happened to your friends." The silence was thick as they remembered Willie's sacrifice.

"We lost a lot of good people." Barbie's voice cracked. She gave them a quick, sad smile. "Goodbye."

"She's the last Hare," Madraeus said after she closed the door.

Thomas rummaged through Barbie's bag and passed out pieces of clothing. He handed the first aid kit to Vivian.

"Do you think she'll start the Hares back up again?" Hamilton asked as he pulled on a pair of pants.

"Hard to say." Madraeus took a long breath and let it out slowly. "Perhaps if she does, the Hares won't be so intolerant."

"Speaking of intolerant..." Fully dressed, Hamilton sat back. "The Races are on the police radar. Agent Milner isn't going to give up."

"It's gonna be cat and mouse for a while," Vivian said as she dabbed at the gash in her leg.

"So then," Sophia looked to Madraeus, "do we hide?"

Madraeus nodded. "At least, lay low. InfiniCorp will have to disappear."

Hamilton leaned forward so he could see Madraeus. "No matter where we go, the authorities will be on the lookout. So, where do we go?"

"North," Madraeus said. "We'll meet up with Lady Douglas."

Hamilton groaned. "She's not going to be happy to see us.

"No," Madraeus glanced pointedly at Philtzer, "but she has doctors and she's close."

Whitney hung over the seat, trying hard to ignore the amount of blood she could smell and see. "Isn't she having a Cecelia purge fest?"

"Ray, Lady Douglas is on a rampage..." Rami turned to his friend.

"I'm sure you can handle it," Madraeus said with a sad smile.

Rami's eyebrows shot up. "What do you mean, *I* can handle it?"

Madraeus glanced at Whitney before turning his sad eyes back to Rami. "I'm resigning from the council."

"What?" Whitney whispered, staring at Madraeus.

Sophia's eyes darted around the van. Everyone railed and protested, except Philtzer, who quietly watched Madraeus.

"You can't!" Hamilton paled. "Who's gonna stop Lady Douglas?"

Vivian glared at Madraeus. "We barely made it through this mess without you!"

"But you did." Madraeus' eyes were filled with pride and sadness as he gazed at each of them. "You all did very well."

"Seriously, boss, you can't leave." Thomas shook his head.

The look on Madraeus' face begged them to understand. "I'm sorry, my friends, but this is what I have to do."

"We've never questioned you before." Philtzer's quiet voice silenced the protests. "We won't question you now."

Madraeus bowed his head, silently thanking Philtzer for his support. The werewolf winked and then closed his eyes.

Rami nodded. "Will you come back?"

"Not for a while." Madraeus shook his head. "I need time. I have to get my head straight."

Whitney climbed out of the passenger seat, grabbed a bandage out of the box next to Vivian, and tiptoed her way back to where Madraeus sat. She squeezed in beside him. Madraeus watched her pull his tattered sleeve aside. She grimaced at the jagged snake bite in his forearm and began wrapping the bandage around it.

"So, if InfiniCorp is no more," Whitney asked, "am I fired?"

"No," Madraeus snorted, "you're not fired."

"Cool." Whitney finished wrapping and tied the ends of the bandage. "I think you're right to take a break." Madraeus raised his eyebrows as Whitney continued. "I think we're both gonna need some time to figure stuff out. I've got a lot to learn."

Madraeus leaned closer so he could whisper in her ear. "My feelings are not going to go away."

Whitney glanced at him.

"But if you want me to leave you alone—"

"I don't!" Whitney grabbed his hand. "I don't want you to leave me! But I've only known you for a couple of months. And ever since I met you, I've been just trying not to get killed. I mean, I can't even deal with the idea of drinking blood, much less think about dating."

Madraeus let out a disappointed sigh. "Hmm."

"But *maybe*, if we stay out of crisis mode for a while, and *maybe*, if we can get past driving each other crazy, we might have a shot." She squeezed his hand. "But I think it's going to take some time."

"Well," Madraeus rubbed his thumb across her knuckles, "we have forever."

Whitney let out a nervous laugh. "Forever?"

Madraeus' lips twitched. "And waiting for you wouldn't be the worst job ever."

Whitney huffed, "I'm still not the kind of girl who dates her boss."

"All right." Madraeus nodded. "You're fired."

"Yeah, well," Whitney bumped Madraeus' shoulder with hers. "This job sucked anyway."

Madraeus let out a deep, rich laugh and kissed her on the forehead. Whitney smiled and rested her head on his shoulder.

Sophia nudged Philtzer. He opened one eye again. She pointed to Whitney and Madraeus.

"About time." Philtzer chuckled, glancing up at Sophia. "Nothing like a happy ending. Now maybe we can get some rest."

EPILOGUE

Sandra stared out the front door of the hospital at the pouring rain.

Nowhere to go and nothing to do, except get wet.

She flipped up the collar of her borrowed jacket and blew out a deep breath. She pushed the door open and walked out into the rain. The nurse had told her there was a bus stop just up the road. Sandra hurried along, keeping her head down.

She glanced up, saw the bus shelter, and dashed the last few yards. Once under the canopy, she shook the water from her hair and wiped her face with her sleeve. As she was lowering her arm, she noticed a black SUV stopped across the road. The door opened, an umbrella unfolded, and Agent Milner stepped out. He gazed at her for a while and then crossed the street.

"I heard you were getting out today."

Sandra glanced at the gray sky. "It's a good day for it."

"I think we have a lot to discuss."

"Do we?"

"Why did you feed her?" Milner's intense, icy gaze bored into her. "She's a vampire."

"Vampire or not, I couldn't just let her die. She was my friend."

"Was?"

Sandra sighed and looked down at her shoes. She rocked back on her heels and tapped her toes together.

Milner leaned forward. "Your sacrifice for your friend was noble, but they're dangerous."

Sandra looked up the street. She could see the bus coming.

"They're not human." Milner looked from her to the bus. "They're something much more dangerous. Someone has to stop them. You're in a unique position."

The bus stopped in front of the shelter. The doors opened.

"You're lost, Miss Conners. You need a purpose. Maybe that purpose is to stand between humanity and the monsters."

Sandra stared at Milner for a long moment, thinking.

"Someone needs to draw the line," Milner pressed.

Sandra looked at the bus and shook her head. The bus closed its doors and drove on. Sandra looked back at Milner. "What did you have in mind?"

AUTHOR'S NOTE

Generally speaking, an author will include a disclaimer that the similarity of the setting of the story to any real place is unintentional. In the case of this story, the settings are very much grounded in real locations. However, I have taken artistic license with the details. The church in Broadclyst is a real place and does have the symbol of the Three Hares carved into the ceiling in nine places. However, to my knowledge, there is no secret society lodged under the town. I have taken equal artistic license with the details of Egyptian mythology in regards to vampire and werewolf myths. However, the stelas, the Bremner-Rhind Papyrus, and the Book of the Dead are real. The spells to overthrow Apep are actually detailed out in those documents. I hope that this sparks an interest in history and architecture while providing a fun escape into fantasy. It was simply fun to tie reality into fiction. Happy reading!

Also By Adriana Pridemore

Council of Races Series
This Job Sucks!
Your Job Bites!

Short Stories
(Available on Amazon KDP)
Just a Little Nap
The Apple's Bite
Flaming Fang

Temp receptionist Whitney Martindale's ex has been turned into a vampire and is trying to kill her. She is forced to rely on Madraeus Ravilla, her boss and a powerful vampire from the Council of Races, to keep her alive. Can they stop her ex from killing again and exposing the Races to the mortal world?

Madraeus Ravilla's psycho nemesis is creating an army to take over the mortal world, and Madraeus is succumbing to his dark side. To save the world, Whitney and the werewolves strike a deal with an ancient enemy, but is it a trap?

ABOUT THE AUTHOR

ADRIANA PRIDEMORE HAS LOVED reading and writing all of her life. She has been a journalist, freelance editor/proofreader, and teacher. She currently lives in Montana with her wonderful husband and family, a fuzzy feline queen, and a moose-sized St. Bernard.